desired

(book #5 in the Vampire Journals)

morgan rice

Cover model: Jennifer Onvie. Cover photography: Adam Luke Studios, New York. Cover makeup artist: Ruthie Weems. If you would like to contact any of these artists, please contact Morgan Rice.

ISBN: 978-0-9829537-6-1

Also by Morgan Rice

turned
(book #1 in the Vampire Journals)

loved
(Book #2 in the Vampire Journals)

betrayed
(Book #3 in the Vampire Journals)

desired
(Book #4 in the Vampire Journals)

FACT:

Montmartre, Paris, is famous for its huge church, the Sacré-Cœur Basilica, built in the 19th century. But sitting beside it, high atop the hill, stands the little known Church of Saint Peter. This small, obscure church is much older than its neighbor, dating back to the 3rd century, and has an even greater importance: it was in this location that the vows were taken that led to the founding of the Society of Jesus.

FACT:

Sainte Chapelle, located a small island in the center of Paris (not far from the famous Notre Dame), was built in the 13th century, and for hundreds of years housed the most precious relics of Christendom, including the Crown of Thorns, the Holy Lance, and pieces of the cross upon which Jesus was crucified. The relics were stored in a large, ornate silver chest….

"Why art thou yet so fair? shall I believe
That unsubstantial death is amorous,
And that the lean abhorred monster keeps
Thee here in dark to be his paramour?
For fear of that, I still will stay with thee;
And never from this palace of dim night
Depart again…"

--William Shakespeare, *Romeo and Juliet*

CHAPTER ONE

Paris, France
(July, 1789)

Caitlin Paine awoke to blackness.

The air was heavy, and she struggled to breathe as she tried to move. She was lying on her back, on a hard surface. It was cool and damp, and a tiny sliver of light came in at her as she looked up.

Her shoulders were squeezed together, but with an effort she just managed to reach up. She stretched out her palms and felt the surface above. Stone. She ran her hands along it, felt the dimensions, and realized she was boxed in. In a coffin.

Caitlin's heart started to pound. She hated tight spaces, and she started breathing harder. She wondered if she were dreaming, stuck in some sort of horrible limbo, or if she had truly awakened in some other time, and some other place.

She reached up again, with both hands, and with all her might, pushed. It moved a fraction of an inch, just enough for her to slide a finger into the crack. She pushed again, with all her might, and the heavy stone lid moved further, with the sound of stone scraping against stone.

She squeezed more fingers into the widening crack, and with all her might, shoved. This time, the lid came off.

Caitlin sat up, breathing hard, looking all around. Her lungs gasped in the fresh air, and she braced herself at the light, raising her hands to her eyes. How long had she been in such darkness? she wondered.

As she sat there, Shielding her eyes, she listened, bracing herself for any noise, for any movement. She remembered how rough her graveyard awakening had been in Italy, and this time, she didn't want to leave anything to chance. She was prepared for anything, ready to defend herself against whatever villagers, or vampires—or whatever else—might be nearby.

But this time, all was silence. She slowly pried open her eyes, and saw that she was, indeed, alone. As her eyes adjusted, she realized it wasn't, actually, that bright in here. She was in a cavernous, stone room, with low, arched ceilings. It looked like the vault of a church. The room was lit only by the occasional burning candle. It must be night, she realized.

Now that her eyes adjusted, she looked around carefully. She had been right: she'd been lying in a stone sarcophagus, in the corner of a stone room, in what appeared to be the crypt of a church. The room was empty, except for a few stone statues, and several other sarcophagi.

Caitlin stepped out the sarcophagus. She stretched, testing all of her muscles. It felt good to stand again. She was grateful that she hadn't awakened this time to a battle. At least she had a few quiet moments to collect herself.

But she was still so disoriented. Her mind felt heavy, like she had awoken from a thousand year sleep. She also, immediately, felt a hunger pang.

Where was she? she wondered again. *What year was it*?

And more importantly, where was Caleb?

She was crestfallen that he was not at her side.

Caitlin surveyed the room, looking for a sign of him anywhere. But there was nothing. The other sarcophagi were all open and empty, and there was nowhere else he could be hiding.

"Hello?" she called out. "Caleb?"

She took a few tentative steps into the room, and saw a low, arched doorway, the only way in or out. She went to it and tried the knob. Unlocked, the door swung open easily.

Before she left the room, she turned and surveyed her surroundings, making sure she hadn't left anything she needed. She reached down and felt her necklace, still around her neck; she reached into her pockets, and was reassured to feel her journal, and the one, large key. It was all that she had left in the world, and it was all that she needed.

As Caitlin exited, she proceeded down a long, arched stone hallway. She could think only of finding Caleb. Surely, he had gone back with her this time. Hadn't he?

And if he had, would he remember her this time? She could not possibly imagine having to go through all that again, having to search for him, and then having him not remember. No. She prayed that this time would be different. He was alive, she assured herself, and they had gone back together. They *must* have.

But as she hurried down the corridor, and up a small flight of stone steps, she felt her pace increasing, and felt that familiar sinking feeling in her chest that he had not come back with her. After all, he had not awakened at her side, holding her hand, he was not there to reassure her. Did that mean he had not made the trip back? The pit in her stomach grew bigger.

And what about Sam? He had been there, too. Why wasn't there any sign of him?

Caitlin finally reached the top of the staircase, opened another door, and stood there, amazed at the sight. She was standing in the main chapel of an extraordinary church. She had never seen such high ceilings, so much stained-glass, such an enormous, elaborate altar. The rows of pews stretched forever, and it looked like this place could hold thousands of people.

Luckily, it was empty. Candles burned everywhere, but clearly, it was late. She was grateful for that: the last thing she wanted was to walk out into a crowd of thousands of people staring right at her.

Caitlin walked slowly, right down the center of the isle, heading towards the exit. She was on the lookout for Caleb, for Sam, or maybe even for a priest. Someone like that priest in Assisi, who might welcome her, explain things to her. Who might tell her where she was, and when, and why.

But there was no one. Caitlin seemed to be completely, utterly alone.

Caitlin reached the huge, double doors, and braced herself to face whatever might be outside.

As she opened them, she gasped. The night was lit up by street torches everywhere, and before her was a large crowd of people. They weren't waiting to enter the church, but rather were milling around, in a large, open plaza. It was a busy, festive night scene, and as Caitlin felt the heat, she knew that it was summer. She was shocked by the sight of all these people, by their antiquated wardrobe, by their formality. Luckily, no one seemed to notice her. But she couldn't take her eyes off of them.

There were hundreds of people, most dressed formally, all clearly from another century. Among them were horses, carriages, street peddlers, artists, singers. It was a crowded, summer night scene, and it was overwhelming. She wondered what year it could be, and what place she could have possibly landed in. More importantly, as she scanned all the strange and foreign faces, she wondered if Caleb could be waiting among them.

She scanned the crowd desperately, hoping, trying to convince herself that Caleb, or maybe Sam, could be among them. She looked every which way, but after several minutes, she realized they simply were not here.

Caitlin took several steps out, into the square, and then turned and faced the church, hoping that perhaps she would recognize its façade, and that it would give her a hint as to where she was.

It did. She was hardly an expert on architecture, or history, or churches, but some things she knew. Some places were so obvious, so etched into the public consciousness, that she was sure she could recognize them. And this was one of those.

She was standing before the Notre Dame.

She was in Paris.

It was a place she could not mistake for any other. Its three huge front doors, ornately carved; the dozens of small statues above them; its elaborate façade reaching hundreds of feet into the sky. It was one of the most recognizable places on earth. She had seen it online before, many times. She couldn't believe it: she was really in Paris.

Caitlin had always wanted to go to Paris, had always begged her mother to take her. When she had a boyfriend once, in high school, she had always hoped he'd take her there. It was a place she had always dreamed of going, and it took her breath away that she was actually here. And in another century.

Caitlin felt herself get jostled in the thickening crowd, and she suddenly looked down and took stock of her clothes. She was mortified to see that she was still dressed in the simple prison garb that Kyle had given her in the Colosseum in Rome. She wore a canvas tunic, rough against her skin, crudely cut, way too big for her, tied over her torso and legs with a piece of rope. Her hair was matted, unwashed, in her face. She looked like an escaped prisoner, or a vagabond.

Feeling more anxious, Caitlin again looked for Caleb, for Sam, for anyone she recognized, anyone that could help her. She had never felt more alone, and she wanted nothing more than to lay her eyes on them, to know that she did not come back to this place by herself, to know that everything would be all right.

But she recognized no one.

Maybe I am the only one, she thought. *Maybe I am really on my own again.*

The thought of it pierced her stomach like a knife. She wanted to curl up, to crawl back and hide in the church, to be sent to some other time, to some other place—any place where she could wake up and see someone she knew.

But she toughened herself. She knew there was no retreat, no option but to move forward. She'd just have to be brave, to find her way in this time and place. There was simply no other choice.

*

Caitlin had to get away from the crowd. She needed to be alone, to rest, to feed, to think. She had to figure out where to go, where to look for Caleb, and if he was even here. Just as important, she had to figure out why she was in the city, and in this time. She didn't even know what year it was.

A person brushed passed her, and Caitlin reached out and grabbed his arm, overwhelmed with a sudden desire to know.

He turned and looked at her, startled at being stopped so abruptly.

"I'm sorry," she said, realizing how dry her throat was, and how ragged she must have appeared, as she uttered her first words, "but what year is it?"

She was embarrassed even as she asked it, realizing that she must have seemed crazy.

"Year?" the confused man asked back.

"Um…I'm sorry, but I can't seem to…remember."

The man looked her up and down, then slowly shook his head, as if deciding there was something wrong with her.

"It's 1789, of course. And we're not even close to New Year's, so you really have no excuse," he said, shaking his head derisively, and marching off.

1789. The reality of those numbers raced through Caitlin's mind. She recalled that she had last been in the year 1791. Two years. Not that far off.

Yet, she was in Paris now, an entirely different world than Venice. Why here? Why now?

She racked her brain, trying desperately to remember her history classes, to remember what had happened in France in 1789. She was embarrassed to realize that she couldn't. She kicked herself once again for not paying closer attention in class. If she had known back in high school that she'd one day be traveling back in time, she'd have studied her history through the night, and would have made an effort to memorize everything.

It didn't matter now, she realized. Now, she was a *part* of history. Now, she had a chance to change it, and to change herself. The past, she realized, could be changed. Just because certain events had happened in the history books, it didn't mean that she, traveling back, couldn't change them now. In a sense, she already had: her appearance here, in this time, would affect everything. That, in turn, could, in its own small way, change the course of history.

It made her feel the importance of her actions all the more. The past was hers to create again.

Taking in her elegant surroundings, Caitlin began to relax a bit, and even to feel a bit encouraged. At least she had landed in a beautiful place, in a beautiful city, and in a beautiful time. This was hardly the stone age, after all, and it was not like she had appeared in the middle of nowhere. Everything around her looked immaculate, and the people were all dressed so nicely, and the cobblestone streets shined in the torchlight. And the one thing she did remember about Paris in the 18th century was that it was a luxurious time for France, a time of great wealth, one in which kings and queens still ruled.

Caitlin realized that the Notre Dame was on a small island, and she felt the need to get off it. It was just too crowded here, and she needed some peace. She spotted several small foot bridges leading off it, and headed towards one. She allowed herself to hope that maybe Caleb's presence was leading her in a particular direction.

As she walked over the river, she saw how beautiful the night was in Paris, lit by the torchlight all along the river, and by the full moon. She thought of Caleb, and wished he was by her side to enjoy the sight with her.

As she walked across the bridge, looking down at the water, memories overcame her. She thought of Pollepel, of the Hudson River at night, of the way the moon lit up the river. She had a sudden urge to leap off the bridge, to test her wings, to see if she could fly again, and to soar high above it.

But she felt weak, and hungry, and as she leaned back, she couldn't even feel the presence of her wings at all. She worried if the trip back in time had affected her abilities, her powers. She didn't feel nearly as strong as she once had. In fact, she felt nearly human. Frail. Vulnerable. She didn't like the feeling.

After Caitlin crossed the river, she walked down side streets, wandering for hours, hopelessly lost. She walked through twisting, turning streets, further and further from the river, heading north. She was amazed by the city. In some respects, it felt similar to Venice and Florence in 1791. Like those cities, Paris was still the same, even to the way it appeared in the 21st century. She had never been here, but she had seen photos, and she was shocked to recognize so many buildings and monuments.

The streets here, too, were mostly cobblestone, filled with horse and carriages, or the occasional horse with a lone rider. People walked in elaborate costumes, strolling leisurely, with all the time in the world. Like those cities, there was no plumbing here either, and Caitlin couldn't help noticing the waste in the streets, and recoiling at the awful stench in the summer heat. She wished she still had one of those small potpourri bags that Polly had given her in Venice.

But unlike those other cities, Paris was a world unto itself. The streets were wider here, the buildings were lower, and they were more beautifully designed. The city felt older, more precious, more beautiful. It was also less crowded: the further she went from the Notre Dame, the fewer people she saw. Maybe it was just because it was late at night, but the streets felt nearly empty.

She walked and walked, her legs and feet growing weary, searching around every corner for any sign of Caleb, any clue that might lead her in a special direction. There was nothing.

Every twenty blocks or so the neighborhood changed, and the feeling changed, too. As she headed further and further north, she found herself ascending a hill, in a new district, this one with narrow alleyways, and several bars. As she passed by a corner bar, she saw a man sprawled out, drunk, unconscious against the wall. The street was completely empty, and for a moment, Caitlin was overcome by the worst hunger pang. She felt like it was tearing her stomach in half.

She saw the man lying there, zoomed in on his neck, and saw the blood pulsing within it. At that moment, she wanted more than anything to descend on him, to feed. The feeling was beyond an urge—it was more like a command. Her body screamed at her to do it.

It took every last ounce of Caitlin's will to look away. She would rather die of starvation than hurt another human.

She looked around and wondered if there were a forest near here, a place she could hunt. While she had seen some occasional dirt roads and parks in the city, she hadn't seen anything like a forest.

At just that moment, the door to the bar burst open, and a man stumbled out of it—thrown out, actually—by one of the wait staff. He cursed and screamed at them, clearly drunk.

Then he turned and set his sights on Caitlin.

He was well built, and he looked at Caitlin with ill intent.

She felt herself tense up. She wondered again, desperately, whether any of her powers remained.

She turned and walked away, walking faster, but she sensed the man following her.

Before she could turn, a second later, he grabbed her from behind, in a bear hug. He was faster and stronger than she had imagined, and she could smell his awful breath over her shoulder.

But the man was also drunk. He stumbled, even as he held her, and Caitlin focused, remembered her training, and sidestepped and swept him, using one of the fighting techniques that Aiden had taught her on Pollepel. The man went flying, landing on his back.

Caitlin suddenly had a flashback to Rome, of the Colosseum, of fighting on the stadium floor while being charged by multiple fighters. It was so vivid, for a moment, she forgot where she was.

She snapped out of it just in time. The drunk man got up, stumbled, and charged her again. Caitlin waited to the last second, then sidestepped, and he went flying, falling flat on his own face.

He was dazed, and before he could get up again, Caitlin hurried to get away. She was glad she had got the best of him, but the incident shook her. It worried her that she was still having flashbacks of Rome. She also hadn't felt her supernatural strength. She still felt as frail as a human. The thought of that, more than anything else, scared her. She was truly on her own now.

Caitlin looked all around, starting to feel frantic with worry about where to go, about what to do next. Her legs burned from the walking, and she began to feel a sense of despair.

That was when she saw it. She looked up, and saw before her a huge hill. On top of that, sat a large, medieval abbey. For some reason she couldn't explain, she felt drawn to it. The hill was daunting, but she didn't see what other choice she had.

Caitlin hiked up the entire hill, more tired than she'd just about ever been, and wishing she could fly.

She finally reached the front doors of the abbey, and looked up at the massive, oak doors. This place looked ancient. She marveled at the fact that, though it was 1789, this church had already been around for what looked like thousands of years.

She didn't know why, but she felt drawn here. Seeing nowhere else to go, she got her courage up, and knocked softly.

There was no response.

Caitlin tried the knob and was surprised to find it open. She let herself in.

The ancient door creaked open slowly, and it took a moment for Caitlin's eyes to adjust to the cavernous, dark church. As she surveyed it, she was impressed by the scope and solemnity of the place. It was still late at night, and this simple, austere, church, made entirely of stone, adorned in stained-glass windows, was lit by large candles, everywhere, burning low. At its far end sat a simple altar, around which were placed dozens more candles.

Otherwise, it seemed empty.

Caitlin wondered for a moment what she was doing here. Was there a special reason? Or had her mind just been playing tricks on her?

A side door suddenly opened, and Caitlin spun.

Walking towards her, Caitlin was surprised to see, was a nun—short, frail, dressed in flowing white robes, with a white hood. She walked slowly, and walked right up to Caitlin.

She pulled back her hood, looked up at her and smiled. She had large, shining blue eyes, and seemed too young to be a nun. As she smiled wide, Caitlin could feel the warmth coming off of her. She also sensed that she was one of hers: a vampire.

"Sister Paine," the nun said softly. "It is an honor to have you."

CHAPTER TWO

Her world felt surreal as the nun led Caitlin through the abbey, down a long corridor. It was a beautiful place, and it was clear that it was actively lived in, with nuns in white robes walking about, getting ready, it seemed, for the morning services. One of them swung a decanter as she went, spreading delicate incense, while others were chanting soft morning prayers.

After several minutes of walking in silence, Caitlin began to wonder where the nun was leading her. Finally, they stopped before a single door. The nun opened it, revealing a small, humble room, with a view overlooking Paris. It reminded Caitlin of the room she'd stayed in in that cloister in Siena.

"On the bed, you'll find a change of clothing," the nun said. "There is a well in which to bathe, in our courtyard," she said. She pointed, "and that is for you."

Caitlin followed her finger and saw a small, stone pedestal in the corner of the room, on which sat a silver goblet, filled with a white liquid. The nun smiled back.

"You have everything you need here for a fresh night's sleep. After that, the choice is yours to make."

"Choice?" Caitlin asked.

"I am told that you have one key already. You will need to find the other three. The choice, though, of whether to fulfill your mission and continue on your journey is always yours."

"This is for you."

She reached out and handed Caitlin a cylindrical, silver case, covered in jewels.

"It is a letter from your father. Just for you. We have been guarding it for centuries. It has never been opened."

Caitlin took it in awe, feeling its weight in her hand.

"I do hope that you will continue with your mission," she said softly. "We need you, Caitlin."

The nun suddenly turned to go.

"Wait!" Caitlin yelled out.

She stopped.

"I'm in Paris, correct? In 1789?"

The woman smiled back. "That is correct."

"But why? Why am I here? Why now? Why this place?"

"I'm afraid that is for you to find out. I am but a simple servant."

"But why was I drawn to this church?"

"You are in the Abbey of Saint Peter. In Montmartre," the woman said. "It has been here for thousands of years. It is a very sacred place."

"Why?" Caitlin pressed.

"This was the place in which everyone met to take their vows for the founding of the Society of Jesus. It is in this place that Christianity was born."

Caitlin stared back, speechless, and the nun finally smiled and said, "Welcome."

And with that, she bowed slightly, and walked away, closing the door gently behind her.

Caitlin turned and surveyed the room. She was grateful for the hospitality, for the change of clothes, for the chance to bathe, for the comfortable bed that she saw lying in the corner. She didn't think she could take one more step. In fact, she was so tired, she felt like she could sleep forever.

Holding the bejeweled case, she walked to the corner of the room, and set it down. The scroll could wait. But her hunger couldn't.

She lifted the overflowing goblet and examined it. She could already sense what it contained: white blood.

She put it to her lips and drank. It was sweeter than red blood and went down more easily—and it ran through her veins faster. Within moments, she felt reborn, and stronger than she'd ever had. She could have drank forever.

Caitlin finally set down the empty goblet, and took the silver case with her to bed. She lay down, and realized how sore her legs were. It felt so good to just lay there.

She leaned back and rested her head against the small, simple pillow, and closed her eyes, just for a second. She was resolved to open them in just a moment, and read her father's letter.

But the moment her eyes closed, an incredible exhaustion overcame her. She couldn't open them again if she tried. Within seconds, she was fast asleep.

*

Caitlin stood on the floor of the Roman Colosseum, dressed in full battle gear, holding a sword. She was ready to challenge whoever attacked her—indeed, felt the urge to fight. But as she spun around, in every direction, she saw that the stadium was empty. She looked up at the rows of seats, and saw that the entire place was vacant.

Caitlin blinked, and when she opened her eyes, she was no longer in the Colosseum, but rather in the

Vatican, in the Sistine Chapel. She still held her sword, but now was dressed in robes.

She looked about the room and saw hundreds of vampires, lined up neatly, dressed in white robes, with glowing blue eyes. They stood patiently along the wall, silent, at perfect attention.

Caitlin dropped her sword in the empty chamber, and it landed with a clink. She walked slowly towards the head priest, reached out, and took from him a huge silver goblet, filled with white blood. She drank, and the liquid overflowed and poured down her cheeks.

Suddenly, Caitlin found herself alone in the desert. She was walking barefoot on the baked dirt, the sun beating down her, and she held a gigantic key in her hand. But the key was so big—unnaturally big—and the weight of it was pulling her down.

She walked and walked, gasping for air in the heat, until finally, she came to a huge mountain. At the top of that mountain, she saw a man standing there, looking down, smiling.

She knew it was her father.

Caitlin broke into a sprint, running for all she was worth, trying to make it up the mountain, getting closer and closer to him. As she did, the sun grew higher, hotter in the sky, bearing down on her, seeming to come from right behind her father himself. It was as if he were the sun, and she were heading right into it.

Her ascent grew hotter, higher, and she gasped for breath as she got close. He stood with his arms are outstretched, waiting to embrace her.

But the hill became steeper and she was just too tired. She couldn't go any further. She collapsed where she was.

Caitlin blinked, and when she opened her eyes, she saw her father standing over her, leaning down, a warm smile on his face.

"Caitlin," he said. "My daughter. I'm so proud of you."

She tried to reach out, to hold him, but the key was now on top of her, and it was too heavy, pinning her down.

She looked up at him, trying to talk, but her lips were cracked and her throat was too parched.

"Caitlin?"

"Caitlin?"

Caitlin opened her eyes with a start, disoriented.

She looked up, and saw a man sitting on her bedside, looking down at her, smiling.

He reached over, and gently brushed the hair out of her eyes.

Was this still a dream? She felt the cool sweat on her forehead, felt his touch on her wrist, and she prayed that it was not.

Because there before her, smiling down, was the love of her life.

Caleb.

CHAPTER THREE

Sam opened his eyes with a start. He was staring up at the sky, looking up the trunk of an enormous oak tree. He blinked several times, wondering where he was.

He felt something soft on his back, and it felt very comfortable, and he looked over and realized he was lying on a patch of moss on the forest floor. He looked back up, and saw dozens of trees high above him, swaying in the wind. He heard a gurgling sound, and looked over, and saw a stream trickling by, just a few feet from his head.

Sam sat up and looked around, glancing in every direction, taking it all in. He was deep in the woods, alone, the only light coming in through the tree branches. He checked himself and saw that he was fully dressed, in the same battle gear he had been wearing in the Colosseum. It was quiet here, the only sound being that of the stream, of the birds, and of some distant animals.

Sam realized, with relief, that the time travel had worked. He was clearly in some other place and time—although where and when that was, he had no idea.

Sam slowly checked his body, and realized he'd sustained no major injuries, and that he was all in one piece. He felt a terrible hunger gnawing at his stomach, but he could live with that. First, he had to figure out where he was.

He reached down, feeling to see if he had any weaponry on him.

Unfortunately, none of it had made the trip. He was on his own again, left to the devices of just his own bare hands.

He wondered if he still carried a vampire's power. He could feel an unnatural strength still coursing through his veins, and it felt like he had. But then again, he couldn't be sure until the time came.

And that time came sooner than he thought.

Sam heard the snap of a branch, and turned to see a large bear hulking towards him, slowly, aggressively. He froze. It glowered at him, raised its fangs, and snarled.

A second later, it broke into a sprint, charging right for him.

There was no time for Sam to run, and nowhere for him to run to. He had no choice, he realized, but to confront this animal.

But strangely enough, instead of being overcome by fear, Sam felt rage course through him. He was furious at the animal. He resented being attacked, especially before he even had a chance to get his bearings. So, without thinking, Sam charged, too, preparing to meet the bear in battle, the same way he would a human.

Sam and the bear met in the middle. The bear lunged for him, and Sam lunged right back. Sam felt the power coursing through his veins, felt it telling him that he was invincible.

As he met the bear in mid-air, he realized that he was right. He caught the bear by its shoulders, grabbed on, spun and threw it. The bear went flying backwards through the woods, dozens of feet, smashing hard into a tree.

Sam stood there and roared back at the bear, a fierce roar, even louder than the animal's. He felt the muscles and veins bulging in him as he did.

The bear got to its feet slowly, wobbly, and looked at Sam with something like shock. It now hobbled as it walked, and after taking a few tentative steps, it suddenly lowered its head, turned, and ran away.

But Sam wasn't going to let it get away so easy. He was mad now, and he felt like nothing in the world could abate his anger. And he was hungry. The bear would have to pay.

Sam broke into a sprint, and was pleased to find that he was faster than this animal. Within moments, he caught up to it and in a single leap, landed on its back. He leaned back, and sunk his fangs deep into its neck.

The bear howled in agony, bucking wildly, but Sam held on. He sunk his fangs deeper, and within moments, he felt the bear slumped to its knees beneath him. Finally, it stopped moving.

Sam lay on top of it, drinking, feeling its life force course through his veins.

Finally, Sam leaned back and licked his lips, dripping with blood. He'd never felt so refreshed. It was exactly the meal he'd needed.

Sam was just rising back to his feet, when he heard another twig snap.

He looked over, and standing there, in a clearing of the forest, was a young girl, maybe 17, dressed in a thin, all-white material. She stood there, holding a basket, and stared back at him, in shock. Her skin was translucent white, and her long, light brown hair framed large, blue eyes. She was beautiful.

She stared back at Sam, equally transfixed.

He realized that she must be afraid of him, afraid that maybe he would attack her; he realized that he must have looked like an awful sight, on top of a bear, blood in his mouth. He didn't want to scare her.

So he jumped down from the animal, and took several steps towards her.

To his surprise, she didn't flinch, or try to move away. Rather, she just continued to stare at him, unafraid.

"Don't worry," he said. "I'm not going to hurt you."

She smiled. That surprised him. Not only was she beautiful, but she was truly unafraid. How could that be?

"Of course you're not," she said. "You're one of mine."

It was Sam's turn to be shocked. The second she said it, he knew it to be true. He had sensed something when he'd first seen her, and now he knew. She was one of his. A vampire. That's why she was unafraid.

"Nice takedown," she said, gesturing at the bear. "A little messy, wouldn't you say? Why not go for a deer?"

Sam smiled. Not only was she pretty—she was funny.

"Maybe next time I will," he said back.

She smiled.

"Would you mind telling me what year it is?" he asked. "Or century, at least?"

She just smiled, and shook her head.

"I think I'll leave that for you to find out for yourself. If I told you, it would ruin all the fun, wouldn't it?"

Sam liked her. She was spunky. And he felt at ease around her, as if he'd known her forever.

She took a step forward, and reached out her hand. Sam took it, and loved the feel of her smooth, translucent skin.

"I'm Sam," he said, shaking her hand, holding it for too long.

She smiled wider.

"I know," she said.

Sam was baffled. How could she possibly know? Had he met her before? He couldn't remember.

"I was sent for you," she added.

She suddenly turned and began heading down a forest trail.

Sam hurried to catch up to her, presuming she meant for him to follow. Not looking carefully where he was going, he was embarrassed to find himself trip over a branch; he heard her giggling as he did.

"So?" he prodded. "Aren't you going to tell me your name?"

She giggled again.

"Well, I have a formal name, but I rarely go by it," she said.

Then she turned and faced him, waiting for him to catch up.

"If you must know, everyone calls me Polly."

CHAPTER FOUR

Caleb held open the huge, medieval door, and as he did, Caitlin stepped out of the abbey and took her first steps out into the early morning light. Caleb at her side, she looked out at the breaking dawn. Here, high atop the hill of Montmartre, she was able to look out and see all of Paris stretched before her. It was a beautiful, sprawling city, a mixture of classical architecture and simple houses, of cobblestone streets and dirt roads, of trees and urbanity. The sky blended in a million soft colors, making the city look alive. It was magical.

Even more magical was the hand that she felt slip into hers. She looked over and saw Caleb standing by her side, enjoying the view with her, and she could hardly believe it was real. She could hardly believe it was really him, that they were really here. Together. That he knew who she was. That he remembered her. That he'd found her.

She wondered again if she had truly awakened from a dream, if she were not still sleeping.

But as she stood there, and squeezed his hand tighter, she knew that she was truly awake. She had never felt so overjoyed. She had been running for so long, had come back in time, all these centuries, all this way, just to be with him. Just to make sure he was alive again. When he hadn't remembered her, in Italy, it had crushed her to the depths.

But now that he was here, and alive, and remembered her—and now that he was all hers, single, without Sera around—her heart swelled with new emotion, and with new hope. She had never in her wildest dreams imagined that it could all work out so perfectly, that it could all actually *really* work. She was so overwhelmed, she didn't even know where to begin, or what to say.

Before she could speak, he began.

"Paris," he said, turning to her with a smile. "There are certainly worse places we could be together."

She smiled back.

"My whole life long, I'd always wanted to see it," she answered.

With someone I love, she wanted to add, but stopped herself. It felt like it had been so long since she'd been by Caleb's side, she actually found herself feeling nervous again. In some ways, it felt like she had been with him forever—longer than forever—but in other ways, it felt like she was meeting him again for the first time.

He reached out his hand, palm up.

"Would you see it with me?" he asked.

She reached out and placed her hand into his.

"It's a long walk back down," she said, looking down at the steep hill, leading all the way down, for miles, and sloping into Paris.

"I was thinking of something a bit more scenic," he answered. "Flying."

She rolled back her shoulder blades, trying to feel if her wings were working. She felt so rejuvenated, so restored from that drink, from the white blood—but she still wasn't sure she was able to fly. And she didn't feel ready to leap off a mountain in the hope that her wings would take.

"I don't think I'm ready yet," she said.

He looked at her, and understood.

"Fly with me," he said, then added, with a smile, "just like the old days."

She smiled, came up behind him, and held onto his back and shoulders. His muscular body felt so good in her arms.

He suddenly leapt into the air, so fast, that she barely had time to hang on tight.

Before she knew it, they were flying, she holding onto his back, looking down, resting her head on his shoulder blade. She felt that familiar thrill in her stomach, as they plummeted, coming down low, close to the city, in the sunrise. It was breathtaking.

But none of it was as breathtaking as her being in his arms again, holding him, just being together. She had barely been with him an hour, and already she was praying that they would never be apart again.

*

The Paris that they flew over, the Paris of 1789, was in so many ways similar to the pictures of Paris she'd seen in the 21st century. She recognized so many of the buildings, the churches, the steeples, the monuments. Despite its being hundreds of years old, it looked almost exactly like the same city of the 21st century. Like Venice and Florence, so little had changed in just a few hundred years.

But in other ways, it was very different. It was not nearly as built up. Although some roads were paved with cobblestone, still others were dirt. It was not nearly as condensed, and in between buildings there were still clumps of trees, almost like a city built into an encroaching forest. Instead of cars, there were horses, carriages, people walking in the dirt, or pushing carts. Everything was slower, more relaxed.

Caleb dove lower, until they were flying feet above the tops of the buildings. As they cleared the last of them, suddenly, the sky opened, and spread out before them was the Seine River, cutting right through the middle of the city. It glowed yellow in the early morning light, and it took her breath away.

Caleb dove low, flying above it, and she marveled at the beauty of the city, at how romantic it was. They flew over the small island, the Ile de la Cite, and she recognized the Notre Dame beneath her, its huge steeple soaring above everything else.

Caleb dove even lower, just above the water, and the moist river air cooled them on this hot July morning. Caitlin looked out and saw Paris on both sides of the river, as they flew above and below the numerous, small arched foot bridges connecting one side of the river to the other. Then Caleb lifted them up, and over to one side of the river bank, setting them down softly, behind a large tree, out of sight of any passersby.

She looked around and saw that he had brought them to an enormous, formal park and garden, which seemed to stretch for miles, right alongside the river.

"The Tuileries," Caleb said. "The very same garden of the 21st century. Nothing has changed. It's still the most romantic place in Paris."

With a smile, he reached out and took her hand. They began strolling together, down a path which wound its way through the garden. She had never felt so happy.

There were so many questions she was burning to ask him, so many things that she was dying to say to him, she hardly knew where to begin. But she had to start somewhere, so she figured she'd just start with what was most recently on her mind.

"Thank you," she said, "for Rome. For the Colosseum. For saving me," she said. "If you hadn't had arrived when you did, I don't know what would have happened."

She turned and looked at him, suddenly unsure. "Do you remember?" she asked worriedly.

He turned and looked at her, and nodded, and she saw that he did. She was relieved. At least, finally, they were on the same page. Their memories were back. That alone meant the world to her.

"But I didn't save you," he said. "You handled yourself quite well without me. On the contrary, you saved me. Just being with you—I don't know what I would do without you," he said.

As he squeezed her hand, she felt her entire world slowly become restored within her.

As they ambled through the gardens, she gazed in wonder at all the varieties of flowers, the fountains, the statues….It was one of the most romantic places she'd ever been.

"And I'm sorry," she added.

He looked at her, and she was afraid to say it.

"For your son."

His face darkened, and as he looked away, she saw genuine grief flash across it.

Stupid, she thought. *Why do you always have to go and ruin the moment? Why couldn't you have waited for some other time?*

Caleb swallowed and nodded, too overcome with grief to even speak.

"And I'm sorry about Sera," Caitlin added. "I never meant to get between the two of you."

"Don't be sorry," he said. "It had nothing to do with you. It was between her and I. We were never meant to be together. It was wrong from the start."

"Well, finally, I've been wanting to tell you that I'm sorry for what happened in New York," she added, feeling relieved to get it off her chest. "I would have never stabbed if I knew that it was you. I swear, I thought you were someone else, shapeshifting. I never in a million years thought it was really you."

She felt herself tear up at the thought of it.

He stopped and looked at her, and held her shoulders.

"None of that matters now," he said, earnestly. "You came back to save me. And I know that you did so at great expense. It might not have even worked. And you risked your life for me. And gave up our child for me," he said, looking down again in momentary grief. "I love you more than I can say," he said, still looking at the ground.

He looked at her with wet eyes.

At that moment, they kissed. She felt herself melting into his arms, felt her entire world relax, as they kissed for what felt like forever. It was the greatest moment she had ever had with him, and in some ways, she felt like she was getting to know him for the first time.

Finally, slowly, they pulled out of it, looking deeply into each other's eyes.

Then they both looked away, demurely, took each other's hands, and continued their walk through the gardens, alongside the river. She looked at how beautiful, how romantic Paris was, and realized that at that moment, all of her dreams were coming true. This was all she'd ever wanted out of life. To be with someone who loved her—who *really* loved her. To be in such a beautiful city, such a romantic place. To feel like she could have a life ahead of her.

Caitlin felt the bejeweled case in her pocket, and resented it. She didn't want to open it. She loved her father very much, but she didn't want to read a letter from him. She knew right then that she didn't want to continue on this mission any longer. She didn't want to risk having to go back in time again, or to have to find any other keys. She just wanted to be here, in this time, in this place, with Caleb. In peace. She didn't want anything to change. She was determined to do whatever she had to to guard their precious time together, to truly keep them together. And a part of her felt that that meant giving up the mission.

She turned and faced him. She was nervous to tell him, but she felt that she had to.

"Caleb," she said, "I don't want to search anymore. I realize I have a special mission, that I need to help others, that I need to find the Shield. And it may sound selfish, and I'm sorry if it does. But I just want to be with you. That's what's most important to me now. To stay in this time, and in this place. I have a feeling that if we continue to search, we'll end up in another time, in another place. And that we might not be together next time..." Caitlin broke off, and realized she was crying.

She took a deep breath in the silence. She wondered what he thought of her, and hoped that he didn't disapprove.

"Can you understand?" she asked, tentatively.

He stared off into the horizon, looking concerned, then finally turned and looked at her. Her own concern mounted.

"I don't want to read my dad's letter, or find any more clues. I just want us to be together. I want things to stay exactly as they are now. I don't want them to change. I hope you don't hate me for that."

"I would never hate you," he said, softly.

"But you don't approve?" she prodded. "You think I should continue with the mission?"

He looked away, but didn't say anything.

"What is it?" she asked. "Are you worried about the others?"

"I guess I should be," he said. "And I am. But I, too, have selfish reasons. I guess…in the back of my mind I was hoping that if we found the Shield, it might somehow help bring my son back to me. Jade."

Caitlin felt a terrible feeling of guilt, as she realized that he equated her giving up the mission with letting his son go forever.

"But it's not that way," she said. "We don't know that if we find the Shield, if it even exists, that it will bring him back. But we do know that if we don't search, we can be together. This is about us. That's what matters most to me." She paused. "Is that what matters most to you?"

He looked off at the horizon, and nodded. But he didn't look at her.

"Or do you only love me because I can help you find the Shield?" she asked.

She was shocked at herself, that she actually had the courage to voice the question. It was a question that had been burning in her mind ever since she'd first met him. Had he only loved her for where she could lead him? Or had he loved her for *her*? Now, she had finally asked it.

Her heart pounded as she waited for the answer.

Finally, he turned and looked deeply into her eyes. He reached up, and slowly stroked her cheek with the back of his hand.

"I love you for *you*," he said. "And I always have. And if being with you means giving up the search for the Shield, then that is what I will do. I want to be with you, too. I want to search, yes. But you are much more important to me now."

Caitlin smiled, feeling in her heart something she hadn't felt in forever. A sense of peace, of stability. Nothing could stand in their way now.

He brushed the hair from her face, and broke into a smile.

"It's funny," he said, "I lived here once before. Centuries ago. Not in Paris, but in the country. It was a small castle. I don't know if it still exists. But we can search."

She smiled, and he suddenly hoisted her onto his back, and leapt into the air. Within moments, they were flying, high up above Paris, and heading into the country, to search for his home.

Their home.

Caitlin had never been so happy.

CHAPTER FIVE

Sam was having a hard time keeping up with Polly as she walked. She talked so fast, and never seemed to stop, racing from one thought to the next. He was still discombobulated from the time travel, from this new place—he needed to process it all.

But they had been walking for nearly half an hour, he tripping over twigs as he followed her through the forest at her brisk pace, and she hadn't stopped talking. He'd barely been able to get a word in. She went on and on about "the palace" and "the court" and about her coven members and an upcoming concert, and a man named Aiden. He had no idea what she was talking about, or why she'd been looking for him—or even where she was taking him. He was determined to get some answers.

"...of course, it's not exactly a dance," Polly was saying, "but still, it's going to be an amazing event—but I'm not quite sure what I'll wear.

There are so many options, not enough for a formal event like this—"

"*Please*!" Sam said finally, as she bounced along merrily through the forest, "I'm sorry to interrupt, but I have questions for you. Please. I need answers."

She finally stopped talking, and he breathed a sigh of relief. She looked at him with something like wonder, as if she were totally oblivious to the fact that she'd been talking all the while.

"All you need to do is ask!" she said happily. And then, before he could respond, she added, impatiently, "Well? What is it?"

"You said you were sent to get me," Sam said. "By who?"

"That's an easy one," she said, "Aiden."

"Who's that?" Sam asked.

She snickered, "My, you have a lot to learn, don't you? He's only been the mentor of our coven for thousands of years. I'm not sure why he's taken an interest in you, or why he'd send me on such a beautiful day tramping all the way through the forest to get you. The way I see it, you could have found your own way, eventually. Not to mention, I had a *thousand* things to do today, including looking at this new dress and—"

"*Please*," Sam said, trying to hold onto his thought before he lost again. "I really appreciate your coming to get me and all, and I don't want to be disrespectful," he said, "but wherever it is that we're going, I really don't have time. You see, I came back here, in this place and time, for a reason. I need to help my sister. I need to find her—and I don't have time for any side trips."

"Well, I would hardly call this a *side* trip," Polly said. "Aiden is only the most sought after man in all the court. If he's taken an interest in you, it's nothing to throw away," she said. "And whoever it is that you're looking to find, if anyone can point the way, it will bc him."

"Then where is it that we're going, exactly? And how much further is it?"

She took several more steps through the forest, and he hurried to catch up, wondering if she'd ever respond, ever give him a straight answer—when, at that moment, the forest suddenly opened up.

She stopped, and he stopped beside her, awestruck.

Before them lay an immense open field, leading, in the distance, to immaculate, formal gardens, the grass cut into elaborate shapes of every size. It was beautiful, like a living work of art.

Even more breathtaking was what lay just beyond the gardens. It was a palace, grander than any structure Sam had seen in his life. The entire building was made of marble, and it stretched as far as he could see in every direction. It was a classical, formal design, with dozens of oversized windows, and a wide, marble staircase leading up to its entrance. He knew that he had seen pictures of this structure somewhere, but he couldn't remember what it was.

"Versailles," Polly said, providing the answer, as if reading his mind.

He looked at her, and she smiled back.

"It's where we live. You are in France. In 1789. And I'm sure that Aiden will let you join us, assuming that Marie allows it."

Sam looked at her, puzzled.

"Marie?" he asked.

She smiled wider, shaking her head. She turned and skipped across the field, towards the palace. As she did, she called out over her shoulder.

"Why, Marie Antoinette, of course!"

*

Sam walked at Polly's side, up the endless marble staircase, heading towards the front doors of the palace. As he went, he took in all the sights around him. The magnitude and proportions of this place were astounding. All around him, strolling the grounds, were people he presumed to be royalty, dressed in some of the finest clothing he'd ever seen. He couldn't get over this place. If someone had told him he were dreaming, he would believe them. He had never been in the presence of royalty before.

Polly hadn't stopped talking, and he forced himself to focus on her words. He liked being around her, and enjoyed her company, even if paying attention to her was really hard. He thought she was pretty, too. But there was something about her that made him unsure whether he was really attracted to her, or whether he just liked her as a friend. With his past girlfriends, it had been lust at first sight. With Polly, it was more like a camaraderie.

"You see, the royal family lives here," Polly said, "but we live here, too. They want us here. After all, we're the best protection they have. We live together in what you might call a friendly harmony. It serves us both. With this huge forest, we have unlimited hunting, a great place to live, and great company. And in turn, we help protect the royal family. Not to mention that a few of them are our kind, anyway."

Sam looked at her, surprised.

"Marie Antoinette?" he asked.

Polly nodded slightly, as if trying to keep it a secret, but unable to.

"But don't tell anybody," she said. "There are a few others, too. But most of the Royals are human. They want to be among us. But there are strict rules here, and it's not allowed. It's us and them, and we're not allowed to cross that line. There are certain members of the royal family we don't want to have too much power. And Marie insists on it, too.

"Anyway, this is just the most fabulous place. I can't imagine it ever coming to an end. There's party after party, endless dances, balls, concerts….There's going to be the most fabulous one this week. An opera, actually. I already have my outfit picked out."

As they approached the doors, several servants scurried to open them. The golden doors were massive, and Sam looked at them, awestruck, as he walked through.

Polly marched right down a huge, marble corridor, as if she owned the place, and Sam hurried to keep up. As they walked, Sam looked all around, amazed by the opulence. They walked down endless corridors made of marble, with enormous crystal chandeliers hanging low, reflecting the light off of dozens of gilded mirrors. The sun poured in and reflected the light in every direction.

They went through door after door, and finally entered a huge parlor, made of marble, with columns all around it. Several guards stood at attention as Polly entered.

Polly just giggled, apparently immune to them. "We also get to train here," shc said. "Their facilities are the best. Aiden has us on a hard schedule. I'm surprised that he let me break to come get you. You must be pretty important."

"So where is he?" Sam asked. "When will I get to meet him?"

"My, you are impatient, aren't you? He's a very busy man. He might not choose to meet you for some time. Or he might summon you right away. Don't worry, you'll know when he wants to see you. Give it time. In the meantime, I've been asked to show you to your room."

"My room?" Sam asked, surprised. "Wait a second. I didn't say I could stay here. Like I said, I really need to find my sister," Sam began to protest—but at that moment, a huge set of double doors opened before them.

An entourage of royals suddenly entered, surrounding a woman in the middle, who they carried on a royal throne.

They set her down, and as they did, Polly bent low, gesturing for Sam to do the same. He did.

A woman who could have only been Marie Antoinette, slowly got down, took several steps towards them, and stopped right before Sam, gesturing for him to rise. He did.

She looked Sam up and down, as if he were an object of interest.

"So, you're the new boy," she said, expressionless. Her green eyes burned with an intensity he'd never seen, and he could, indeed, sense that she was one of theirs.

Finally, after what seemed like forever, she nodded. "Interesting."

With that, she walked right past them, and her entourage quickly followed.

But one person lingered behind, clearly one of the royals. She looked to be about 17, and was dressed in a royal blue, velvet gown, from head to toe. She had the fairest skin that Sam had ever seen, set against long, curly blonde hair, and piercing aqua eyes. She fixed them right on Sam, locking them onto his.

He felt helpless in her gaze, unable to look anywhere else.

She was the most beautiful girl he had ever seen.

After several seconds, she took a step forward, and stared even closer into his eyes. She reached out her hand, palm down, clearly expecting him to kiss it. She moved slowly, proudly.

Sam took her hand, and was electrified at the touch of her skin. He pulled her fingertips close, and kissed them.

"Polly?" the girl said. "Aren't you going to introduce us?"

It wasn't a question. It was a command.

Polly cleared her throat, reluctantly.

"Kendra, Sam," she said. "Sam, Kendra."

Kendra, Sam thought, staring into her eyes, taken aback by how aggressively she stared back at him, as if he were already her property.

"Sam," she echoed, smiling. "A bit simple. But I like it."

CHAPTER SIX

Kyle smashed through the stone sarcophagus with a single punch. It smashed into a million bits, and he walked right out of the standing coffin, on his feet, and ready for action.

He wheeled and looked about, ready to fight anyone who approached. In fact, he was hoping that someone approached him for a fight. This time travel had been particularly annoying, and he was ready to let his rage out on someone.

But as he looked around, to his disappointment, he saw that the chamber was empty. It was just him.

Slowly, his rage began to cool. At least he'd landed in the right place, and he could already sense, the right time. He knew that he was more of a veteran of time travel than Caitlin, and he could place himself more specifically. He looked around, and to his satisfaction, saw that he landed exactly where he'd wanted to be: Les Invalides.

Les Invalides was a place he'd always loved, one that had been important to the more evil of his kind. A mausoleum, deep underground, it was made of marble, beautifully adorned, sarcophagi lining its walls. The building had a cylindrical shape, with a soaring, hundred foot ceiling, culminating in a dome. It was a somber place, the perfect resting place for all of France's elite soldiers. It was also the place, Kyle knew, that Napoleon would one day be buried.

But not yet. It was only 1789, and Napoleon, that little bastard, was still alive. One of Kyle's favorites of his own kind. He would be about 20 years old now, Kyle realized, still starting his career. He wouldn't be buried in this place for some time to come. Of course, being of his race, Napoleon's burial was just a ruse, just a way to let the human masses think he was one of theirs.

Kyle smiled at the thought of it. Here he was, in Napoleon's final resting place, before Napoleon had even "died." He would look forward to seeing him again, to reminiscing about old times. He was, after all, one of few people of his kind that Kyle semi-respected. But he was also an arrogant little bastard. Kyle would have to slap him into shape.

Kyle walked slowly across the marble floor, footsteps echoing, and checked himself. He had seen better days. He had lost one eye from that horrible little child, Caleb's son, and his face was still disfigured from what Rexius had done to him back in New York. If that weren't enough, he now had a large wound in his cheek from the spear that Sam had hurled at him in the Colosseum. He was a wreck, he knew.

But he also kind of liked it. He was a survivor. He was alive, and no one had been able to stop him. And he was madder than ever. Not only was he determined to stop Caitlin and Caleb from finding the Shield, but now he was determined to make them both pay. To make them suffer, just as he had suffered. Sam was on his list now, too. All three of them—he would stop at nothing until he tortured each of them slowly.

With a few leaps, Kyle bounded up the marble staircase, and into the upper level of the tomb. He circled around, walking down to the end of the chapel, beneath the huge dome, and reached behind the altar. He felt its limestone wall, searching.

Finally, he found what he was looking for. He pushed a hidden latch, and a secret compartment opened. He reached in, and pulled out a long, silver sword, its hilt encrusted with jewels. He held it up to the light, and studied it with satisfaction. Just as he remembered it.

He slung it over his back, turned, and headed down the corridor, reaching the front door. He leaned back, and with one huge kick, the large oak door when flying off its hinges, the crash of it echoing throughout the empty building. Kyle felt satisfied that he had his full strength back already.

Kyle saw that it was still night, and he relaxed. If he wanted to, he could fly through the night, head right for his target—but he wanted to savor his time. Paris in 1789 was a special place. It was still, he remembered, rife with prostitutes, alcoholics, gamblers, criminals. Despite the nice veneer and architecture, there lived an underbelly that was long and wide. He loved it. The town was his for the taking.

Kyle lifted his chin, listening, sensing, closing his eyes. He could sense Caitlin's presence strongly in this city. And Caleb's. Sam, he wasn't so sure about, but he knew that at least the two of them were here. That was good. Now all he had to do was find them. He would come upon them by surprise, and, he imagined, kill them both quite easily. Paris was a much simpler place. There was no grand vampire Council, like in Rome, that he had to answer to. Even better, there was a strong evil coven here, led by Napoleon. And Napoleon owed him.

Kyle decided that his first order of business would be to track down the little runt and make him reciprocate. He would enlist all of Napoleon's men to do whatever they could to track down Caitlin and Caleb. He knew Napoleon's men could be useful if he should run into resistance. He would leave nothing to chance this time.

But he still had time. He could feed first, and get both his feet planted firmly on the ground. Plus, his plan here was already set in motion. Before he'd left Rome, he'd tracked down his old sidekick, Sergei, and had sent him back here ahead of him. If all had gone as planned, Sergei was here already, and hard at work executing their mission, infiltrating Aiden's coven. Kyle smiled wide. There was nothing he loved more than a traitor, than a little weasel like Sergei. He had become a most useful plaything.

Kyle bounded down the steps like a schoolboy, filled with joy, ready to plunge right into the city, to take whatever he wanted.

As Kyle headed down the street, a street artist approached him, holding out a canvas and brush, gesturing for Kyle to allow him to paint his picture. If there was anything Kyle hated, it was someone wanting to draw his picture. He was in such a good mood, though, he decided to let the man live.

But when the man pressed his case, following Kyle aggressively, thrusting his canvas towards him, he pushed it too far. Kyle reached over, grabbed his brush, and jabbed it right between the man's eyes. A second later, the man dropped dead.

Kyle took the canvas and tore it up over his corpse.

Kyle continued on, quite happy with himself. This was already turning out to be a great night.

As he turned down a cobblestone alley, heading into the district he remembered, everything began to feel familiar again. Several prostitutes lined the streets, beckoning him. At the same time, two large men stumbled out of a bar, clearly drunk, and bumped hard into Kyle, not looking where they were going.

"Hey, you jerk!" one of them yelled at him.

The other turned to Kyle. "Hey, one-eye!" he yelled. "Watch where you're going!"

The big man reached out to give Kyle a hard shove to the chest.

But his eyes opened wide in surprise when his shove didn't work. Kyle hadn't been budged at all; it had been like pushing a stone wall.

Kyle shook his head slowly, amazed at the stupidity of these men. Before they could react, he reached back over his shoulder, extracted his sword with a cling, and in one motion, swung it, chopping off both their heads in a fraction of a second.

He watched with satisfaction as their heads rolled, and both of their bodies began to slump to the ground. He put back his sword, and reached out and pulled a headless corpse to him. He sunk his long fangs right into the open neck, and drank hardily as the blood squirted.

Kyle could hear the screaming of the prostitutes erupt all around him, as they saw what had happened. This was followed by the sound of doors slamming, window shutters closing.

The whole town was already scared of him, he realized.

Good, he thought. This was the sort of welcome he loved.

CHAPTER SEVEN

Caitlin and Caleb flew away from Paris, over the French countryside in the early morning, she holding tightly onto his back as he cut through the air. She felt stronger now, and felt that if she wanted to fly, she could. But she didn't want to let go of him. She loved the feel of his body. She just wanted to hold him, to feel what it was like to be together again. She knew it was crazy, but after being apart for so long, she had a fear that if she let him go, he might fly away forever.

Beneath them, the landscape was ever-changing. Pretty quickly the city fell away and the landscape shifted to dense woods and rolling hills. Closer to the city, there were occasional houses, farms. But the further they got, the more the land opened. They passed field after field, rolling meadows, an occasional farm, sheep grazing. Smoke rose from chimneys, and she guessed that people were cooking. Clotheslines spread out over lawns, and sheets hung from them. It was an idyllic scene, and the July temperature had dropped just enough so that the cooler air, especially up this high, was refreshing.

After hours of flying, they rounded a bend, and the new view took Caitlin's breath away: there, on the horizon, sat a shimmering sea, vibrant blue, its waves smashing into an endless, pristine shoreline. As they got closer, the elevation rose, and rolling hills went right up to the shoreline.

Nestled in the rolling hills, amidst the tall grass, she saw a single building set against the horizon. It was a glorious, medieval castle, designed of an antique limestone, covered in ornate sculptures and gargoyles. It was nestled high on a hill, overlooking the sea, and surrounded by fields of wildflowers as far as the eye could see. It was breathtakingly beautiful, and Caitlin felt as if she were in a postcard.

Caitlin's heart beat with excitement, as she wondered, as she hoped to dream, that this could be Caleb's place. Somehow, she felt that it was.

"Yes," he called out, over the wind, reading her mind, as always. "This is it."

Caitlin's heart pounded with delight. She was so excited, and felt so strong, she was ready to fly by herself.

She suddenly jumped off of Caleb's back, and went flying through the air. For a moment, she was terrified, wondering if her wings would sprout. A moment later, they did, supporting her in the air.

As the air ran through them, she loved the feeling. It felt great to have them again, to be independent. She rose and dove, swooping up, close to Caleb, who smiled back. They dove down together, then up, swerving in and out of each other's flight paths, the tips of their wings sometimes touching.

As one, they dove down, closer to the castle. It looked ancient; it felt worn in, but not in a bad way. For Caitlin, it already felt like home.

As she took it all in, looked at the landscape, the rolling hills, the distant ocean, for the first time in as long as she could remember, she felt a sense of peace. She felt, finally, like she was home. She saw her life together with Caleb here, living together, even starting a family together again, if that was possible. She would be happy to live out her days here with him—and finally, at long last, she didn't see anything that stood in their way.

*

Caitlin and Caleb landed together in front of his castle, and he took her hand and led her to the front door. The oak door was covered in a thick layer of dust and sea salt, and clearly hadn't been opened in years. He tried the knob. It was locked.

"It's been hundreds of years," he said. "I'm pleasantly surprised to find that it's still here, that it hasn't been vandalized—that it's even still locked. There used to be a key…"

He reached up, way above the door frame, and felt the crevice behind the stone arch. He ran his fingers up and down it, and finally stopped, extracting a long, silver skeleton key.

He slipped into the lock, and it fit perfectly. He turned it with a click.

He turned and smiled at her, stepping aside. "You do the honors," he said.

Caitlin pushed the heavy, medieval door, and it opened slowly, creaking, encrusted salt falling off in clumps as it did.

They walked in together. The entry room was dim, and covered in cobwebs. The air was still and dank, and it felt like it hadn't been entered in centuries. She looked up at the high, arched stone walls, the stone floors. There were layers of dust on everything, including the glass windows, which blocked a lot of the light, making it seem darker than it was.

"This way," Caleb said.

He took her hand and led her down a narrow corridor, and it opened up into a grand hall, with high, arched windows on both sides. It was much lighter in here, even with the dust. There was some furniture left over in here, too: a long, medieval oak table, surrounded by ornate, wooded chairs. At its center sat a huge, marble mantel, one of the largest fireplaces Caitlin had ever seen. It was incredible. Caitlin felt as if she had walked right back into the Cloisters.

"I had it built in the 12th century," he said, looking around himself. "Back then, this was the style."

"You lived here?" Caitlin asked.

He nodded.

"For how long?"

He thought. "Not more than a century," he said. "Maybe two."

Caitlin marveled, once again, at the huge increments of time in the vampire world.

Suddenly, though, she got worried, as she thought of something else: had he lived here with another woman?

She was afraid to ask.

He suddenly turned and looked at her.

"No, I did not," he said. "I lived here alone. I assure you. You're the first woman I've ever taken here."

Caitlin felt relieved, though embarrassed at his reading her mind.

"Come on," he said. "This way."

He led her up a spiral stone staircase, and it twisted and turned, and let them out on the second floor. This floor was much brighter, with large, arched windows facing every direction, sunlight pouring in, reflecting the distant sea. The rooms were smaller here, more intimate. There were more marble fireplaces, and as Caitlin wandered from room to room, she saw a huge four-poster bed dominating one of them. Chaise lounges and overstuffed velvet chairs, were spread throughout the other rooms. There were no rugs, just a bare stone floor. It was very stark. But beautiful.

He led her across the room, to a set of huge, glass doors. They'd been covered in so much dust, she hadn't even known they were there. He stepped up and tugged hard at the locks and knobs, and finally, with a bang and a cloud of dust, they opened.

He stepped outside, and Caitlin followed.

They stepped out onto a huge, stone terrace, framed by an ornate limestone, column railing. They walked together up to the edge, and looked out.

From here, they had a commanding view of the entire countryside, of the ocean. Caitlin could hear the crashing of the waves, and smell the sea heavy in the air on the rolling breezes. She felt like she were in heaven.

If Caitlin had ever imagined a dream house, this would definitely be it. It was dusty, and it needed a woman's touch, but Caitlin knew that they could fix it up, could get it to the state that it once was. She felt that this was truly a place they could call home together.

"I was thinking about what you said," he said, "the entire flight here. About our building a life together. I would like that very much."

He put an arm around her.

"I would like for you to live here with me. For us to start our life over again. Right here. It's quiet here, and safe, and protected. No one knows about this place. No one will ever find us here. I see no reason why we can't live out our lives safely, as regular people," he said. "Of course, it will need a lot of work to fix it up. But I'm game, if you are."

He turned and smiled at her.

She smiled back. She had never been more game in her life.

More than that, she felt deeply touched that he'd invited her to live with him. Nothing had ever meant more to her. The truth was, she would have lived with them anywhere, even if it was just a hut in the woods.

"I'd love to," she answered. "I just want to be with you."

Her heart pounded as they came together in a kiss, the sound of the waves in the background, the ocean breezes rolling over them.

Finally, everything was perfect in her world again.

*

Caitlin had never been so happy as she ambled through the house, going room to room, carrying a washcloth. Caleb had left, had gone out hunting, excited to bring them both home dinner. She was thrilled, because it gave her some time alone to walk through the house, to take it all in, by herself, and to look at it, with a woman's eye, for how she could fix it up and make it a home for them both.

She walked through the rooms, opening windows, letting in the ocean air. She'd found a pail and rag and had gone down to the stream she'd seen running through the backyard, and had returned with an overflowing pail full of water. She'd run the rag through the stream until it was as clean as could be. She'd found a large crate to stand on, and as she opened each of the huge, medieval windows, she stood up on the crate, and wiped each pane. There were a few windows which were simply too high for her to reach, and for these, she activated her wings, fluttering high in the air, and hovering before the windows as she cleaned them.

She was shocked at the immediate difference it made. The room transformed from being dark to being completely flooded with light. There must've been hundreds of years of caked dirt and salt on both sides of the pane. Indeed, just opening each window was a feat in itself, taking all her might to yank them free of rust and debris.

Caitlin looked carefully and was in awe at the craftsmanship of each window. Each window pane was several inches thick, and had the most beautiful design. Some of the glass was stained, some was clear, and some had the slightest tint of color. As she wiped each one down, she could almost feel the house's gratitude, as it slowly, inch by inch, came back to life.

Caitlin finally finished and surveyed it again. She was shocked. What had before been a dark, uninviting room, was now an incredible, sun-filled room, with a view of the ocean.

Caitlin turned to the floors next, getting down on her hands and knees and scrubbing them foot by foot. She watched with satisfaction as inches of dirt came off, and the beautiful, huge stones began to shine through.

After that, she turned to the enormous marble mantelpiece, wiping off years of dust. Then she turned to the huge, ornate mirror above it, wiping it down until it shone. She was bummed that she could still not see her reflection—but she knew there was little she could do about that.

She turned to the chandelier next, wiping each and every one of its crystal laden candle holders. After that, she set her sights on the four-poster bed. She wiped down each of its posts, and then its frame, slowly bringing back to life the ancient wood. She grabbed the aging blankets and went to the terrace and shook them hard, clouds of dust flying everywhere.

Caitlin returned to the room, her would-be bedroom, and surveyed it: it was now magnificent. It shone as brightly as any room in any castle. It was still medieval, but at least now it was fresh and inviting. Her heart soared at the idea of living here.

She looked down and realized that the water in the bucket had turned completely black, and bounded down the steps and out the door, eager to refill it in the stream.

Caitlin smiled as she thought of what Caleb's reaction would be when he came back. He would be so surprised, she thought. She would clean out the dining room next. She'd try to create an intimate environment in which they could have their first meal together in a new home—the first, she hoped, of many.

As Caitlin arrived at the waterbank, sinking to her knees in the soft grass, emptying and filling the bucket, she suddenly felt her senses on high alert. She heard a rustling noise, close by, and sensed an animal approaching her.

She quickly spun, and was surprised at what she saw.

Approaching her slowly, just feet away, was a wolf pup. Its fur was all white, except for a single streak of gray running down its forehead and back. What struck Caitlin most was its eyes: they stared back at Caitlin as if it knew her. What's more: they were the same eyes as Rose.

Caleb felt her heart pounding. She felt as if Rose had come back from the dead, had been reincarnated in some other animal. That expression, that face. The fur color was different, but otherwise, this could have been Rose reborn.

The wolf pup, too, seemed startled to see Caitlin. It stopped, staring at her, then slowly, cautiously, took a few tentative steps towards her. Caitlin scanned the woods, looking to see if other pups were around, or its mother. She didn't want to end up in a fight.

But there was no other animal anywhere in sight.

As Caitlin examined the pup more closely, she saw why. It was limping badly, blood coming from its paw. It look injured. It had probably been abandoned by its mom, Caitlin realized, left to die.

The wolf pup lowered its head, and walked slowly, right up to Caitlin. Then, to Caitlin's surprise, it lowered its head and rested it in her lap, whining softly as it closed its eyes.

Caitlin's heart leapt. She had missed Rose so badly, and now she felt as if she'd come back to her.

Caitlin set the bucket down, reached out, and took the pup in her arms. She held it close to her chest, crying as she did, remembering all the time she'd spent with Rose. Despite herself, the tears rolled down her cheeks. The pup, as if sensing it, suddenly looked up at her, leaned back, and licked the tears from her face.

Caitlin leaned down and kissed it on its forehead. She held it tight, cuddling it to her chest. There was no way she could let it go. She would do whatever she had to to help it heal and bring it back to life. And, if the wolf wanted, to keep her as a pet.

"What shall I call you?" Caitlin asked. "We can't do Rose again….How about…Ruth?"

The pup suddenly licked Caitlin's cheek, as if responding to the name. That was as definitive an answer as Caitlin could have asked for.

Ruth it was.

*

Caitlin, Ruth at her side, had just finished cleaning the dining room, when she spotted something interesting along the wall. There, beside the fireplace, were two long, silver swords. She picked up one of them, dusted it off, and admired the hilt, encrusted with jewels. It was a beautiful weapon. She set down the rag and pail, and couldn't resist giving it a go. She swung the sword wildly, left and right in circles, switching hands, all throughout the cavernous room. It felt great.

She wondered how many other weapons Caleb had here. She could have a field day training with them.

"I see you found the weapons," Caleb said, suddenly walking in the door. Caitlin immediately set down the sword, self-conscious.

"Sorry, didn't mean to pry into your stuff."

Caleb laughed. "My house is yours," he said, as he walked into the room carrying two huge deer slung over his shoulder. "Whatever I have, you're welcome to. Besides, you're a girl after my own heart. I would have went right for the swords, too," he said with a wink.

He strutted through the room, carrying the deer, then suddenly stopped and turned, doing a double take.

"Wow," he said, in shock. "It looks like a new place!"

He stood there, staring, wide-eyed. Caitlin could see how impressed he was, and she felt happy. She looked at the room herself, and saw that it was indeed transformed. They now had a gorgeous, dining room, replete with table and chairs for their first meal.

Ruth suddenly whined, and Caleb looked down, and saw her for the first time. He looked even more surprised.

Caitlin suddenly worried if he'd mind having the pup here.

But she was relieved to see that his eyes opened wide in delight.

"I can't believe it," Caleb said, staring, "those eyes...she looks just like Rose."

"Can we keep her?" Caitlin asked, hesitantly.

"I'd love to," he answered. "I'd give her a hug, but my hands are full."

Caleb continued with the deer, through the room, and down the corridor. Caitlin and Ruth followed him, and watched him set down the deer in a small room, atop a huge slab of stone.

"Since we don't really cook," he said, "I thought I'd drain the blood for us. Then we could drink together, for dinner. I thought I'd take care of the messy work in here, so we could just sit before the fireplace and drink in style."

"I'd like that," Caitlin said.

Ruth sat at Caleb's heels, looking up and whining as he carved. He laughed, cut a small piece for her, and reached down and fed it to her. She snapped it up and whined for more.

Caitlin headed back to the dining area, and began wiping down the goblets she'd seen. Before the mantle sat a pile of furs, and she gathered them up and took them out to the terrace, shaking them out in preparation.

While Caitlin waited for Caleb to finish, she looked out at the sunset, breaking over the horizon. She could hear the sound of the waves, breathed in the salt air, and had never felt more relaxed. She stood there and closed her eyes, and she wasn't even aware of how much time had passed.

When Caitlin opened her eyes again, it was nearly dark.

"Caitlin?" came the voice, calling out for her.

She turned and hurried back inside. Caleb was already in there, carrying two huge silver goblets of the venison blood. He was in the process of lighting candles, all throughout the dim room. She came over and joined him, setting the furs back down.

Within moments, the room was completely lit, glowing with candlelight in every direction. The two of them sat together on the furs, before the fireplace, and Ruth ran up and set beside them. The windows were open and a breeze wafted through, and it was actually getting cool in here.

The two of them sat beside each other, and looked into each other's eyes as they toasted.

The liquid felt so good. She drank and drank, as he did, and she had never felt so alive. It was an incredible rush.

Caleb looked rejuvenated, too, his eyes and skin shining. They turned and faced each other.

He reached up, and slowly touched her cheek with the back of his hand.

Caitlin's heart started to pound, and she realized she was nervous. It felt like it had been forever since she had last been with him. She had imagined a moment like this for so long, but now that it was here, she felt like it was her first time with him, all over again. She could see that his hand was trembling, and she realized he was nervous, too.

There remained so many things she wanted to say, so many questions she had for him, and she could see that he was brimming with questions, too. But at this moment, she didn't trust herself to speak. And apparently, he didn't either.

The two of them kissed passionately. As his lips met hers, she felt overwhelmed with emotion for him.

She closed her eyes as he came in closer, as they met in a passionate embrace. They rolled onto the furs, and she felt her heart surge with emotion.

Finally, he was hers.

CHAPTER EIGHT

Polly strode quickly down the corridors of Versailles, heels echoing on the marble floor, rushing down an endless corridor with soaring ceilings, moldings, marble fireplaces, enormous mirrors, and chandeliers hanging low. Everything shone.

But she barely noticed it; it was second-nature to her. Living here for years, she could hardly imagine any other form of existence.

What she did notice, though—very much—was Sam. A visitor like him was not at all a part of daily life—and, in fact, was most unusual. They hardly ever had vampire visitors, especially from another time, and when they did, Aiden never seemed to care. Sam must be very important, she realized. He intrigued her. He seemed a bit young, and he seemed to be bumble around a bit.

But there was something about him, something she couldn't quite place. She felt like, somehow, she had some connection to him, that she'd met him before, or that he was connected to someone who was important to her.

Which was so strange, because just the night before, she'd had the most vivid dream. About a vampire girl named Caitlin. She could see her face, her eyes, her hair, even now. In the dream, she was told that this girl had been her best friend for life, and throughout the dream, it seemed like they were friends forever. She woke up feeling it was so real, that it was more a meeting than a dream. She couldn't understand it, but she woke up remembering everything about this girl, remembering all the times they'd spent together.

It didn't make any sense, because Polly knew she'd never been to any of those places. She wondered if maybe, somehow, she had been looking into the future? She knew that vampires visited each other in dreams, and that they occasionally had the power to see into the future and the past. But these powers were also unpredictable. It could be a world of illusions. One never knew: was one seeing the future, seeing the past, and was one merely dreaming?

After the dream, Polly had awakened looking for Caitlin, as if she really knew her. She found herself missing her as she walked down the hall. It was crazy. Missing a girl she'd never even met.

And then this boy showed up, Sam. And for some crazy reason, Polly felt his energy to be connected to hers. How, she couldn't possibly know. Was she just imagining that, too?

Aside from all of this, she found herself feeling something for Sam. She wouldn't say that she was head over heels for him. But she was not unattracted to him either. There was something about him. It wasn't the feeling of being in love. It was more a feeling of being…intrigued. Wanting to know more.

Which made her all the more agitated that Kendra had already laid her eyes upon him. Not necessarily that she wanted him for himself. It was way too early for her to know that. But more because he seemed so innocent, naïve, impressionable. And Kendra was a vulture. She was a member of the royal family, one who had never been told No in her life, and she had a magical way of getting whatever she wanted, from whomever she wanted.

Polly had always sensed that Kendra had some sort of sinister agenda. For years, she'd been trying to get every vampire in her coven to turn her. Of course, it was forbidden, and no one would oblige her. But now, she could tell, she'd set her sights on Sam. Fresh blood had arrived, and she was determined to try again. Polly shivered, not liking the idea of what could happen to Sam if Kendra was determined.

Yes, this was certainly an unusual day for her. Her mind swarmed with emotions as she marched down the hall, and she realized she was already late. The new singer everyone had been talking about was giving a private concert for Marie and her entourage. The singer had been here for weeks, and all the other girls were going on about not only his voice, but his looks. She was eager to get a glimpse of him for herself. Polly had been looking forward to this, and now she was doubly annoyed that she'd come in at the tail end of it.

That was the problem with this place, she thought, as she marched down yet another corridor. It was just too big. It was impossible to get anywhere on time.

Polly stepped up her pace, and finally reached the end of another corridor, and two guards opened the immense double doors for her. She walked right through, and as they closed behind her, she was immediately embarrassed.

The entire room turned and looked at her; as the singer continued his performance, she realized she'd interrupted the concert. Her face reddened, as she sank to the back of the room, taking a seat among her friends.

Everyone turned back slowly, and as they did, she settled in, and realized the concert was almost over.

She looked up, and watched, and as she caught the first glimpse of the singer's face, she was shocked. He was even more gorgeous than everyone had said. He had dark features, with dark eyes and dark, wavy hair. His face was perfectly chiseled. He was so regally dressed, from head to toe, in a black velvet coat, with white stockings, and shiny black shoes. He stood in the center of the small stage, and looked so confident, so in control. He looked like he might be…Russian.

But even more than that: his voice was mesmerizing. As he sang, Polly was transfixed. She was completely riveted, helpless to do anything but listen, helpless to look anywhere else.

Polly was lost in a daze as the singing ended, still staring, still hearing his final notes, while everyone else got up, clapping, and approached him. The entire room crowded around him, and he stood there, smiling, basking in the attention.

Polly slowly made her way through the crowd. She could see the adoration of all the other girls, and she stepped up herself and took a look.

He turned and looked at her, fixing his eyes on her. He seemed to look at her with a bit of disdain, with a brazen, arrogant look, as if to say suggest that she should look up to him.

"I…enjoyed your concert," Polly said, realizing she was nervous.

"Of course you did," he said. "Why wouldn't you?"

The other girls giggled, and Polly thought his comment was somewhat rude. Still, she couldn't bring herself to look away.

"Well, if you're just going to stare like that, you might as well tell me your name," he said.

Polly stammered, caught off guard. No one had ever talked to her like that before. Part of her told her she should just walk away; but another part just couldn't bring herself to.

"Polly," she said breathlessly.

"Polly," he mimicked back, with a giggle. "Like a bird."

Polly reddened, as the other girls giggled. She did not know whether she was in love with this man, or hated him. How could he be so arrogant?

"Well, Polly," he said, with a faint accent, "I'll have you know my name."

He slowly held out his hand, which was pale and soft, like a girl's.

"Sergei," he announced proudly, as if she should be thrilled to know it.

She took her hand in his, staring, unable to look away.

"Sergei," she repeated, breathlessly.

And despite herself, despite the fact that he suddenly turned away and talked to the other girls, despite every red flag that screamed for her to walk away, she knew that she was already, hopelessly, in love.

CHAPTER NINE

Caitlin woke gently, slowly opening her eyes, feeling completely rested and relaxed. It was the first night in as long as she could remember in which she hadn't dreamt of her father—in fact, in which she hadn't dreamt at all. It was also the first time night in as long as she could remember in which she hadn't been awakened abruptly, when she was able to sleep as long as she would like.

Caitlin woke to sunlight streaming in through the windows on all sides of her, and to the sound, through the open windows, of crashing waves. She could smell the fresh ocean pouring through the room.

She looked over and realized she was sleeping with her head resting on Caleb's chest. They were both undressed, under the covers, and she was sleeping in his arms.

She looked up, and saw that his eyes were closed, and he was still fast asleep.

For the first time in as long as she could remember, Caitlin felt completely at ease. Here, in this place, in this time, in Caleb's arms, she felt that nothing could ever go wrong. She wanted to freeze the moment, to hold onto it. Finally, it felt like there was nothing threatening on the horizon, nothing looming that could make life change.

Caitlin looked around the room, and glanced at the silver case with her father's letter inside, still unopened. As she looked at it, she had a moment of worry: she felt that if she opened it, if she read it, it would lead her somewhere, and things would change. She looked away from it, more determined than ever *not* to open it.

She got up from bed and walked across the room, her bare feet nice and cool on the stone, and took the bejeweled case, and hid it behind a drape. She didn't want to look at it. She didn't want anything to change. She was *determined* for nothing to change.

Caitlin slowly got dressed, putting on the new clothes that the nun had given her. She had washed them the night before in the stream, and had hung them out to dry on the edge of a gargoyle outside her window. She was surprised by how fast they had dried, how fresh they had become, as she put them back on. She felt ready to face the day.

Caitlin had to figure out what to do to replace her wardrobe. Now that she was finally settled—and in an enormous castle with endless closet space—she was sure she could figure something out. If need be, she would take up sewing, knitting—whatever was necessary. With all the sheep everywhere, she was sure there had to be a local farmer who sold some kind of clothing. It wouldn't be 21st century fashion, but then again, that wasn't what she wanted. She wanted to blend in, to become a part of this time, this place, these people. More than anything, she just wanted to live here, to make this her home. Whatever they wore, she would be happy to wear, too.

Caitlin opened the huge double glass doors, and stepped out onto the patio. The sun-baked stone felt nice on her feet, and she lifted her chin and felt herself being warmed by the sun. The nun had given her fresh skin wraps, and fresh drops for her eyes, and the sun didn't bother her at all. On the contrary, it felt good.

She walked to the edge of the banister, placed her hands on it, and gazed out at the horizon. She was caressed by the ocean breezes as she looked out at the endless blue sky, past the rolling hills, and saw the waves crashing in the distance. The beach was completely empty. This seemed to be such a remote place, she wondered if anyone ever came to the beach.

"There you are," came the voice.

Caitlin turned, and was delighted to see Caleb up, already dressed, heading towards her.

He walked right up to her, a huge smile on his face, and she broke into a smile, too. She took two steps towards him, and they met in a long kiss, followed by a hug.

It felt so good to be in his arms, especially first thing in the morning.

Slowly, they pulled back and looked into each other's eyes.

"I dreamt of you," he said.

"Good dreams, I hope."

He smiled wider. "Of course."

She was curious what he'd dreamt, but he didn't offer any more, and she didn't want to pry. That was the thing about Caleb: he could sometimes mysteriously fall into silence, and it was sometimes hard to read his thoughts. Of course, they both had the power to read each other's thoughts, but she also noticed that, paradoxically, when they were at their closest, it became harder to hear what each other was thinking. It was almost as if the more in love they were, the more that their power was obscured the power. As if certain things were meant to be kept hidden.

She desperately wanted to know everything he was thinking now, but again, she found his thoughts obscured.

She took his hand, and they walked together to the balcony, looking out.

"I love it here," she said. "I'm already thinking of all the ways we can fix it up."

As she spoke the words, she noticed the smile on his face drop, ever so slightly. It was a subtle change of expression, but she was close to enough to him now that she could see it. She also felt the grip of his hand loosen, just the slightest bit. She couldn't read his mind, but as a woman, she could sense the slightest pulling away.

Why? she wondered.

"That would be great," he said.

But there was something in the tone of his voice, some subtle thing she detected, that told her that something was bothering him. That he was troubled by something.

Was she imagining it?

What had gone wrong? she wondered. *Is he changing his mind about us?*

She stared at him, looking into his eyes, which looked off at the horizon, trying to figure out what he was thinking.

"Are you happy to be back here?" she asked, gently prying.

"Yes, very much," he answered.

She wanted to say: *Then why do I see sadness behind your eyes? Is it me? Do you not love me as much as you thought?*

But she was too scared to say it. And she didn't want to push him away.

So instead, Caitlin fell silent. But she felt her heart slowly beginning to break.

She thought back on their relationship, of all the places they'd been. New York City. Boston. Edgartown. Venice. Rome. They had always been on the run; there had never been time for them just to be quiet, to be together. To enjoy themselves as a couple.

Now, that time had come. Maybe now that there were no more obstacles, that there was nothing between them, it was not as exciting for him. Maybe he was scared by being so close. Maybe the only thing that had made him love her, she worried, had been the circumstances, the fact that they could not be together.

Maybe now that they were together, he didn't know what to do.

And was Caleb really the type of man that could live a domestic life, not on the run, not heading into battle? Content to just sit there and make a home and live in it?

She started to worry. Maybe he wasn't. After all, look at how he had lived his life for the last thousand years. How could he possibly change all that now? Just for her?

Or, Caitlin wondered, was her mind just playing tricks on her? Was she just imagining the whole thing? Was she blowing it all out of proportion? Was she just being too sensitive, looking into things that weren't there? After all, he did say it would be great. Had he really meant it?

Caitlin knew she had to get the bottom of this. She couldn't live a lie. If for some reason he wasn't interested in her, she had to know. She *had* to.

She felt herself slowly shaking, as she geared up to ask.

"Caleb," she began softly, her throat going dry, her voice trembling, "Is everything okay?"

He looked at her, as if puzzled.

"You seem…sad," she said. "Like you're not entirely happy."

"I…" he began, then trailed off. He stopped himself, and sighed deeply. "I am very happy to be with you."

That was all he could say. And it sounded forced to her.

"Would you excuse me for just one moment?" he asked politely.

Caitlin nodded back, too upset to speak.

And with those few words, he turned and walked off the patio, and was soon out of sight.

Where had he gone? Why had he suddenly left?

Caitlin had no idea, but it confirmed her suspicions. He couldn't just stand there, with her, and enjoy the view. Something was going on inside him. Something strong enough to make him want to walk away.

Caitlin slowly felt her world shattering.

What could it possibly be?

Then it dawned on her. Sera. The last time Caitlin had seen him, he'd been married to her. Maybe it was still fresh in his mind. Did he still have feelings for her? Was he thinking of her right now? Did their sleeping together last night bring back his feelings for her?

That must be it, Caitlin realized. She couldn't imagine any other explanation. Caleb must miss her. She was on his mind. Maybe he was gearing up to tell her that he had to leave, to go find Sera.

Caitlin couldn't read his mind, but she was a woman after all. And like any other woman, she felt her heart beginning to break into a million little pieces.

*

Caleb hurried off the balcony and through the rooms of his castle, overcome by emotion. Despite himself, he couldn't stop thinking about his son, Jade. He couldn't stop flashing back to the image of holding his dead body in his arms.

As he walked quickly into the other room, he burst into tears. He couldn't let Caitlin see him like this. He'd had to get away from her quickly.

He had loved Jade so much. The boy was just like him in so many ways, and had been growing not only into a fine warrior, but into a fine young man. Caleb had never imagined not spending a life without him in it.

Now, he felt the grief of it suddenly weighing on him heavily. Once Jade had passed, Caleb had no regrets about coming back in time. On the contrary, he was thrilled to be away from Sera, whom he was never really close with, and thrilled to be back with Caitlin. He was thrilled to have had a chance to save her in the Colosseum, and thrilled to be at her side now. In fact, it was the only thing that was keeping him going.

He been so caught up in the whirlwind of events, in finding her and bringing her to this place, that he'd not had a moment until now to really feel the impact of Jade's loss. But now it came out of nowhere, when he least expected it, and it overwhelmed him. Which was why he'd left Caitlin's side so quickly. It was her first day here, they had just had an amazing night together, and he wanted her to be happy. He didn't want to drag her down into his sadness.

Caleb walked from one room to the next, then went through a hidden door, leading to a narrow twisting staircase. He took it up, turning and twisting, heading up a small circular turret to the third and highest floor of the castle. Here, at the top, was a small sitting room, an open-air, stone gazebo, which he used to retreat to in times of worry. He sat on the ledge of the stone, in a well-worn groove, and looked out at the ocean.

He reflected on his life. He was happy to be here, in this time and place. He was happy beyond belief to be with Caitlin again. He was racked by grief over Jade, but the more he sat, calmly listening, the more he felt that Jade was still with him, even now. He knew that he could not travel forward in time, and he knew he could not see him again. He realized, with resolve, that he just had to accept how things were now, and let him go. He breathed deeply, slowly starting to feel better.

The more he thought about it, the more he realized that he wanted to have another child. This time, with Caitlin. The child that they never had. He knew that it was impossible for two vampires to have a child. But maybe, just maybe, there was some way.

Ever since he'd seen her again, he'd been trying to find a moment to tell her how much he cared for her. And to tell her that he wanted to spend the rest of his life with her.

He was about to raise the topic, in Paris, by the river, but he'd gotten nervous at the last second, and hadn't been able to summon the courage to tell her.

But now that he was here, in this place, the timing felt right to him.

He searched the walls of the stone gazebo, looking for the secret compartment that he remembered.

He ran his fingers along the stone, and eventually he found it. He pushed the lever, and a small crack opened in the stone. He pulled it with his fingertips, and a stone loosened.

Caleb reached in, and found what he was looking for. He had placed it here, hundreds of years ago. It was a small, silver box, encrusted with jewels.

Inside it, was his mother's wedding ring.

She had given it to him once, and had told him to only give it to the one he truly loved, the one that he was sure he would be with forever. Being of his race, "forever" took on a whole new meaning.

Caleb had never given it to Sera, despite their marriage. Somehow, something inside him had prevented him from doing so. Somehow, even then, he knew it was not a relationship that was meant to last.

But with Caitlin, things were different. He wanted her to have this ring. He was certain that he wanted to spend the rest of his life with her. And now, he felt ready.

It was time for him to propose.

Caleb slowly opened the box, hoping the ring was still there.

It was. It was as magnificent as he remembered: a huge, six carat sapphire, perfectly cut, mounted on a band of sparkling rubies and diamonds.

He felt overwhelmed with emotion, as he thought of his mother, of Jade, and now, of Caitlin.

Of the family they might one day, some way, have together.

Now, he only hoped that she would say Yes.

*

Caitlin walked through the entire house again, looking everywhere for Caleb. She was baffled as to where he might have gone.

Just then, she heard a creaking door, and saw him coming down from a spiral staircase. She hadn't even known that staircase existed. She realized he had been coming from the roof, and wondered why he would go up there.

And then she realized. There was no reason why he would, unless he wanted to get as far away from her as he could. To be alone. Her presence was bothering him, she realized. He wanted to distance himself from her, perhaps even prepare himself to tell her something she did not want to here. That he had changed his mind about their living together. Like asking her to leave.

Caitlin felt her heart sink, as Caleb approached and as she caught a glimpse of his troubled face. She felt that he was getting ready to break up with her. He was going to tell her that he had invited her here too quickly, that he hadn't really thought it through. That it had all happened too fast. That he wasn't cut out for domestic life. That he wanted her to leave.

As he walked closer, she could see the redness in his eyes, and her heart pounded. Had he been crying? Then there was no doubt about it. He was bracing himself to tell her something that she did not want to hear.

Caitlin felt herself trembling with upset.

"Caitlin," he said softly, looking down at the floor.

He could not even look her in the eye. That could only mean one thing.

Caitlin had never felt more upset. Where would she go now?

"Caitlin—" he began again.

But she held out a hand, and stopped him. Whatever words he was about to speak, she didn't want to hear them. She didn't want to have his words of rejection echoing in her mind forever.

"I know what you're going to say," she said, her voice shaking.

His eyes opened wide in surprise. "You do?" he asked.

Caitlin nodded. "And I don't want to hear it."

Caleb looked disappointed. She couldn't understand why. She was saving him the trouble of having to break up with her.

"I'm sorry this all happened so fast," Caitlin said. "Maybe if it happened slower, things would've worked out better."

Caleb looked puzzled.

"Don't worry," she said. "I'm leaving now."

And with those words, she turned and marched out on him.

"Caitlin!" he called out behind her.

But she didn't want to hear it. She didn't want to hear him tell her that he loved her, but that he loved Sera more. She couldn't bear to hear those words.

Caitlin found herself crying as she hurried through the main hall and then out the door of his house that she had grown to love so quickly.

She looked down and saw Ruth at her feet, whining, and she picked her up, and held her tight, kissing her, as tears ran down her cheeks.

Caleb followed her out the front door.

"Caitlin, wait, please!"

But she couldn't. She took a few running steps and leapt into the air, Ruth in her arms, and within moments, she was flying, flying, far away from this place.

CHAPTER TEN

Kyle strutted right down the middle of a wide, cobblestone boulevard, late at night, cutting through the center of Paris. He felt relatively satisfied, having just come from the red light district, and having fed on several more prostitutes. He could still feel their blood swirling through his veins, and slowly, he was beginning to feel himself again.

He hated time travel. Hated it. And he hated Caitlin for making him do this. He thought of all the fun he was missing back in New York, of the raging war—*his* war—and fumed at her. He fantasized of all the ways he would exact revenge upon her. Gradually, his spirits began to lift.

Kyle turned down alleyway after alleyway, keeping an eye open for any more victims, but finding the streets empty. It was nearly daybreak, and it seemed most people had gone to sleep. He had already drank his fill. If he killed any more victims at this point, it would just be for pure recreation.

Kyle thought back, through thousands of years, when he and his friends would go hunting humans for recreation. Those were the days. He remembered times when they would fill the streets with corpses, not even bothering to feed. They had such fun watching them die. It had been one of his favorite games.

Nowadays, vampires were so conservative. They only killed to feed. And they only fed as much as they had to. When Kyle killed Caitlin and figured out a way to return to the future, things would change. He would make killing humans a national sport once again.

Kyle turned down the street, and finally found what he was looking for: a massive, round building, with huge stone columns and marble steps. It had a grand dome, and looked ancient. In fact, it didn't look that different from the Pantheon in Rome. Which was fitting, because this was a Pantheon, too. The Pantheon of Paris.

Kyle remembered the building well. It was an important place for his coven, a place they had always been. It was very different from the Pantheon in Rome: the vampires here were much more chaotic, more disorderly, more democratic. In New York, or Rome, if someone stepped out of line, the leaders would step forward and have them killed on the spot. Here, the covens were run by committee. On the one hand, Kyle respected that, because he hated authority. On the other, he also enjoyed watching people get punished who were out of line, and watching them get killed before his eyes.

Kyle thought of his old friend Napoleon, and guessed that he'd already have taken control of this coven. They were probably all inside it, arguing about something right now. They were a contentious bunch.

Kyle bounded up the marble steps three at a time, eager to see him, to let them know who was boss. Napoleon had power, but not nearly as much as Kyle. After all, Kyle had survived for thousands of years, while Napoleon was still a child.

Kyle kicked open the massive doors and strutted inside.

As he suspected, the huge marble building was completely packed with his own kind. It was chaotic. The enormous, marble room was shaped in a circle, with huge columns framing it in every direction. It had a marble floor, and an arched ceiling, culminating in an oculus. It was as grand as the Pantheon in Rome.

Except this one was filled with vampires screaming and yelling over each other, pushing and shoving. As he suspected, they were in the midst of a heated debate.

And at the center of the crowd, standing on a podium, was Napoleon, yelling to be heard.

Kyle pushed and shoved his way through the crowd, elbowing people as he strutted right to the center.

As he did, the huge crowd slowly began to gain awareness of him. He was so tall, he towered over everyone else, a foot above the crowd, and his scarred face gave people pause. Slowly, the room began to turn his way.

Kyle had no intention of waiting his turn. He had urgent business. He had an agenda to fulfill, and Napoleon and his people could be of service to him.

Kyle took two huge steps and leapt up onto the platform. As he did, he reached up, grabbed Napoleon by his shoulders and hoisted him high in the air, until he was at eye level with Kyle.

The entire crowd gasped, and grew quiet in shock.

Kyle stared down at Napoleon with his disfigured face, with his one good eye, and he saw Napoleon stare back, recognition and fear in his eyes.

"Kyle," he whispered, startled.

Kyle broke into a crooked smile. He was happy to see his old friend again. He couldn't help admiring his audacity.

"You little bastard," Kyle answered.

And then, in one swift move, he threw him, flying, into the crowd.

A gasp raced through the room, as several guards scurried to catch his fall. They caught him, and looked up at Kyle in shock, wondering who on earth could have the audacity to do such a thing to their leader.

Kyle smiled.

"I have returned," he said.

CHAPTER ELEVEN

Caleb stood at the entrance of his castle, watching Caitlin fly away, completely baffled. He could not understand why she had left so abruptly, or what he had done wrong. He thought the night before had gone so well, and she had seemed so happy to be there. Why her sudden change of mind? He racked his brain, trying to think what it might be.

Maybe she blames me, Caleb thought, *for having to come back in time for me. For losing our child of the 21st century. If it weren't for me, she wouldn't have had to come back, she would be safe and sound in the 21st century, with everyone she knew, with everything that was familiar, with that child.*

Or maybe, he thought, she was still blaming him for turning her. She had asked him, she had begged him, to turn her, and he had urged her not to. But he had relented. Did she resent him for that? For a life stuck in immortality?

Or maybe she just doesn't love me anymore, Caleb thought, *at least not like she used to. Maybe she loved the idea of me, but the reality of being here, with me, settling down for a life together—maybe it scared her away.*

Whatever the reason, Caleb had to know. He couldn't just let it go until he at least had an answer.

He set out from the house determined to find her, to discover the reason, and to do whatever he could to make wrongs right. In some ways, it was like heading off into a battle. In fact, he wished he was heading into battle instead. This, he realized, was harder. Love, caring for someone, he was realizing, could sometimes be the hardest battle of all.

*

Caitlin walked on the sand, barefoot, alongside the crashing waves, Ruth beside her. The day grew overcast, and the strong wind pushed back her hair. She had never felt so sad. Just at the moment when she thought she'd finally found peace, had finally found true love, she had discovered that he didn't truly love her the way she thought he had. She'd been so stupid. Living in a fantasy all this time.

But now what? Without Caleb in her life, she felt like she had no purpose. She had no idea where to turn, or where to go next. She could go back to searching for her father, but what was the point? Whether she found him, or found the Shield, Caleb would still not be there.

She could go off in search of Sam. But again, without Caleb there, none of it really meant much to her.

Caitlin looked out at the waves, and wondered how life could be so cruel. She felt completely, utterly hopeless.

She suddenly heard a noise, and turned.

She was shocked to see Caleb walking towards her.

He walked barefoot in the sand, and in his hand he held a rope, by which he led two beautiful, white horses.

He had a small, hopeful smile on his face.

Her heart pounded in her chest, as she wondered what had happened. Had he changed his mind?

Within moments he stood just a few feet away from her. Ruth ran over to them, looked up at, and yelped. In return, the horses lifted their heads and slowly lowered them.

Caitlin couldn't help smiling.

"I'm not sure what happened back there, or whatever I said to offend you," he said, "but whatever it is, I'm sorry."

"It's not what you said," Caitlin said. "It's what you *didn't* say."

Caleb looked back, puzzled.

"I guess…" Caitlin added, "…I just realized that your heart was somewhere else."

He looked even more puzzled. "What do you mean?"

Caitlin studied him, wondering if he was being truthful. She could tell that he was.

Now, she was confused.

"I… I know that you still want to be with her," Caitlin said, now not so sure of herself. "That you regret leaving her. Sera."

Caleb broke into a laugh.

"Is that really what you thought?" he asked. "And here I am, thinking that you were mad at me because I turned you."

Now it was Caitlin's turn to be confused. "Are you saying you're not interested in her?"

Caleb laughed again. "Not in the least," he said. "I have never felt so free as I do now, being away from her. In fact, she hadn't even crossed my mind."

"Then what was it?" Caitlin asked. "I saw your expression change. You became so sad. I know that I wasn't seeing things. I thought it was because you didn't want to be with me anymore."

Caleb looked down for a moment, his expression darkening.

"I was thinking of Jade," he said, somberly. "I still miss him very much."

Caitlin felt a huge sense of relief overcome her; she felt her entire body relax, felt her heart slowly get filled up again. She had been so stupid. Why had she judged him so quickly? Why couldn't she have given him the benefit of the doubt?

She was so mad at herself. She would've thought that she would've grown up already, after all this time, after all these misunderstandings. But she was still the same old Caitlin, fearless when it came to battle, but still overcome by fear when it came to matters of love, and when it came to expressing what was on her mind.

"Is that what that was all about?" Caleb asked. "I thought that you were upset with me over our child."

Caitlin looked at him, confused.

"I thought you regretted leaving him, the 21st century," Caleb continued, "and that you regretted giving it all up to come back for me."

Caitlin suddenly understood. He had misunderstood her completely. The same way she had misunderstood him.

She shook her head.

"I do miss that child, very much, whoever he or she would have been," she said. "But I don't, for a second, regret coming back for you."

The two of them came together and kissed. It was a long, comforting kiss, and when they came out of it, they both smiled.

Ruth ran over and yelped up at them. They both looked down and laughed. The tension had finally lifted, and the air had been cleared.

"Well," Caleb smiled, "I remembered Edgartown, and so I thought I'd bring these horses, in case you'd be willing to ride with me again."

"Willing?" Caitlin asked. "There is nothing I'd love more."

"There is a place I'd like to take you," Caleb said. "We could fly, but I think it'd be more romantic to ride, and to hike."

Caitlin smiled wide. She couldn't wait.

They both mounted the horses at the same time, Caitlin picking up Ruth as she did, and they took off at a trot along the beach.

The waves crashed all around them as they rode, and Caitlin couldn't help thinking of Edgartown. A different time, a different continent, a different century, a different life. Yet still, somehow, it all felt so connected, as if it were right here, and as if it had only happened yesterday.

They rode and rode, along the beach, in and out of the waves. There was not a person in sight.

It eventually became late in the day, and the sun finally broke through the clouds, spreading out in a gorgeous sunset.

Caleb led them around a bend, and then turned away from the water, up to the base of a hill. He stopped, and Caitlin came up beside him.

They dismounted, and as they did, the horses galloped away.

Caitlin watched them go with concern.

"Don't worry," Caleb said. "They're wild. They'll always come when I call for them. And from here on in, we won't need them."

He took her hand and led her away from the beach, onto a narrow trail, winding its way up the hillside. They hiked through beautiful dune grass, lit up by the sun, Ruth on their heels. Caitlin wondered where he was taking her.

As they walked in silence, Caitlin had so many questions she wanted to ask him. But for now, she was content to just be with him. It felt so good just to be by his side, to have her life restored to her again.

Finally, they reached the hilltop, and Caitlin was awestruck by the sight.

From this vantage point, high atop the hill, on a grassy plateau, she could see for miles. She saw the ocean stretching into the horizon, and in the other direction saw endless rolling hills and fields of wildflowers.

Caleb sat on the grassy plateau, and she sat beside him. Ruth came up and sat with them, too.

They lay back together, and looked up at the sky, and she put her head in his arms. The sky was so blue, unlike any sky she had ever seen, as it began to enter that magical time between day and night.

Caitlin lost track of time as they lay there, quietly, taking in the universe.

Eventually, Caleb slowly sat up. Caitlin did, too.

He looked at her with a seriousness and intensity that scared her, as if he were preparing to say something really important.

He cleared his throat, and she thought for a moment that he even looked a bit nervous.

"Caitlin," he began. He paused. "I just want to tell you how much you mean to me. I've never really had a chance, with just the two of us, to look back and reflect. I just want you to know, that even if it weren't for all this, even if we hadn't met the way we had, I still would have fallen just as much in love with you."

Caitlin felt her heart soar. It felt so good to hear the words, to know that he loved her as much as she loved him. Now, with him at her side, and feeling the same way she did, she felt like they could do anything. Nothing in the world could hold them back.

Caleb cleared his throat again, and she thought he looked even more nervous. She couldn't understand why.

"Caitlin," he said, clearing his throat again. "There's something I've been meaning to ask you."

Caitlin wondered why he didn't just come out and say it, whatever it was. They had known each other long enough. Why was he standing on ceremony? Why was he so nervous?

Caleb opened his mouth to speak again, and at the same time he appeared to be reaching back for something in his pocket.

Suddenly, at just that moment, there was a tremendous screech in the sky, and they both stopped and looked up.

Right overhead, there was a huge falcon, circling them, and diving fast right towards them.

The bird came in so fast, seeming to dive right for their heads, that they had to both duck at the last second to keep from getting clawed. It landed just feet from them, on the grass.

It turned and stared at them with defiant eyes.

Then, after a moment, it suddenly took off again, its huge wings flapping so close to their faces, that Caleb and Caitlin had to duck again.

They both looked at each other in shock, as the huge bird flew off into the horizon.

They then turned and looked back in the grass, where the bird had been, and saw that it had left something.

It was a scroll. A message, Caitlin realized.

And as she looked closely at it, her heart stopped within her.

On the outside, in delicate, feminine handwriting, it read: "For Caleb. My love."

CHAPTER TWELVE

As Sam walked with Kendra down the marble, gilded halls of Versailles, he was having a hard time concentrating. After the two of them had met, and Polly had rushed off, they had been left alone. Kendra hadn't said anything else to him, but she had looked at him in such a way, that he felt she was beckoning him to stay with her.

So when she had turned, without a word, and had begun to slowly walk away, he felt like he should accompany her. He hurried to catch up, and had been walking beside her ever since. She hadn't looked surprised that he had done so, and she had not asked him to leave. At the same time, she had not explicitly invited him, either.

She was a confusing person, hard to read. Sam marveled at how this woman—if he could even call her that at 17—already had such an effect upon him. After being transfixed by her eyes, a light, mysterious aqua blue, he had fallen hard, and had a hard time thinking of anything else. It was as if she'd had a power to transfix him.

And yet, he could sense, she was not one of his kind. She was a mere human. How could she have this kind of power?

He also could feel the huge sense of entitlement coming off of her. Clearly, she was a member of the royal family. It was apparent in the way she moved, the way she held her chin, the way she carried herself. She was clearly the type of person, he could tell, who was used to giving people orders since birth. He, too, felt that it was hard to do anything but fulfill her command while in her presence.

Not that he minded. His heart had beat faster at his first sight of her, and he didn't especially want to be anywhere else but by her side. It was literally as if he had been struck by a lightning bolt. He could not understand how she had captured his interest so quickly. He didn't even know her. And up until now, he had never even believed in love at first sight.

He thought of the first time he had met Samantha, of the feelings he had felt. He had been so attracted to her, too. But it was also different. With Kendra, it was something deeper, stronger.

The timing was so weird, too, because, before he'd met her, he had just been starting to warm up to Polly. Upon first seeing Polly, he had been struck by how pretty she was. But she was not ravishingly beautiful, like Kendra was, nor did she have the same power to hypnotize him. And once Kendra appeared, it was hard for him to think of anything else.

As they walked, their footsteps echoing in the cavernous marble corridors, passing huge floor-to-ceiling windows that looked out over the formal gardens of Versailles, Sam finally began to come back to his senses. He wondered where they were going. Being around Kendra, he was having a hard time remembering why he was here. He was even having a hard time remembering what his mission was at all, and why he'd come back in time.

A wave of her perfume came his way, and Sam felt even more lightheaded. He willed himself to think. To remember.

Caitlin. He'd wanted to find her. To help her.

Aiden. Polly had brought him here. To meet him.

But as he turned the corner with her, and walked down yet another corridor, it all seemed to fade to the back of his mind. Somehow, none of it seemed so pressing anymore. Strangely enough, he now felt as if he had all the time in the world. And that nothing was more important than being by Kendra's side.

As the silence between them continued, Sam finally began to wonder if he should say something. He cleared his throat.

"Where are we going?" he asked.

They walked several more feet in silence, and Sam began to wonder if she would even bother to answer him.

"*I* am going to the court," she said slowly, haughtily.

Now Sam felt embarrassed. Was he intruding? Had he misread the signs? Should he leave her be, go in another direction?

"Do you want me to come with you?" Sam asked.

He watched her expression, and caught the slightest flicker of a smile at the corner of her lips. "As you will," she said.

He didn't know what that meant, but he decided he would take that for a Yes. He wasn't ready to leave her side so quickly, at least not until she explicitly told him to go.

"So, like, who are you?" he asked.

They walked in silence, she not bothering to answer. Finally, Sam figured he should rephrase the question.

"I mean, like, do you live here? How do you know Polly? I've never been here," he said. He knew that he sounded lame, but he didn't know what else to say.

"That is obvious," she said, as she suddenly stopped before a door.

She looked at Sam, waiting there, impatient.

He could not figure out what she was waiting for.

Then he realized. The door. She expected him to open it for her.

Clumsily, he hurried forward and yanked it open.

She turned and walked through the open door, without even a thank you.

Sam rushed through it, hurrying to keep up beside her.

They were now outside, walking through the immaculate, formal gardens. It was a beautiful day, but very sunny and hot.

Sam felt something in his hand, and looked down, and saw her place a long, slim, black parasol into it.

He couldn't figure why she had handed him an umbrella, since it wasn't raining, but then, he realized. She expected him to open it for her. To block the sun.

He assumed she expected him to hold it over her head, so he did. She continued to walk, as if his holding it over her were the most natural thing in the world. He was starting to feel like he was her servant.

"To answer your question," she said slowly, in a dignified voice, "yes. I am of the royal family. I am Marie's cousin. Younger than her, obviously, but still, we practically grew up together," she said. "In fact, all things being equal, I am as entitled to the crown as she. But because of legitimacy questions, she retains the glory."

Sam looked at her in a whole new light. A would-be Queen. That explained it. She certainly carried herself like one.

But even if he didn't know this, even if she wasn't a royal, he still would have felt equally attracted to her.

"Life here can be very dull," she added, with a sigh. "Yes, there are the parties and balls and visitors and dignitaries. But there are also endless formalities, etiquettes, mind-numbing dinners, ceremonies. I'd much prefer to be elsewhere. Horseback riding, like the men do. Archery was something I liked as a child, but which is forbidden for me now. Life here is restrictive for a woman. Our best hope is to find a man. That is the sum of all our ambition. Quite boring, if you ask me. In fact, I think it should be reversed. I think the sum of all ambition should be for a man to find a woman. And that *she* should be free to do as she wishes."

Sam marveled at her strange combination of total silence, then opening up in a long, detailed monologue. He wondered if she had opened up to him because she felt close to him in some way, or if she was just like this with everybody.

"Well, at least you're not opinionated," he said with a smile.

She turned and gave him a cold look, and he realized he fumbled. Clearly, sarcasm wasn't her thing.

"Just kidding," Sam said, trying to ease the tension.

"That is apparent," she said, coldly.

They walked down a long row of perfectly trimmed hedges, workers all around them, hard at work trimming and pruning, tending to an endless row of roses.

"The only thing that brings life to our party is your kind," she said, as they turned down yet another trail, and passed a huge bubbling fountain.

So, Sam realized. At least she knew he was a vampire. That was a relief. It meant less explaining for him.

"You bring an element of unpredictability to the equation," she added. "An element of freedom. I like to watch your kind train. I like to see the battles. The techniques. Your kind keeps our kind on edge. If truth be told, it is the only thing that keeps the Royals in their place."

They walked for a while in silence, as Sam thought over their conversation, everything she said.

"So, what about you?" he asked finally, without really thinking in advance. "Do you have a boyfriend?"

He realized right away it was a mistake. He was too blunt, as always. He should have been more subtle.

She turned and stared right through him, looking appalled.

"I beg your pardon?" she said. "You're very forward. And rude."

"Just asking," he said quietly, feeling dejected.

"I don't see what business that is of yours," she added.

They continued to walk in silence, the tension increasingly awkward between them, and they finally came to another immaculate palace. Sam was confused. He had always thought that Versailles was just one palace. He hadn't realize that there were several palaces on the property. Each one seemed grander than the next.

As they reached the front door, several servants rushed to open the door for her. Sam returned her parasol, and she stopped, and faced him. He was surprised she had stopped; he had assumed that she didn't like him, that he had messed up, and that she would just walk away.

She looked at him, and once again, her eyes struck him, held him in place as if hypnotized.

Sam felt his heart beat faster, as her eyes locked onto his. He was certain this time that she was giving him a message.

"You're different than the others," she said quietly, out of earshot of the guards. "The others are ancient. They've been around forever. They're more predictable. You're younger. More naïve. That's a good thing."

Sam didn't know what to say to that.

"Well," he said, smiling, "I guess you're not half bad yourself."

Once again, his sarcasm fell flat. She stared back coldly, and he thought that he blew it for sure this time.

But suddenly, she added: "To answer your question: No. I don't. But maybe, quite soon, I will."

Then, without another word, she turned and walked away.

Sam stood there staring after her, speechless.

CHAPTER THIRTEEN

Caitlin sat there, her heart pounding, as Caleb sat across from her, reading the scroll with concern on his face.

She couldn't believe it. It had been such a magical moment, one of the peak moments of their relationship, and she had felt that she and Caleb were on the brink of getting so much closer. And then that stupid bird had to appear, out of nowhere, diving down like a messenger of death.

Whatever the letter had to say, she couldn't stand the suspense anymore. Her heart now pounded, not with love and excitement, but with fear and dread.

With love, it had been signed. That could only mean one thing. It was from Sera. Who else would sign it that way?

Caitlin's body shook with anger. Always, at every turn, Sera somehow managed to be a thorn in her side.

"Well?" Caitlin finally asked, with more anger in her voice than she would have liked. But she couldn't stand waiting anymore.

Caleb finally looked up, a mix of concern and sorrow across his face.

"It is from Sera," Caleb said. "It says that Jade is alive. That she has managed to resurrect him, and to bring him back in time. That he is here, now. That he wants to see me."

Caitlin's heart plummeted. She felt as if she'd been stabbed with a knife. She could see already, from the look on Caleb's face, that an offer to see Jade was something he could not refuse. And that if she tried to get in the way, he would resent her forever, would always view her as the person who prevented him from seeing his son.

"How is that possible?" Caitlin asked. "How could she possibly resurrect him?"

Caleb looked down at the letter again, shaking his head, looking puzzled himself. "I don't know," he answered. "I really don't."

He looked at her with sorrow and guilt.

"Caitlin," he said, and she could hear the grief and longing in his voice. "I'm so sorry. I would never ever want to leave you. And I never would. But this is different. It is my *son.*"

Caitlin suddenly stood, overwhelmed with anger. Caleb stood, too.

"You *have* to understand," he said, reaching out and grabbing her as she turned to walk away. He turned her to face him. "He is my *son.* And this is a chance for me to see him alive again. How can I walk away from that?"

"You love her," Caitlin said. "You still do."

"No," he insisted. "I promise you, I do not. This has nothing to do with Sera. It is only about Jade."

Despite herself, Caitlin burst into tears.

"How can I prove it to you?" he asked. "You met Jade. You know what a special human being he is. How can I turn my back on him? How can I never see him again?"

Caitlin stood there, crying, not knowing what to say.

"You can accompany me," Caleb said. "I will prove it to you. I will prove to you that this is not about Sera. We can go together. We will see Jade. And then we can bring him back here, to live with us."

"And you think Sera would allow that?" Caitlin asked. "Allow us to take her son away from her?"

Caleb furrowed his brow.

"He's *my* son, too. And regardless of what she wants, I don't plan on spending any time with her. I'm going to see my son. I don't need to be with her to be with my son. Come with me. You will see. We will get Jade together, and we will leave."

Caitlin shook her head, again and again.

"I could never go with you. You know that. I could never stand to see Sera. And I don't want to be involved in your relationship with her."

"I have no relationship with her," Caleb insisted. "You have to believe me."

"Is that why you're going to leave me and see her?"

"Caitlin," he said softly. "Please, understand. It's not like that."

Caitlin turned, wiping away her tears. With her back to him, she said, "You don't need my permission. If you want to go—go."

Several seconds followed. He stepped up close, laid a hand on her shoulder.

"Will you wait for me? Will you be here when I return? It will only be a few days. I promise you. I will return, with Jade in hand. And then we can start our lives together. Will you wait? Please, promise me!"

She turned and looked at him, straight in the eye, feeling scorned, and her sadness hardened to resolve.

"I won't promise you anything."

CHAPTER FOURTEEN

Kyle stood opposite Napoleon in the small side chamber of the Pantheon. After his dramatic entrance, Kyle had marched Napoleon off, fuming like a chided schoolboy, surrounded by a dozen of his closest followers.

Napoleon's men had wanted to come inside, but Kyle had ordered them to wait outside. They looked to Napoleon for approval, and he grudgingly lowered his gaze and nodded, clearly embarrassed he was no longer the one giving orders.

One of them wouldn't budge, though, so Kyle walked up to him, picked him up, and threw him with such force that he went flying through the air, out the door, and into the hallway.

"Wait outside," he said to the others.

They abruptly turned, and hurried out, leaving just Kyle and Napoleon facing each other in the small chamber.

"You needn't always be so dramatic," Napoleon fumed. "I would have followed you here if you had only asked. You needn't order around my people."

"*Your* people?" Kyle asked. "The only reason you are in power is because of me. I'll do anything I wish. Including stripping you from power."

Napoleon finally softened, as if ready to take orders from his commander.

"Why are you here?" Napoleon asked. "I thought you were waging your war in New York?"

"I was," Kyle snapped. "But a girl got in the way. A very annoying girl named Caitlin. And her boyfriend, Caleb. And her brother, Sam. The three of them—they have ruined my plans. I've come back myself to take care of them all."

"So?" Napoleon snapped. "What do you want from me?"

"They've come to *your* time and place, unluckily for you," Kyle said. "You and your men are going to help me find and kill them."

Napoleon stared back, indignant. "You have chosen the worst possible time. We have no time for such distractions now. We are in the midst of a revolution. My men—I can barely control them. They want a revolution. They want democracy. They want to be entirely out in the open."

"Perfect," Kyle said. "We will give them the war they want. We will attack Versailles."

Napoleon raised his eyebrows.

"Impossible," he snapped. "We'd never win. They have ranks of vampire soldiers protecting the place. Aiden's people. My men could not possibly win an attack."

"That's because you're not as good a strategist as I," Kyle retorted. "We will attack. And we will defeat them. For that is where Caitlin's people will be. And once I kill them, I can kill her. But I agree, that we will not attack head on. Instead, we will create a diversion."

"What diversion?" Napoleon asked, impatiently.

"The savage seven," Kyle stated.

Napoleon's eyes opened wide.

"Impossible. They've been locked up for centuries. No. That's way too dangerous."

"That's precisely why we're going to break them free," Kyle answered with a smile.

Napoleon paced, thinking.

Kyle knew it would be a shock. It was an unexpected plan. Which was precisely why it was brilliant. The savage seven, he knew, were some of the most vicious vampires to ever walk the earth. They had not belonged to any coven, and they had been captured in Paris centuries before. They sat rotting in jail, in the bowels of the Bastille. If unleashed, they could wreak endless havoc. Exactly what he needed.

But they were also a liability: they were just as likely to turn on Kyle and his men as they would on the humans. They were machines of destruction. It had taken hundreds of years to catch them, and both the vampire and the human races were happy to keep them where they were.

Which was precisely why Kyle would free them. They would never expect it. And it could create exactly the sort of diversion he needed.

"We will free them," Kyle commanded. "And then we will attack. And your people can also have their revolution."

"Even if we wanted to," Napoleon said, "it is impossible. They are deep in the Bastille. There are legions of guards surrounding them. And I hear they are contained in a special cell, unbreakable. It's better for us to wait," he added. "I have infiltrators in Versailles. A spy, who reports back to me. She will tell me all I know. We just need to wait for her."

"I have an infiltrator there, too," Kyle said.

"Who is yours?" Napoleon asked.

"Who is yours?" Kyle asked.

Neither answered, both distrusting of each other.

"It doesn't matter," Kyle finally said. "We will not wait for them. We never wait. We initiate. This is our war to begin."

"I don't like it," Napoleon said.

Kyle stepped forward, bearing down on him with his full height.

"Well then I'm glad you're not the one in charge."

CHAPTER FIFTEEN

As Caitlin walked through the fields, heading back alone to Caleb's castle, she felt the world falling out from under her. She was in a daze, barely paying attention to where she was going. She barely glanced at the sea, barely heard the crashing of the waves, barely noticed that Ruth skipped alongside her, craving attention. Caitlin was oblivious to it all. Once again, she had let her guard down, had been ready for love, and had let Caleb back in. Once again, her heart had been broken.

She was so mad at herself. How many times would she allow herself to become vulnerable, only to be crushed again? When would she ever learn her lesson?

And how had it all fallen apart so quickly?

Caitlin wondered why her life could never just be normal. She felt as if she were always ascending to the highest peaks, only to be brought down to the lowest depths. All she wanted was a normal life, a steady relationship, a place to call home. And she had thought she'd finally found it. This place had seemed so imperturbable; it had felt as if nothing from the outside world could ever reach them here.

And then, like lightning in a clear blue sky, that awful bird had appeared, carrying that letter. From Sera. In her awful handwriting. It was so unfair. It made her want to scream at the world.

As quickly as Caleb had taken her to that hilltop, in that beautiful moment which she thought would never end, he had just as quickly departed. She remembered watching him flying off, his huge wings flapping, heading off to Sera. As if he couldn't wait another minute to be with her.

Maybe she wasn't being fair. Of course, he had said it was to be with his son. But had he really meant it?

And did that even matter? After all, he would be seeing her, regardless. He would be running to answer her letter, the second she came calling.

It was hard for Caitlin to know what to think.

It just wasn't fair, Caitlin thought again, as she bunched up her face, flooding with anger.

Just as quickly, her anger morphed to sadness, as she felt fresh tears streaking down her cheeks.

Where would she go now? What would she do? She had embarked on time travel for Caleb. *He* had become her mission. And now, with him gone, what was her life's purpose?

Had she made a mistake to make love her life's mission? To make this relationship her central purpose?

At the time, nothing had seemed more important. And deep down, she still felt as if love was the ultimate purpose in life.

But now, at this moment, in her heartbreak, she couldn't help feeling as if she'd made a mistake. As if she should have focused on more important things.

On anything, except love.

*

Caitlin arrived at Caleb's empty castle at dusk, Ruth limping at her heels. It felt to her like hours had passed since she'd left the hilltop. The long walk had cleared her mind, and now she just felt hollowed out, depressed. Empty. Alone.

Now, instead of looking up at the castle as her new home, as a place she looked forward to fixing up, a place where she could spend her life in peace, she just saw it as a reminder of Caleb, and of his leaving her alone.

As she walked inside, she lit a few candles, just enough to see by. The dim environment suited her mood.

Ruth whined, and Caitlin went instinctively to the room that held the leftover deer; she took some scraps and hand-fed them to Ruth, who snapped them up. For such a small animal, she was ravenous.

Caitlin herself was not. She had lost all desire for food.

She wandered upstairs alone, trying not to think of Caleb, and made her way to the bedroom. She sat at the small, medieval desk, and looked out the window. Before her, the last light of day was fading. In the distance, she could see the moon begin to rise.

Caitlin lit a candle and pulled it close, as she reached over and opened her journal. This was what she needed right now. The one friend she could turn to, she could voice all her frustrations to. This journal had really become a trusted friend, the one common denominator in all her travels.

She turned back the heavy leather cover, and the pages crinkled. She looked at her handwriting, flipping through the pages, and noticed how it had already changed. All the different types of inks, of pens….Some of the pages were soiled by now, covered in dirt stains or wine spills. The pages had become thick, too, from water stains and dampness. The journal already felt as if it were a thousand years old.

She was shocked at how thick it had become. Had she really done all this?

The pages were getting completely filled, and Caitlin had to keep turning to find a blank page. Finally, she did. She took out the quill and ink blot she'd found, sharpened the edge, dipped it, and leaned in to write.

*

I don't know how I've let myself end up in this position once again. I promised myself I wouldn't let it happen, wouldn't let myself fall in love with someone who might not be there for me. This time, though, it seemed so different. Caleb had seemed so sincere. And that's the hardest thing—a part of me still thinks he is. That if that letter hadn't come, we would still be here, together.

Sera. I hate her. She's always there, ready to split us apart.

But I'm getting ahead of myself. I need to take a step back, to figure out how this all began. How I even got here in the first place.

It all started in New York. New York, my God. It feels like a thousand lifetimes ago. I was just a normal, typical teenager, living with a mom who didn't like me, and who I didn't like either, and with an annoying little brother, who I loved. But, of course, nothing was normal. I was a hybrid, or so I would learn. A half-breed. Half human, half vampire. And coming of age at exactly the wrong time.

There was that awful public high school, there was Jonah, the first boy I really had a crush on. There was our first date, my first feeding. I'd been so embarrassed to run out on that date, and even more embarrassed to find myself waking up the next day in a place I didn't know. And having fed on I didn't know what.

Overnight, my life changed. I was hunted down by a dark coven of vampires, who captured me, and were determined to kill me. I broke free with Caleb's help, and that was the first time I met him. I'd loved him from the first moment I saw him—and I haven't stopped loving him since.

He took me to his people, to his coven, to the Cloisters. But they refused to have me. I was on my own, and almost killed again, until Caleb saved me again, and turned his back on his own people to take me away.

Then there came the searching for my father, my true father, for the mythical vampire sword that he would lead me to and which would save mankind. Or something like that. The way I saw it, it was really a search to find out who I was. Or what I was.

Caleb and I searched together, from one town to the next, all up the East Coast. From the Hudson Valley to Martha's Vineyard to Boston. There was our night of riding horses on the beach, of spending the night with him for the first time….It was amazing.

But just as our romance began to take off, danger came for us. I found the Sword, and I was attacked by Sergei, Kyle's awful sidekick, who stabbed me in the back with it. Dying, I begged Caleb to turn me.

He listened.

I was brought to Pollepel, an island in the Hudson River, to recover—once again, saved by Caleb. He left me, though, to go back with Sera, to go back to his people. He said it was just to help them, to save them from the war. I had been so jealous. Instead of giving him the room he needed, I believed he loved Sera.

I trained on that island, and met Polly, my best friend, and Aiden, my mentor and teacher, and Blake, a mysterious boy who I loved but never really understood. I trained and fought and became a much better warrior. Became more of myself.

And then I found out that I was pregnant, and that rocked my world. I just knew that Caleb was in danger. I left the island, to save him. Aiden told me that if I left, I could never come back. I chose Caleb. He was more important to me.

I joined Sera, and together, we fought to rescue Caleb, who'd been captured in the vampire wars. We found him, captured in Kyle's coven. And we were about to free him.

But Sam had been caught in the grip of Kyle's terrible influence, and he used his shapeshifting powers in an evil way. He tricked us, and he even tried to kill me. But Sera had stepped in, and gave up her life for mine.

But Sam had actually killed me, because he tricked me to kill Caleb. With my own hands. With the Sword.

Aiden had told me that there'd be one chance to save Caleb: if I went back in time. I had agreed to lose our child, to give up everything, to try. Aiden told me I could never come back. I let it all go for Caleb.

I found myself in Italy, in 1791. Assisi. Venice. Florence. Rome. It was a whirlwind. In Venice, at first I couldn't find Caleb, and then when I did, I had my heart broken to discover that he didn't remember me. I fell in love with Blake, though, and in Florence, I finally found a clue to lead me to my father. But again, Kyle appeared, and stole it away, and captured us both.

In Rome, I fought for my life, in the Colosseum, in Kyle's cruel games. It was because of me that Blake died, taking a stab for me. Nothing hurt worse than that.

How many people will have to die to keep me alive?

Then their came Sam. I thought he would try to kill me, but he saved me instead. As did Caleb, who finally remembered. The three of us fought our way out together, and made it to the Vatican.

There, I met my people. My true people. They gave me the first of four keys I need to find my father. And then sent us back in time. Yet again.

And here I am now. In this new time and place. Finally reunited with Caleb—or so I thought. I felt sure that this could be the time and place where we could finally be together. When everything was perfect.

And now, it all seems to be falling apart, once again.

And who am I now? A daughter without a father? A sister without a brother? A girl without a boyfriend?

Should I be searching for the Shield? Should I be searching for my father? Should I be chasing after Caleb? Should I wait for him here?

Or should I leave this place forever?

*

Caitlin burst out the front door of the castle and ran in the night, through a waist high field of grass. As she ran, she tried to set off, to fly into the air, but her wings wouldn't work. She ran faster, trying to jump, to lift off, but nothing happened. As she continued to run, nearly out of breath, she finally realized that she didn't have the power she used to.

In the distance, on the horizon, stood a lone figure, his body silhouetted against the full moon. The sky was alight with an enormous moon, illuminating thousands of small clouds. Caitlin ran towards the figure, feeling that it might be her father. Or possibly, Caleb.

As she ran, suddenly, the landscape sloped downward, and she found herself running down, into a valley. Eventually, she was running up the other side again, up a huge hill. But the hill became so steep, and she grew tired. The lone figure stood atop it, beckoning, but it was too hard for her to reach him.

The landscape became rocky, and Caitlin found herself slipping on huge rocks as she was trying to run up the side of a mountain. She was losing her grip and as she did, a rockslide began.

She slid downward. She grabbed hold of a large rock, hanging precariously, and looked up, hoping for help.

Her father looked down, holding out a hand.

"Help!" Caitlin screamed.

"Find me, Caitlin," he responded, as his hand nearly reached hers. "Don't give up the search."

Caitlin reached up, trying to touch her father's hand, but she lost her grip, and suddenly, she was sliding down the mountain, further and further down, until she was falling endlessly into a black hole. She screamed for all she had, knowing that she was plummeting to her death.

Caitlin woke screaming.

She looked all around, breathing hard, trying to remember where she was.

She spotted a dying candle in the corner of the room, and saw Ruth lying on her bed, looking at her with concern. She saw the huge window, open to the moonlight, and realized it was just a dream. She was still in Caleb's castle.

Caitlin got out of bed, covered in sweat, and paced, barefoot, on the stone floor. It felt so weird to be in this huge place alone, to be in his bed alone. She felt like an intruder here, and felt disoriented.

The dream had seemed so real. Her heart was still pounding as she crossed the room, then through the huge doors and out onto the open terrace. She grabbed a jug of water and gulped it down as she stood on the terrace, looking out. Her throat was parched.

She heard a whining noise, and looked down and saw Ruth at her feet, looking up. She put down what was left of her water, and Ruth quickly lapped up the rest.

Caitlin studied the sky, lit up in the moonlight. As much as she had loved being here the day before, now, she hated it. It felt wrong to her. Despite the unusual circumstances, she still felt as if she had been spurned by Caleb. She felt he should have refused, that he should have just been happy with her, and had stayed put. That he shouldn't have gone flying off the second that Sera contacted him. She knew that she was being selfish, and she understood that he missed his child. But still, she felt like she deserved better than that.

Caitlin zoned out, standing there for she didn't know how long, as she slowly watched the horizon begin to break, the dark blue gradually melt into a softer, lighter blue. She felt so confused about so many things. Maybe her dream had been a message. Maybe she *should* focus on the search. Maybe it was time to let Caleb go from her life.

After all, Caitlin did desperately want to find her father. She did want to have all the searching behind her, to have her life return to whatever state of normalcy there might be. And somehow, she felt, as long as the Shield was out there, as long as her Dad still loomed on the horizon, her life would never quite be normal.

As dawn began to break, Caitlin realized she needed to clear her head, to stop the thousands of racing, conflicting thoughts swirling through it. Ruth whined again, and this time, Caitlin picked her up. Ruth clearly needed to take a walk, and so did she.

Caitlin walked down the stairs and out the castle, into the dawn, and followed the trail through the fields. The trail wound its way right into a patch of woods, and Caitlin realized that would be a perfect place for a long walk.

Caitlin wound her way into the woods, and already felt more relaxed. It was darker here, still night, and more peaceful. All around her were towering trees, blocking out most of the sky, and she could hear the songs of a few early morning birds, just waking. It was tranquil.

Caitlin thought of where she might go next. She found herself thinking of the unopened scroll, of her father's letter. Maybe now was the time to open it. Maybe something in there would lead her, show her the way. Maybe she was being punished for not following her mission to begin with. Maybe she had needed all this drama to force her back on track.

Suddenly, there was the sound of a twig snapping. Caitlin spun.

She was shocked to discover that there, following her, was a large man, about twice her size. He was overgrown, with missing teeth, and a half open mouth. He looked like a real brute, very mean. She could see trouble in his large, black eyes.

Caitlin heard another snap, and turned the other way to see two more ruffians approaching her. They were nearly as big as the first man, and, covered in scars, had even meaner expressions, if possible.

Her heart started to pound as she realized she was being ambushed. Probably local thieves, or rapists, waiting to pray on passersby. She had been so stupid. She should have been more vigilant. Just because she was in middle of nowhere, didn't necessarily mean it was safe.

Normally, Caitlin would have been fearless, but she hadn't had a real chance to test her full powers since she'd arrived back in time. Did she still have them? She knew she could fly. But did she still have the strength? The rage? The reflexes? The speed and agility and fighting skills?

Now was hardly the time to be experimenting, she realized, with a pit her stomach.

"Take off your clothes," one of them barked.

It was the big one, and as she looked, she saw him pull something small and shiny from his waist. It was a dagger.

Clearly, these men didn't just want to rob her.

Ruth snarled beside her.

"I'm only going to warn you once," Caitlin said, in as loud and firm a voice as she could muster. But deep inside, she was trembling. "Don't come near me."

A short, harsh laugh came out from the two other men, as they each pulled out daggers of their own.

"This one has a mouth on her, doesn't she?" one of them asked.

At that moment, the first one, several feet closer, reached for her. Caitlin waited, not wanting to show her hand.

Ruth suddenly lunged at the man, and bit as hard as she could on his ankle. Ruth was small, but her teeth were sharp, and as she clamped down hard, the man screamed in agony. He shook his leg furiously, swinging Ruth in the air, but she would not let go. Finally, he swung hard, and Ruth went flying.

Caitlin saw her chance. She lunged forward, sending the heel of her hand up high and hard, right into the base of the man's throat.

It was a perfect strike. She hit him in the vocal cords, and he immediately raise both hands to his throat, and dropped to his knees.

Caitlin grabbed him by the back of the head, and brought his face into her knee, breaking his nose. He fell into the ground.

Caitlin suddenly felt her arm burn with pain, as she heard the slicing of a knife.

She grabbed her arm in pain and felt the hot blood pour out of her—and realized she had been sliced by a dagger. Stupid of her. She had left herself open to attack from the other men, who were faster than she'd thought.

Before she could react, she was grabbed from behind by the other man. She struggled, but the man was strong, and no matter what she did, she was unable to break free.

The other man came around and faced her, wiping his lips with the back of his hand, as if looking at his next meal. He quickly pulled down his pants.

"Undress her," he commanded the other.

The other began to reach around and grab Caitlin's shirt.

That was when it happened. Caitlin closed her eyes and suddenly thought of all the times in her life she'd been attacked, abused, bullied. She thought of New York, back in the alley. She thought of Cain, on Pollepel. She remembered Venice. She even thought of her mother, who never had a kind word for her. And more than anything, she felt all the frustration and anger that had built up in her from Caleb's leaving her. The heartbreak. The depression. She was overwhelmed with rage. She could scream at the world. It wasn't fair. She deserved better.

It just wasn't fair.

A sudden, inexplicable rage flooded through her. She felt her arms and hands and shoulders bulge, and suddenly felt the strength of a hundred men. She leaned back, broke free of his grasp and roared. It was the vicious snarl of an animal, of a wolf. Of a vampire.

Caitlin turned, grabbed the man and threw him, and he went flying at full speed, until he smashed into a tree, unconscious.

The other man, his pants down, suddenly stared at her wide-eyed, in shock, as if staring at a wild tiger that had just been unleashed from its cage. His expression changed from audacity to fear and cowardice. She could see him trembling.

But Caitlin had no sympathy left. She had transformed, into a beast, and she couldn't hold back her primal urge. She lunged into the air, and kicked him hard in the chest with both feet. The man, his pants down, went flying through the air, and cracked his head hard against a tree. He slumped to the ground, unconscious.

Caitlin spun in time to see the big one charging at her. She waited, then at the last second, bent down, easily picked up, and hurled him through the air. He went flying headfirst, this time into a branch, impaling and killing him on impact.

Caitlin walked over to one of the unconscious men, her rage still not satisfied.

One of them began getting up slowly, and she kicked him as hard as she could in the face.

It still wasn't enough for her. She wanted blood. She wanted revenge. Revenge for every act of cruelty in her life.

Sinking to one knee, she began to choke him. He awoke from his unconsciousness, and grabbed her wrist with both of his huge hands, trying to get it off. But he was no match for her. Her single, thin wrist held him pinned down in a vice-like grip, and his eyes bulged out of his head, as his face turned blue. It was clear he would be dead in moments.

"CAITLIN!" yelled a voice.

Caitlin spun, shocked to recognize the voice.

Out of the forest, holding a staff, dressed in a long robe, a single man hiked towards her.

She released her grip, and slowly stood and faced him.

He came close, lowered his hood, and stared at her with his piercing blue eyes.

She looked at his timeless face, his long, silver beard, and knew it could only be one person. Only one person in the world had that sort of affect upon her.

Caitlin faced her old master.

It was Aiden.

CHAPTER SIXTEEN

Polly had been unable to stop thinking about Sergei. It felt like a drug had been injected into her veins. No matter what she did—walked, slept, ate, trained—the thought of him was always with her. His dark, Russian features; the sound of his voice; his translucent skin, his sharp features; and his incredible, hypnotic singing voice. She had never met anyone remotely like him.

She also couldn't stop thinking about the way he had treated her. He had been so brazen, so arrogant. No boy had ever treated her like that before. What was it about him? What made him feel so entitled? Why had she allowed him to treat her that way? And more importantly, when he had, why hadn't she just walked away?

She couldn't understand it. Logically, she should hate him. Yet, for some crazy reason she couldn't understand, she couldn't stop thinking of him.

Polly strode down the hall at a quick pace. She had chosen her finest dress, a lightweight, light blue, with a white lace trim, elaborate white collars, and which flowed from her neck down to her feet. She wore a large hoopskirt beneath it, making it flare out at her hips. It was hot in this July weather, and she had chosen the thinnest material she had, but still, it offered little relief from the heat. She patted at the perspiration on her forehead as she went, which grew with each step she took.

Polly wanted to arrive early this time. Sergei was giving another concert, at the far end of Versailles, in the Grand Trianon, and this time, she didn't want to miss a note. She wanted to get a good seat, in the front, and be able to look up and stare into his eyes. She wanted to see if her vision of him matched her memory, or if it had all just been an illusion. She wanted to know for sure if she still felt the way she thought about him. And she desperately wanted to hear that voice of his again.

Everyone, humans and vampires alike, had been talking about him for weeks. The palace was practically buzzing with his name. She hadn't really paid attention before, as it had just been at the periphery of her consciousness.

But now, she really wondered. She could sense that he was of her race, one of her kind. But where was he from? Which coven did he belong to? And why was it that, no matter how many people she asked, no one seemed to know? Everyone seemed to think he came from somewhere else. And no one seemed to know when he was leaving, or even why he was here. He had just, seemingly overnight, become an accepted fact of Versailles. It all seemed so mysterious to her.

Even more mysterious, he seemed to blend in effortlessly, as if he had always been here. Particularly the way he carried himself, so arrogant, one would have thought he was royalty. The accepted rumor about him was that he was a young Russian Prince, traveling through France, and was visiting Versailles for a few weeks to grace them with his presence. That he was the most celebrated vocalist in all of Russia, that he was close personal friends with composers like Mozart and Clementi and Salieri.

Polly glanced at her watch as she turned down another corridor, and realized that she was, in fact, quite early. Now, she was embarrassed. She certainly didn't want to be the first one to arrive in that big, empty room, and she didn't want to seem too desperate.

She deliberately slowed her pace, and just as she began to wonder where to go to idle the time, she suddenly heard footsteps coming up behind her. She looked over and saw somebody else walking down the corridor.

Her heart dropped. It was him.

Sergei, his thick, wavy hair perfectly styled, dressed this time in a royal, red satin coat, white breeches, and shining black shoes, caught up to her at a quick pace, matching hers. He looked straight ahead, as if not bothering to look her way, or to even acknowledge that the two of them were the only ones in this huge corridor. He seemed to lack even the basic decency and grace to turn and say hello. Was he so arrogant that he was waiting for *her* to acknowledge *him*?

Polly gulped. Up close, in this light, right beside him, he was even more gorgeous than she had remembered. She found herself completely frazzled by his sudden appearance, and had a hard time collecting her thoughts.

"Hi," she said, finally.

He glanced at her.

"I presume you're coming to my concert," he stated, not smiling, looking away.

Polly stammered, not sure how to respond. "Um…I was heading in that direction, yes."

He smirked, as if catching her in a lie.

"Quite early, aren't you?" he snipped.

She racked her brain for a response, but none came.

"Of course you are. You don't want to miss a note, do you?" he asked.

Again, Polly was unsure how to respond. He had a way of making her feel so nervous and on edge with every word he said.

"That's all right, I don't blame you," he said, "I wouldn't want to miss me, either."

Polly cleared her throat. "You're…a very talented singer," she said.

"I'm a *vocalist,*" he corrected. "*Singers* are common. *Vocalists* are rare. And yes, I know that already."

Polly fumed. She hated being corrected. And she hated how conceited he was. A part of her just wanted to turn and storm away, to forget the whole thing.

But another part of her, a part she couldn't understand, felt so attracted to him, felt drawn to him like a magnet. Why, she wondered? She had never allowed herself to be poorly treated by anyone in her life. The fact that she couldn't stand up for herself bothered her more than anything else.

"Where are you from?" she asked. "How long will you be here?"

"As long as I like," he said. "I don't put time limits on myself. Why? Would you rather see me go?" he asked, glancing her way with his disdainful dark eyes.

But instead of seeing the disdain, all Polly could notice was the way the sun hit his eyes as he looked at her. It made him all the more attractive.

"No," Polly stammered, "I...um...wasn't saying anything like that. I was just curious."

"People here are so trivial," he said. "Few here can really appreciate my talents. I'm beginning to think I'm wasting my time at this place. I will move on soon."

They both turned down a corridor, and were now getting close to the venue.

"You seem to be one of the few who appreciates my talents," he said. "That bodes well for you."

She looked at him, but he was still not looking her way as he walked. Was that his version of a compliment? She assumed that it was, and felt flattered, in a strange way. Maybe he liked her after all. Maybe he was just socially awkward.

The two of them reached a massive door, and as they did, the waiting servants opened it for them. It wasn't the door to the main room, but a side door, to the backstage area, Polly could see. As the doors opened, she saw a small dressing room, a vanity in its center, with a large white and gold stuffed chair before it.

Polly stopped at the door, ready to turn away.

She was shocked to feel his hand touch hers. She looked down, and saw Sergei holding her hand.

"Why are you leaving?" he asked, looking at her this time. He stared at her with an intensity unlike any she had ever seen.

"Well," she began, finding it hard to think clearly, "I didn't know…um..."

"Come inside. You can have the privilege of watching me prepare."

He let go and turned his back on her, and strutted into his dressing room.

Polly didn't know what to do. The rational part of her screamed for her to walk away; but some other part of her just couldn't let this go. She just had to see where this went. And she had to understand for herself why she would be compelled to be near such a person who treated her like this.

As if in a trance, she found herself walking inside, following him, and felt the two huge doors close behind her.

Sergei sat in his dressing chair, looking back at himself in his huge mirror. No reflection showed, but two servants immediately set to work on powdering his face and fluffing his already perfect hair. He lifted his chin as they did, smiling. Polly had never met anyone so in love with himself.

Since he ignored her, she felt like a fool just standing there, watching him get ready. She wondered why he had invited her in. After several moments of silence, she was about to turn around and leave.

Suddenly, he said: "So tell me, Polly, why do like me?"

Polly felt her cheeks redden.

"I never said I like you," she said.

He smirked, and looked back at himself in the mirror, even though there was no reflection. "You don't need to say it. It's obvious."

Polly felt herself redden even more. She'd had just about enough. She was about to storm out, when suddenly, Sergei snapped his fingers, and the servants rushed out of the room.

Polly followed them, ready to leave herself, when Sergei hurried up behind her and grabbed her wrist. He held it firm this time, and turned and pulled her to him, as the door closed, leaving them alone.

He faced her, inches away, staring into her eyes, with a surreal intensity. His features were so perfect, it was like staring at a statue.

"Kiss me," he said, reaching out and holding her face with his palms, just inches away.

Polly felt herself trembling, more nervous than she could ever remember. Her throat grew dry. She was too nervous to even speak, and had no idea what to do.

Despite herself, she began to slowly lean in towards him, when suddenly, he leaned into her, kissing her hard on the lips, which tremendous force. Taken aback, startled, she didn't even enjoy it.

After several seconds, he pulled back.

Then suddenly, without a word, he turned and brushed past her, walking out the room, and slamming the door behind him.

Polly stood there, all alone, completely shocked by what had just happened. And despite herself, she began to cry.

CHAPTER SEVENTEEN

Caitlin walked with Aiden in the early morning light, winding their way slowly through the forest, Ruth at her heels. They had been walking like this together, silently, for what felt like hours. On the one hand, no words needed to be exchanged. As always, when she was around Aiden, she felt like she already knew everything he was going to say.

Yet at the same time, she rarely knew precisely what he was thinking. What she wanted to know most of all was if he remembered everything. From the look in his eyes, she sensed that he did.

Aiden had a funny way of showing up at the strangest moments in her life. Every time she felt like she was at a crossroads, every time she felt unsure of what direction to take, he seemed to appear. And each time he led her back on the path, and she realized he was right—that she should not give up the search for the Shield, for her father, for her own identity. But once she got away from him, once other things happened, it became harder to see clearly. Just being around him helped her to focus.

Being around him also made her feel guilty. When she was around him, she wanted to be a better person, a better warrior; she wanted to train, to be the best she could be. She thought of their unfinished training on Pollepel, and remembered how sharp her skills were becoming. A part of her missed the training, and wanted to go back to it. Seeing him made her think of her unfulfilled ambition.

Caitlin felt such a mix of emotions as she walked with him. Was he disapproving of her? Was he mad at her for not continuing her search? How much did he know already? How had he found her? In some ways, he felt like a father to her. And she was nervous to hear what it was he had to say.

Caitlin knew better than to initiate conversation. She just had to walk, to be with him in the silence. Aiden was always about *being*, not talking. About tuning in to what someone else was thinking and feeling it without needing to say it.

So she respected his way of being, and just walked with him. After what felt like hours, she almost felt as if she were walking alone. She was contemplating her future, wondering where to go from here, wondering if Caleb would return—wondering all these things, when suddenly, the silence was broken by the sound of Aiden's voice:

"Does your arm hurt?" he asked.

Caitlin looked down and saw her bleeding arm, and remembered.

"Yes," she admitted.

"Come here."

He stopped, and she approached, and he lay his hands on the wound and closed his eyes.

When he removed them, she was shocked to find it completely healed.

Ruth whined, and Aiden reached down and with a smile, picked her up, and lay his hands on her injured paw. He then set her back down, and she walked perfectly, without a limp.

Caitlin was shocked.

Aiden sighed, turning to her.

"I had hoped to find you elsewhere," Aiden said.

Caitlin thought about that. As usual, with Aiden, everything he said could be interpreted so many ways. It was so hard to know what he ever really meant. Did that mean he had hoped that she wouldn't be fighting? Or that she wouldn't be with Caleb? Or that she would be searching for the Shield? She assumed he meant the latter.

She thought about how to respond.

"I'm sorry," she said. "I couldn't continue the search."

He didn't respond, and they continued in silence.

Finally, he said: "Maybe you've been searching all along."

That, too, made her think. What did he mean, exactly? Did he mean that some part of her had never stopped the search? That she was searching inside her mind?

"Sometimes you search for an object," he said, "and sometimes it searches for you."

Again, she wasn't quite sure what he meant. But it felt true to her, on some level. She had felt overwhelmed by the search, and even when she'd decided to stop searching, she had felt it was still always there, in the back of her consciousness.

"It's not that I don't want to find it," she said. "I do. And I want to help. I just...I also want to live a normal life. I was tired of running. And then... I found Caleb again."

"And you thought it would work out forever," Aiden said.

Caitlin turned and looked at him, searching his face for some sort of clue. Did he know what their future held?

But all she could see was his slowly shaking his head in disappointment.

She felt embarrassed, as if Aiden had known all along that it would not work out—and that she had been foolish to hope that it would.

"Some things are more important than forever," Aiden replied.

Caitlin thought. Had she been selfish to stay with Caleb? To give up the search? Was she being punished for it now? Was all of this, her meeting Caleb, his leaving—was it all preordained? Had she been a fool to think that she could change their destiny?

"Some things are fated," Aiden said, reading her thoughts, snapping her out of it. "We can never change our destiny. We can try. We can run from it. But life has a way of bringing it back to us.

"And yours, Caitlin," he said, as they finally emerged from the woods, into an open meadow, "is a very special one."

Caitlin looked up, feeling relieved to be out of the dark, heavy woods, into the open.

The two of them continued to walk, and she saw Caleb's castle in the distance. Her heart soared for a moment, as she hoped beyond hope that Caleb might have returned.

Aiden shook his head.

"You haven't listened," he said. "You won't find him there."

Caitlin turned to him.

"Will he return?" she asked. She scrutinized Aiden's face, waiting for any reaction.

But he was expressionless, staring off into the horizon with his large, light blue eyes.

"The question isn't whether he comes back for you," he said. "It is what *you*, Caitlin, decide to do. You are stronger than one man. You are stronger than one relationship. You have a mission. A destiny. And you have free will. It is not your place to wait for anyone. Is your place to *create* your fate. To take action."

He finally stopped, turned and looked at her. She looked up at him, and was taken aback at the intensity of his eyes, which looked both prophetic and scolding.

"When will you stop running from your destiny, Caitlin? When will you accept who you are?"

She looked at him, wondering.

"Who am I?" she asked. She wasn't sure she knew herself anymore.

He stared back. "A warrior," he said flatly.

A warrior, she thought. She didn't always feel like it. On some days, yes. But on others, she felt just like everybody else. She had moments of courage, but she felt like they were only moments.

"A warrior is defined by moments," Aiden said. "A single moment can make you a warrior. A warrior is also defined by decisions. By courage. But a warrior, otherwise, is normal. A warrior cannot be a warrior every moment of the day. But, a warrior's *spirit* is always there."

Caitlin thought about that. She felt flattered by the term, and the more she pondered it, the more she liked the label, the identity. But she also felt it came with a responsibility.

"You need to choose," Aiden said. "You can stay here, give up the mission, and live a very happy domestic life with Caleb. It will be a life of the heart. But not of the spirit. We are brought to this planet to choose between two lives: a life of the heart, or a life of the spirit. Our heart can tie us down to domestic matters. But our spirit must soar. It must follow its calling.

"You're calling, Caitlin, is to find the Shield. To help save us all. To find your father. And most importantly, to find out who you really are."

Caitlin stared at him, her mind reeling with all the implications.

"But what if I never find the Shield?" she asked.

"What if the Shield is not something to be found?" he asked back.

She looked at him puzzled. "What do you mean?"

"You assume that the Shield is an object."

She was baffled.

"Of course I do. What else could it be?"

Even as she asked the question, her mind spun with a million possibilities. Was the Shield something else? And if it wasn't physical, what else could it be?

But Aiden didn't help. He stared, expressionless.

"I'll tell you this," he said, finally. "A warrior's mission is never about finding an object, or completing a task. It is about the *journey*. It is not about what you find in the journey, but about what you *become*."

She looked at him. "What am I becoming?"

But Aiden turned and continued walking in silence, and she followed him, all the way up to Caleb's castle. The door was wide open, and she looked and saw that it was clear he had not returned.

The two of them stood there, before the open door.

"The price of being a warrior is leaving behind family. Home. The ones you love. It is the journey that every warrior must take. And one you must do alone.

"The choice is yours," he said. "You can go inside, and stay here, and live happily. Or you can come back with me. And train. And fulfill your mission."

Caitlin stood there, thinking. On the one hand, the thought of leaving Caleb broke her heart. The thought of him coming home and not finding her saddened her beyond belief, as did the thought of her giving up what could be the perfect life.

On the other hand, she felt something deep inside her stirring. It was her warrior instinct. She felt a primal urge to train. To become whatever it was she was meant to be.

As Caitlin stood there, staring back at Aiden, she felt as if this were one of the peak crossroads of her life. She felt how monumental the choice was before her, and felt how it would irrevocably change her life forever.

And strangely enough, she, in a flash, felt certain of her decision.

She knew, deep down, what she had to do.

CHAPTER EIGHTEEN

Sam walked the grounds of Versailles alone, trying to collect his thoughts. He walked down an ambling path, twisting and turning its way through perfectly trimmed hedges. Ever since he'd met Kendra, he had been able to think of little else. There was something about her: she was so young, and her skin was so smooth and flawless, and her aqua eyes completely hypnotized him. When she looked at him, with the full power of those eyes on him, he had been able to think of nothing else.

And even now, after an entire day had passed since he'd seen her, he still could think of little else. He was intoxicated by her.

He had been shown his room, and was still waiting for Aiden to summon him, and in the meantime, he didn't know what else to do, other than wait. So he had shown himself the grounds. He had stopped and watched for a while, with interest, as his fellow vampires sparred. He admired their techniques. But even as he watched them, he felt his own strength surging within him, and he knew that he was stronger than them all.

Then why hadn't Aiden summoned him? Why had he been kept waiting here, on the sideline?

Sam walked, trying to remember his sense of direction. Caitlin. He had come back to find her, to help her. Then that Polly girl had appeared, and had led him to this place. Sam sensed somehow that Polly and Aiden might be connected to Caitlin. He felt intuitively that he was here for a reason, and exactly where he should be.

Yet still, he was antsy. He wanted to find her. To help her, if need be, especially on her mission. He wanted to find his Dad. He had a feeling that Aiden might know where she was, and he was anxious for him to summon him. Without that, he didn't know where else to even begin to look for her.

In the meantime, while waiting, his thoughts of Kendra had overtaken him so much, he was having a hard time trying to stay focused on finding Caitlin. He found himself, instead, dreaming of Kendra, of wanting to be with her, wanting to see her again. He even found himself daydreaming of staying here with her. Of not even searching for Caitlin or his father anymore.

He chastised himself for even having the thought. How could a girl have such an impact on him so quickly? How could she affect him so much to make him feel loyal to her, over his own family? Whatever it was, he could not understand it. He felt that when he was around her, he was in the grip of something more powerful than himself, something even he didn't understand. He felt that it was dangerous.

At that moment, Sam resolved not to seek her out again, and not to spend any more time with her. If she looked his way, he would look away, and if she tried to talk to him, he would ignore her. That was the only thing to do with someone like this.

At just that moment, as if the universe were playing tricks on him, Sam looked up to see Kendra standing there. He stopped in his tracks, shocked. There she was, standing on the outskirts of the crowd, out of sight from everyone, on the edge of the woods. She was sitting proudly on a horse, looking down at him, and loosely holding the reins of a second horse beside her. She looked down at Sam, expressionless. She wasn't smiling.

But then again, she was looking at him.

Despite himself, he found himself approaching her.

"What are you doing here?" he asked her.

"I'm going for a ride," she said. "Women are not allowed to ride around here. At least not the way I would like to ride. So I take my horse of sight from the others."

Sam looked over and saw the vacant horse beside her, and saw her still staring at him. He couldn't figure out her expression; she was just too hard to read. Was she inviting him to join her? Or was she waiting for him to walk away, to leave her alone? And if so, who was the second horse for?

"I hope I'm not intruding," Sam said, trying to figure it out. "I didn't mean to startle you."

"I'm never startled," Kendra said. She stared at him, then looked away, as if watching something on the horizon.

"I'm going for my afternoon ride," she announced, then suddenly turned her back, and began walking away on her horse. She dropped the reins of the other horse. "You can join me—that is, if you're unafraid," she added, her back to him as she rode off into the woods.

Sam looked at the vacant horse, and he could not believe it. Had she just invited him to join her? Was it a date? She sure had a funny way of asking. Maybe she was just too proud, too embarrassed to really ask him.

Whatever it was, he didn't want to miss his chance. Despite his new resolve, when he was actually in her presence, all his resolve went out the window. He *had* to be with her. It was a physical thing, something he could not stop if he chose.

He hurried up to the horse, jumped on, and kicked it, so that it was trotting after her. Within seconds, he caught up.

She broke into a trot, and moments later, the two of them were trotting through a broad, winding forest trail.

*

It felt like they had been riding for hours when Kendra finally stopped. It had been a challenge for Sam to keep up with her, as she was so unpredictable: at some points, she had broken into a gallop, across open fields, without notice. At other moments, they had trotted together beside streaming brooks, in and out of the forest, clearings, meadows.

Finally, she had turned and taken a narrow path up a gently sloping hill, covered in fields of flowers. She'd found a spot under an ancient tree, and had dismounted and tied her horse to a branch. Sam did the same, and as he saw the well-worn marks in the branch, he guessed she had been to this spot many times before.

Ignoring him, she turned her back and walked to a bubbling stream nearby. She knelt and splashed cold water on her face. She ran it through her hair and as she did, she pulled her hair out of its bun and let it fall around her shoulders.

Sam watched, mesmerized, as the sun shone through her hair. He had never seen anyone more beautiful. He could not believe his luck in being here right now. Why had she chosen him? She hadn't exactly invited him, but she hadn't exactly told him *not* to join her either. And even though she did a great job of ignoring him, and had barely said a word to him the entire afternoon, he still sensed that deep down she liked having him with her. He only wondered if it was because some company for her was better than no company at all, or if she really wanted him there.

Kendra turned to him.

"I'd like to sit in the grass," she said. "There is a blanket in the saddle."

Sam at first didn't realize what she was talking about; but then he looked over at her horse, and saw a large silk blanket sitting in a pouch. He realized she expected him to unfold the blanket and lay it out for her.

It annoyed him a bit. He was not her servant. At the same time, he just figured that this was the treatment she was used to, and he didn't want to rock the boat over it. Plus, he really didn't mind. So he took out her large, pink blanket, and laid it out on the grass.

Kendra walked over and sat down gingerly, smoothing her skirt, and lay back, resting her head in her hands, and staring at the sky.

Sam looked down, and saw the big empty space on the blanket beside her. He wondered if she wanted him to join her.

"Um…" he began, "can I sit with you?"

He watched her shrug, ever so slightly, as she stared at the sky. His legs were hurting from all that riding, so he decided to take that as a yes.

He went over and sat on the blanket beside her, and laid on his back beside her, resting his head in his hands, too.

The sky was beautiful from this perspective, a crystal clear blue, with small white clouds, broken into a million pieces, drifting overhead.

They both lay like that for what felt like forever, and Sam finally wondered if he should say something. The silence, he felt, was a bit awkward.

"That was fun," he said. "Thanks for bringing me."

"I didn't bring you," she answered. "You brought yourself."

Sam was indignant. He'd had enough of this, and he felt it was time to confront her.

He sat up.

"Okay then," he said, "I'll leave."

He was preparing to stand, when he felt a cold hand on his wrist. He turned, and saw her staring at him.

"Don't be so dramatic," she said. "I didn't tell you to leave."

He stared back at her, puzzled. Clearly, she wanted him to stay. But why couldn't she just come out and say it? Was she afraid? Was she nervous? Was she that proud?

Everything inside of Sam screamed at him to leave, to go back to the training ground, seek out Aiden, and stay focused on his search for Caitlin.

But something inside him, something he could not control, forced him to stay.

He slowly lay back down. This time, he propped himself on his elbow, turning and looking at her.

She went back to laying on her back and looking up at the sky.

Sam couldn't stop staring at her sculpted features. They were perfect.

"I come here, to this spot, to get away from Versailles," she said, after a while. "There are no humans here. No vampires. No one to gossip or slander me." She turned and looked at him. "Have you heard them talking about me?"

Sam shrugged. He had, indeed, already heard things—rumors, whispers. But he didn't want to upset her.

"Tell me," she said. "What did they say?"

"They say that you want to be turned. And that you'll use anyone to get it."

Kendra looked back at the sky, and for the first time in the day, she broke into a smile.

"Do you believe them?"

Sam shrugged. "I don't know. I don't even know you."

"Well, don't. It's all gossiping. Backbiting. The only way they can get at me. It's because I'm superior to them. They know they can never be like me. So they pretend that I want to be like them."

Sam studied her. He didn't know what to believe. All he knew for sure was that he was completely enamored of her. And whether she was being truthful or not, he still felt sorry for her.

She turned to him, finally, propped herself on her elbow, and looked him right in the eyes. She was only inches away, and he felt his heart race faster.

"Do you think that's the only reason I want to be with you?" she asked.

Sam shrugged. She was so close, he could smell her skin, her perfume. He could hardly concentrate, and didn't trust himself to speak.

As she came in closer, he felt his heart pounding. She was now only inches away.

"Well, it's not," she said.

And then, suddenly, she moved in, ever closer, until both of their lips were touching.

And from that moment on, Sam knew that he was completely, utterly, lost.

CHAPTER NINETEEN

Kyle stood before the Bastille, hiding in the shadows in that special moment between darkness and light. He knew this would be the time of the changing of the guard, when the night shift vampires would be replaced by the day ones. He knew this would be the moment when they were most vulnerable to attack, and when they would least expect it.

He only needed one entry point. One weak, young, vulnerable, and inexperienced vampire. He could take him out, and get inside. It was a crucial first step. Before he could direct Napoleon and his men in a full-fledged attack, he needed to do his reconnaissance first. He needed to make sure that the savage seven were still down there, and he needed to find the angle to set them free.

He watched, and waited.

This was a funny building, the Bastille, a circular, stone tower that rose right up to the sky. It almost looked like a lighthouse in the center of the city. There were no windows—just a few iron bars here and there. Kyle spotted the multiple layers of silver bars, and knew why they were there. Inside, deep underground, lay seven of the most vicious creatures that had walked the planet. He had heard that, in addition to the silver, there was another layer of a special metal installed, to contain them. He needed to find out exactly which type of metal it was. Once he did, he would know what he needed to break it.

Kyle saw his opportunity, and moved quick. As the shift changed, one of the guards moved just a little bit slower than the others, on the far side of the building. Kyle crept up behind him, and before he could react, reached up and snapped his neck.

The man collapsed, lifeless, and as he did, Kyle grabbed the key off his waist. It was a long, silver skeleton key, and Kyle turned and opened the lock on the silver door. He could have kicked it down, but he didn't want to call attention to himself. He was still vastly outnumbered, and he didn't know the extent of their protection and didn't want to risk a confrontation.

Kyle dragged the body so that it would not be detected, and shut the door behind them.

Kyle turned and surveyed his surroundings. It took a moment for his eyes to adjust to the darkness. The only light that came in came from way up high, through bars high above. It was a circular structure inside as well, with the corridors shaped in steep circles, rising and falling from the top of the tower to the basement. It was all stone.

Kyle headed down. He knew that down there, deep in the bowels of the earth, would be where they were locked up.

As he descended level after level, deeper than he imagined possible, hundreds of feet beneath the earth, finally, the staircase ended in a wall. He knew there had to be something behind it.

Kyle took several steps back and charged, putting his shoulder into it. The wall gave way, stone collapsing everywhere in a big crash. He hadn't wanted to call such attention to himself, but he saw no other choice.

As he suspected, he saw the staircase continue of the other side, descending even further down. He took off at a sprint, knowing there was no time to lose.

Finally, he reached it. The staircase ended in massive columns of silver bars, thicker than he had ever seen. More important, he could tell right away that they were coated in some kind of material. As he reached out to touch them, he felt a burning in his palms, and felt himself being repelled. This metal was too toxic, even for him.

He gazed closely, trying to detect what it was. Finally, he realized: titanium. The most toxic of all metals for vampires.

He looked past them, and saw additional layers of bars behind them.

He had no doubt now that the savage seven were being kept here.

Kyle heard a faint rumbling noise. As he leaned in, suddenly a long, yellow claw reached out of the blackness, towards the bars. This was followed by a hideous face, with long, orange fangs, drooling. He could smell its rotten breath, even from here. Ancient, primordial creatures, the savage seven were too hideous too look at, even for Kyle, and he had to turn away. For a moment, he felt relieved that they were locked up, and he second-guessed releasing them.

Would he be unleashing a danger greater than even he could control?

But he had no choice. These creatures were just what he needed to unleash a monumental chaos upon the city, and to catch and kill Caitlin. He'd have to risk it.

Don't worry, he thought, I'll come back for you and set you free.

As if reading his mind, the other six suddenly appeared, too, snarling back.

Suddenly, Kyle heard a rattling behind him. He spun to see several guards bearing down on him. He was surprised they were so close: they had been quicker than he'd expected.

Before he could react, Kyle felt himself being picked up and slammed into the silver bars. He felt pain rack through his entire body. He was shocked, more than anything else, to realize how powerful these vampire guards were. Paris had certainly spared no expense in guarding this place.

But Kyle was no slouch. He'd been alive for thousands of years longer than most, and he had plenty of tricks up his sleeve. He summoned his primordial rage, and managed to grab two of the four guards facing him and smash their heads together.

They collapsed, but the other two jumped Kyle, knocking him down and kicking him several times. He was stunned by their speed and strength, but he managed to catch his breath just long enough to grab one of their feet, break his ankle, and swing him into the other guard.

But it barely phased them. The four guards immediately recovered, and were pouncing back for Kyle. He couldn't believe how fast they were.

He didn't want to risk fighting them any longer. Now was not the time. He saw his chance, and he leapt through the crowd, taking off at a sprint, back up the staircase.

They were right on his heels.

Kyle realized he could not outrun them, and he leapt into flight. Using his wings, he flew higher and higher, up the staircase, up the shaft, aiming right for the ceiling. He knew he couldn't risk stopping, so he gained speed and braced himself for impact.

He smashed through the stone ceiling, and seconds later was in the air, flying fast away.

He flew off into the horizon, and turned back to see the guards standing on the roof, watching him. But luckily for him, they wouldn't follow. Their orders were to guard the Bastille.

Kyle was stunned from the ordeal as he flew away, and realized he'd need more manpower than he needed. He looked forward to returning, to storming the place with Napoleon's men, and demolishing the place down to the ground.

CHAPTER TWENTY

Holding Ruth in her arms, Caitlin flew beside Aiden, high over the country.

She looked down and watched as the landscape changed. At first, they had flown over the shoreline, and she had watched the crashing waves, the magical cliffs and beaches; then they had turned towards land, and the landscape changed to rolling hills, then to woods. It was an entirely new part of France, one she had never seen, and she couldn't believe how endless this country seemed.

Caitlin felt torn with mixed emotions as she flew. On the one hand, she was happy to be beside Aiden, beside someone she knew and trusted, someone who, she knew, would not abandon her. She was excited to see wherever it was he would take her, and excited to begin her training and her mission anew. She wondered if she might see Polly there, and the thought warmed her. She also wondered if Blake could be there, and the thought left a pit in her stomach. She wasn't sure how she would react to that.

At the same time, her heart still broke at the thought of leaving Caleb. She imagined him arriving home, at his empty castle, and finding her gone. She had never promised him she would stay. But still, he seemed to hope she would. He would not know where to find her. Would this be the last time they ever saw each other?

Had she turned her back on a perfect life? If she'd waited just wait a few more days, it was possible that all would be peaceful and tranquil with Caleb, for the rest of their lives. Was she leaving prematurely?

Caitlin couldn't help feeling as if she was were swept up in an endless tide of events; it felt like an undercurrent in an ocean, taking her out further and further, to more clues, back to another time, another place, another artifact, another key. She prayed that this might be the final time and place, that this time, for sure, she would find her father and the Shield. Then maybe, after it was all done, she could stay in one place. And maybe even stay with Caleb. Would her father like Caleb? It was a question that had often crossed her mind.

Caitlin looked down and watched as the thick woods eventually gave way to open fields, and as eventually, these, too, gave way, to formal, well-tended roads. The sky opened up, and in the distance, on the horizon, Caitlin spotted the most magnificent structure she had ever seen.

It wasn't just one structure but several—huge marble buildings, spread out over an enormous compound, separated by formal, ornate gardens, with a huge fountain in the middle. Flying over it, circling, again and again, Caitlin marveled that anything manmade could be that perfect. It looked like a palace fit for a king.

As she followed Aiden, circling, getting lower, she began to realize that this was where his coven lived. She was shocked. Pollepel had been magnificent, and so had his island outside of Venice. But this place outdid them all. She vaguely recognized the buildings, and wondered if she had seen pictures once somewhere.

"Where are we?" she yelled out, as they circled lower.

They dove in low, and landed on a road on the edge of the woods.

As they landed, he turned and looked at her:

"Versailles," he said. "Your new home. At least, while you choose to train here."

A servant stepped forward from behind a horse and carriage, dressed in royal finery. He took several steps towards Aiden, and bowed.

"You will now receive your formal introduction to the palace," he said. As he did, the servant hurried around and opened the gilded door to the carriage for Caitlin, waiting for her.

She was confused. "What about you? Aren't you coming?"

"I have important matters to attend to. You'll be shown your room, and when you are ready, you'll meet me on the training field."

And with that, he took several steps and leapt into the air, flying off.

Caitlin turned to the servant, who still stood there, holding the door.

"Thank you," she said, embarrassed to be waited upon. "You don't need to hold the door. I'm not royalty, after all."

He smiled back as Caitlin stepped up into the carriage, and then closed it behind her.

It was small and cozy in here, as Caitlin settled back on velvet cushions, Ruth in her lap, and looked out the dainty glass window. The servant jumped on board, whipped the horses, and they were off, the horses trotting, taking Caitlin through the manicured road leading to the palace.

Caitlin leaned forward and looked, and Ruth did, too. She marveled at the perfectly cut grass, the endless, formal gardens designed in every shape, the huge fountain bursting at its center, the perfectly trimmed hedges. She marveled at how smooth the roads were, how white they were, how well taken care of. It was like riding on air.

As they pulled up to the main entrance, Caitlin saw several people come out to greet her. She felt embarrassed. The sleek, marble steps, were already crowded with servants, royals, all sorts of people teeming, waiting to get a glimpse of her. They all watched with expectation as the carriage pulled up.

They came to a stop and the servant opened the door for her, and she slowly climbed out.

As she looked at the crowd, at all their fine outfits and elaborate hats, she suddenly felt self-conscious of what she was wearing. She looked down and was mortified to see that she still wore the simple wardrobe the nuns had given her.

Caitlin ascended the steps—there seemed to be hundreds of them—until she finally reached the top. The crowd stared back. She wondered who exactly was supposed to introduce her, to show her around, now that Aiden had left her to her own devices. She scanned the faces, hoping to find someone familiar, and especially hoping to find Polly.

But she didn't recognize anyone. And she suddenly felt like a stranger here.

Caitlin heard a giggling, and turned to see several girls, dressed in incredible finery, whispering and laughing at her, as they eyed her from head to toe. Caitlin felt her cheeks redden. Clearly, they were making fun of her.

Caitlin suddenly felt under scrutiny, and wanted to leave this place. Everyone here seemed so formal, so uptight, so judgmental. And she didn't recognize anyone. She was thinking of turning around and leaving, when suddenly, someone stepped forward from the crowd.

She was one of the most beautiful women Caitlin had ever seen. She was dressed in a long, green, satin dress, with high collars that framed her perfect cheekbones. She had dark skin, standing out amidst all the pale, white faces, and she looked to Caitlin to be of African descent, and maybe 18. She had large, emerald green eyes and long lashes, and she stood so erect, with such a straight posture, so regal. Caitlin wondered if she were a princess.

She turned to the girls who were giggling and scowled at them.

"Silence yourselves!" she snapped. "That is not how we treat our guests!"

The group of girls quieted.

The woman took two steps towards Caitlin, and curtsied.

Caitlin curtsied back, trying her best to remain dignified. She was so grateful for this woman's intervention, whoever she was.

"It is a great pleasure to meet you, Caitlin," she said. "Aiden has told us all about you. I am Lily."

Caitlin shook her hand. "Thank you," she said.

"I've asked Aiden for the honor of escorting you, and showing you our grounds. Would you like to accompany me?"

"I'd be delighted," Caitlin said, relieved to be away from this crowd.

Caitlin stepped up, linked arms with Lily, and the two of them began walking away from the steps, Ruth at her heels.

"Don't mind them," Lily whispered to Caitlin as they walked, the crowd parting ways. "They are young. And bored."

Caitlin couldn't help smiling. She really liked Lily already, and already felt that they would be close friends.

"Caitlin!" suddenly came an excited voice.

Caitlin recognized the voice immediately.

She turned, and there, rushing at her, dressed in a royal gown but otherwise looking exactly as she'd remembered her, was Polly.

Polly came rushing towards her and embraced her in a huge hug, before Caitlin could even react.

Ruth whined hysterically, until Polly leaned down and hugged her, too.

"Oh my God, I can't believe it!" she said in a rush. "I had a dream about you last night. It was so weird. I mean I know I've never met you before. At least not formally. But in the dream it was like, I remembered everything. Pollepel, Venice—the whole thing. Was it really you? I can't believe it!"

Caitlin couldn't help smiling back. She was delighted to see Polly, and even more delighted that she remembered.

"Yes, it was me. It *is* me. The same old Caitlin. I'm so happy you're here."

Polly embraced her in a second hug. Judging from the stares of all the formal people around them, it seemed that Polly was breaking etiquette.

"Oh my God, it's incredible!" she said. "We have so much catching up to do. I have to show you around," she said, as she grabbed her arm and began to lead her away.

Caitlin stopped and turned to Lily, who seemed disappointed.

"Lily was just about to," Caitlin explained to Polly. "I'd like for her to join us."

"Oh my god, of course!" Polly said. "Lily is awesome!"

And with that, Polly locked one arm with Lily and one with Caitlin, practically dragging the two of them away from the crowd.

They walked towards the huge marble entrance of the palace. Caitlin had never been in such a magnificent place in her life. Not only was everything built in such a grand scale, but everything was so well-maintained. Everywhere she looked, she saw freshly cut flowers. The floors were draped in magnificent rugs, there were endless wall hangings, tapestries, oil paintings; there were rare china vases.

If that were not enough, huge crystal chandeliers hung everywhere, their light reflected by dozens of ornate mirrors. The sun shone through rows of windows larger any she had ever seen. The three of them walked so far just to get down one corridor, that her feet already hurt—and there was still no end in sight.

Polly had not stopped talking the entire time. Caitlin had never seen her so excited. She went on and on, hardly taking a breath, as she filled Caitlin in on everything about the palace, the grounds, Aiden, their training, the Royals, the local gossip, Marie Antoinette—and most of all, her new crush. She would not mention his name. All she'd say that he was a singer. A vocalist.

"You *have* to meet him," Polly said, grabbing Caitlin's wrist in enthusiasm, "oh my God, he's so amazing. I mean, he can be a little brusque at first, but he doesn't really mean it. It's just like how he warms up for his art, you know what I mean? I can't stop thinking about him. I'm really falling for this guy!"

Caitlin examined Polly's face, and couldn't believe it. She had never seen Polly so in love. She was happy for her. She was a little worried by the way she described this guy, though. A bit brusque? No one should be brusque to Polly, Caitlin thought. She felt the need to check out this guy for herself, to see if he was truly the right one for Polly. Especially since Polly seemed to be so in love.

"I'm so happy for you," Caitlin said. "Just be careful. Take it slow. Make sure he treats you well. You deserve that."

"Of course he treats me well, why wouldn't he?" Polly shot back, sounding defensive.

Caitlin was shocked. Polly had never snapped at her before, in all the time she had known her. Caitlin sensed that she had changed—that this guy, this singer, was having some sort of weird influence over her. It made her worry even more.

"I'm just saying," Caitlin said softly, trying to backtrack, "you deserve the best."

Polly seemed to soften at that. She looked down and checked her watch. "Oh my god!" she exclaimed, suddenly wide-eyed. "I'm almost late. He's giving a performance at the far end of the palace. I have to go!"

And with that, Polly suddenly took off down a corridor.

Caitlin stopped, watching her go, completely baffled. She had never seen Polly like this. She couldn't believe that she would just take off like that, so soon after barely seeing her. It seemed like she was totally under the control of this guy. Caitlin had a sinking feeling about it.

"Was she always like this?" Caitlin asked Lily.

Lily shook her head. "No. It's only since she met him. He's a real jerk, too, if you ask me. Full of himself."

Caitlin sensed that Lily was right. That Polly was under the spell of a guy who was wrong for her. She remembered all the times she'd had to watch her girlfriends date guys who were jerks, and their friends were too clouded to see it. It was painful for her to have to watch them go through that, especially when there was nothing she could do about it. Whenever she tried to help them, give them advice, they didn't want to listen, and inevitably, it just seemed to backfire on their friendship.

"That's not the Polly I know," Caitlin said.

"Me either," Lily said.

Caitlin sighed as Lily took her arm, and the two of them continued walking down the corridor, Ruth following.

Caitlin missed Polly, but at the same time, it felt good to have a chance to walk with Lily in the calm and silence. Polly could sometimes be a bit overwhelming.

Around Lily, though, Caitlin fell totally peaceful.

"So you and Polly have known each other a long time?" Lily asked.

"Centuries," Caitlin said, but immediately after she said it, she realized it must have sounded weird to a human. She wondered if Lily would think she was crazy.

But Lily nodded, seeming to take it all in stride.

"Don't worry," Lily said, "I know all about your kind," she said. "I've been living with you guys all my life here. Nothing surprises me."

"So you've lived here your whole life?" Caitlin asked.

Lily nodded. "I'm a member of the royal family. Marie is my second cousin. Adopted, if you're wondering. These people certainly didn't give birth to an African child like me," Lily said, and burst into laughter. She had a warm, infectious laugh. "My birth parents are from Kenya. But they died when I was an infant, and I was adopted by one of the Royals while they were on their African vacation. And here I am. A member of the royal family. Isn't that ironic?"

"No, I don't think it's ironic at all," Caitlin said, seriously. "In fact, you seem to be the only one here with real class."

Caitlin could see Lily's expression change. Her face seemed to fold into appreciation, and at that moment, Caitlin could tell that she had just made a friend for life.

"That's the nicest thing anyone here's ever said to me," she said. "All the others do here is backbite and gossip about each other. You're different."

They walked out the rear palace door, down a set of marble steps, and through the formal gardens.

"You better pick up your pace, girlfriend," Lily said. "We've got miles to go to show you this place."

They walked for what seemed like forever, through garden after garden, as Lily pointed out all the different buildings. They walked around a large pond, and Lily pointed out where Marie's private residence was.

"At least she's fun," Lily said. "Lots of parties. It's never dull around her. It's the people who surround her that are the problem. Of course, Marie's one of yours, though. That's the big thing around here: who's vampire and who's human. All the humans here want to be vampires. But the vampires will never turn them. So we live in a sort of harmony together. The vampires watch our backs, protect this place from attack, and we give them a place to live. We guard the palace by day, and they by night. So far, it's working out. But there've been a few close encounters over the years."

"What do you mean?" Caitlin asked.

"I mean, a human falling for a vampire, or vice versa. People almost getting turned. That's a big no-no for Aiden. If that happens, they're out. It's always a source of tension around here. We can be friends, but we can't cross that line. Which is fine with me. All the guys I like are human anyway. But that's not true of all of my human girlfriends. Some of them set their eyes on a vampire, and just won't let it go, if you know what I mean."

Caitlin thought about that, and remembered back to when she was human, and she knew how they felt.

"Anyway, all your kind do is train all the time anyway. They spend the whole day on the training ground. Every day it seems like they've got a new weapon to try out, or some new skill. It's fun to watch. Us royals gather around, and watch you guys square off. It's probably the greatest entertainment around here."

They walked down a set of grass steps, across another formal courtyard, and approached a low, marble building, set back from the rest of the palace.

"That's where you guys live," Lily said. "I trust you've seen worse accommodations?"

Caitlin was in awe. It looked like a miniature palace. She couldn't believe she'd be staying here. In the fields all around her, she saw dozens of vampires training, sparring with bamboo swords, their click-clack heard from yards away.

She suddenly had a pang of worry, as she wondered if Blake were among them. She was going to ask Lily, but was afraid to hear the answer. That was the last thing she wanted to deal with right now. As it was, her heart was still hurting over Caleb, wondering if she'd made the right decision to leave.

Lily stopped before the door, and faced Caitlin. "Well, this is far as I go," Lily said.

Caitlin stepped up and gave her a hug. "Thank you," Caitlin said. "For everything."

Lily hugged her back.

"I'll see you soon," Lily said. "After all, humans and vampires always feast together. I'll save you a seat next to mine."

"I'd like that," Caitlin said.

*

Caitlin surveyed her room, taken aback by its opulence. Other rooms she'd stayed in, like the one in Pollepel, had been beautiful but simple—

medieval and stone, almost monastic. This room was the opposite. It was huge, grand, ornate, decorated with a rug and drapes and a chandelier and mirrors and a vanity, and a huge four-poster bed. Everything about this room was oversized, overdone, piling opulence on top of opulence.

Caitlin didn't necessarily mind. After being on the run for so long, after sleeping in one place after the next, she appreciated being in such a quiet, comfortable place. She certainly could get used to living in a palace. It just felt so foreign to her, as if this were all a dream. She tiptoed through the room as if she were in a museum, afraid to touch the shining oak of the bedframe, or the perfectly smoothed silk linens on top of it.

Ruth, on the other hand, had no qualms. She happily wagged her tail as she ran about the room, smelling everything.

Caitlin made her way over to the huge dresser in the corner. It had a shining, white marble top, with golden drawers. On top of it, there had been laid out already several sets of clothing options for her. She could not believe it. Each outfit was more beautiful and extravagant than the next. There was a long, formal gown, in a black silk; there was the Versailles version of casual clothing, which was just a slightly shorter gown, but which still looked formal to Caitlin, in a light blue, with yellow buttons.

Then there were all sorts of hats. And beside these, there was what looked like a training outfit. It was made of a material she had never seen, like a thin leather, all-black. It looked like a skintight battle uniform, padded, with long pants and a tee shirt. Caitlin recognized. It was the sparring gear of Aiden's coven. It was lightweight and durable, and allowed her to fight, and at the same time, it managed to look elegant, with its shiny black coat and high collars.

Caitlin immediately pulled off all of her dirty clothes and was about to change, when she spotted a luxurious bathtub in the corner of the room. It was already filled with water, and she could see by the steam rising off of it that it had been heated for her. There were bubbles in it, and it was surrounded by all sorts of soaps.

Caitlin closed the drapes of her sun-soaked room, went over to her tub, and stepped slowly inside it, naked. She felt the luxurious feeling of the steaming hot water, and felt every muscle in her body relax. She had never appreciated it more.

Caitlin leaned back, closed her eyes, and breathed. Images flashed through her mind, and she tried to stop them. But it was of little use. She saw Caleb's face, how he looked in the morning, as they sat on his terrace together. She saw him laughing, as they were horseback riding on the beach. She saw them flying together, dipping, swerving. And she saw him on the hilltop, the beauty and serenity of his expression, right before that falcon landed.

She tried to push the image out of her head. That moment when everything had changed for her.

She willed herself to think of anything else. She thought of Aiden. Of their walk in the forest that morning. What he had said. *What if the Shield is not something you find? What if it is something that finds you? What if it's about what you are becoming?*

She opened her eyes and stared up at the ceiling as she thought about that. What did he mean by that? What exactly was she becoming?

Caitlin looked over at the end table, where she'd placed her father's scroll. It lay there, in its gilded case, as if luring her to open it. She wondered what he could have possibly written to her. She wondered if she should open it now. A part of her desperately wanted to. But another part of her knew that if she did, and if it suggested a clue, she would have no choice but to follow. And she didn't want to leave this new place so quickly. She was happy here. And she needed to train.

Still, Caitlin's curiosity was beginning to get the best of her. She slowly got up from the bath, covered in bubbles, wrapped herself in a huge bath towel, and walked barefoot across the marble floor. She reached out and picked up the case. She held it up, examining it, feeling its energy.

With her heightened senses, she could feel how powerful it was. A jolt of electricity ran through her hands. She was on the verge of opening it.

Suddenly, there was a knock on the door. Caitlin quickly put down the scroll, tied the towel tighter around her, and crossed the room. She slid back the latch and looked out, and saw a pair of blue eyes looking back at her, framing a freckled face, bright red hair, big ears, and a large smile. She was taken aback. It was Patrick.

"Caitlin? Are you ready yet?" she recognized that voice. It was definitely him.

"Ready for what?" she called back, confused.

"Aiden sent me. It sparring time. Let's go. We're gonna be late!"

"Just a minute!" she yelled.

She crossed the room, dried herself, and quickly changed into her sparring gear. She pulled her hair back, tied it in a bun, and tucked what was left of it underneath her high collar, so it would be safe for battle.

She crossed the room, Ruth at her heels, and opened the door.

There stood Patrick, his back to her. He quickly spun, and broke into that huge, boyish smile of his.

Caitlin could not help smiling back. There was something about him, so boyish and goofy, that always made her smile.

"God, you girls take forever to get ready!" he said, smiling.

She came out, Ruth trailing, and followed him as he headed off across the field.

As they walked, he thrust a bamboo sword into her hand. She loved the feeling of it, and ran her hand along its hilt.

"I'm Caitlin," she said, not sure if he remembered.

He laughed.

"Don't you think I know?" he asked. "Everyone's talking about you already. They want to see what you got!"

They turned the corner, through the formal garden, and there, in the open field, were dozens of Aiden's vampires. They were lined up neatly alongside a huge sparring ring, while two of them sparred in the middle. In the distance, on the marble steps, sat a crowd of royals and onlookers, watching the scene.

The click-clack of the bamboo swords filled the air.

"I hear you're pretty good," Patrick said. "But not as good as me, I'm sure," he said, with a wink.

He increased his pace and so did she, and soon they were standing with the others. They stood off to the side, and Caitlin watched as the two vampires in the middle sparred.

Caitlin couldn't believe it. It was Taylor and Tyler. The twins. After all these centuries, here they were, still sparring with each other. As she watched, Tyler came in for a lunge, but Taylor used her wings and flew right over his head; as she did, she cracked him hard in the back with her bamboo sword.

There was a roar among the crowd.

"No fair!" Tyler yelled to Aiden, who watched patiently. "She used her wings!"

Aiden stepped forward.

"Taylor, you know better," he said.

"It was more of a leap than a flight!" she said.

Aiden shook his head slowly. "Disqualified."

Taylor, dejected, walked off to the side.

"Caitlin!" Aiden yelled out.

All eyes turned to her, as she felt her face flush with embarrassment.

"You're up!" he yelled.

As Taylor left, a space opened on the sparring floor. Tyler stood there, waiting for his next opponent.

Caitlin walked slowly, feeling the eyes on her, and faced off with him. She squeezed the hilt of her sword tightly, assured by its weight.

As she faced off with Tyler, about ten feet away, she studied him. He looked exactly as she remembered. If she remembered, he was fast, and liked to jab more than swing. He also had a tendency to sweep his opponents. She looked into his eyes, and saw a blend of mischievousness and ego. She could tell from his glance that he expected this would be an easy victory.

Tyler jumped into action. He lunged right for her with the sword, and if he'd been successful, he would have poked her hard, right in the gut.

Luckily, Caitlin's reflexes kicked in. At the last second, she dodged, stepping to the side, and Tyler went flying passed her. But he only missed her by a hair. Caitlin was surprised by his speed. She focused. She had to get her game on.

She let him charge again, preferring a defensive position. This time, he struck from above, coming right down for her shoulder blades. She grabbed both ends of her sword and held it above her head, and blocked the strike. Locked in a sword clash, inches away, she could see him sweating, grunting, as he struggled to bring his sword straight down, to break her grip, to overpower her.

Instead of fighting his strength, which was considerable, Caitlin decided to use it against him. She suddenly leaned backwards, ducking down, letting his sword come down, landing back on her shoulder blades.

She saw her opening. She kicked him hard, with a front kick, right in his solo plexus. She could've kicked him even lower, but she didn't think that would be fair.

Still, her kick did considerable damage. He collapsed to his knees, winded, clearly not expecting it. Caitlin stood over him, and held the tip of the sword to his exposed throat. She needn't do anymore. Clearly, she was the winner.

There was a muted roar of approval among the coven, as Tyler, ashamed, got up and limped off the battlefield.

"Who will stand and fight her?" Aiden called out.

There was a momentary silence among the group. No one seemed to want to.

Finally, a voice called out. "I will!"

Caitlin looked over, and was surprised to see who it was. Cain. Except now, he had a shaved head, and looked much meaner and larger than she had remembered.

If he remembered Caitlin at all, it clearly was not with joy. He had a meanness, a coldness in his eyes, that she hadn't remembered. He wore a cut-off version of their uniform, and his muscles were bulging through skin. He looked like a hardened warrior.

He held in his hands two bamboo swords—one long, one short. He also had several other sparring weapons on his belt. Clearly, this was unfair. She was outmatched. She should have been given the opportunity to have equal weapons.

She glanced over at Aiden, indignant, but he looked in the other direction, indifferent. He knew she was mismatched with the weaponry. Apparently, he wanted her to be.

Caitlin didn't have much time to reflect, because Cain burst into action. He grabbed something from his belt and in a flash of an eye, pulled it back and swung it at her.

Caitlin was startled by it, but even more startled by her own reaction. Somehow, using some sense she didn't even know she had, she managed to bring up her sword and swing it down, and strike away with the object in mid-air, before it hit her in the head. She looked down, and realized he had slung an object at her with his slingshot, a material that looked something like hardened rubber. She was shocked not only at his speed, but his treachery. It was a cheap way to open a fight.

Cain charged right at her, a scowl on his face, leapt into the air, and aimed his two feet right for her chest. At the last second, Caitlin managed to dodge his kick—but she didn't dodge the strike. His feet, she realized too late, had been a distraction. At the same time, he had swung with his long sword, and hit her hard, right on her hip. The pain of the bamboo stung, reverberating right through her.

She spun to face him again, and now she was mad.

All of his moves had been cheap, she thought. He didn't have the courage to stand and fight her, head-on. She felt the indignity of it all coursing through her, and before she knew it, her veins ran with fire. She wouldn't wait for him to charge again.

Caitlin charged, and leapt into the air for her own kick. As she predicted, he dodged himself, but she spun in the air at the same time, and backhanded him hard across the face.

The crowd oohed as the smack reverberated.

He looked at her with eyes meant to kill.

He charged head-on, swinging both swords wildly. This was just what she'd wanted. She got him off balance. Now he was out-of-control.

With her single sword, Caitlin managed to parry every single blow of his, click for clack, back and forth. He was fast, but, she was happy to realize, she was faster. She realized that she was, in fact, so fast, it was like she was in another dimension, almost like he was moving in slow motion.

She began to enjoy it. Every time she blocked one of his blows, she spun around, and cracked him in the side of the shoulder. She followed blow for blow, and cracked him on the shoulder, then the hip, then the stomach. She was toying with him.

Soon, she could see how confused he was, that he could not understand what was happening. As he spun another time, she grabbed one of his wrists, then grabbed the other, and kicked him hard the chest, stripping him of both of his weapons. He went flying back, onto the ground.

The crowd roared in approval. Clearly, Caitlin was the victor.

But Cain was furious. Apparently, he was not used to losing. Instead of gracefully admitting defeat, he got up and charged her again.

Caitlin hadn't expected that. It happened so fast, before she knew it, he had his arms wrapped around her waist, tackling her, driving her hard to the ground. It knocked the wind out of her, and momentarily stunned her. He got on top of her, pinning her down.

Aiden stepped forward. "CAIN!" he yelled out.

But Cain didn't care. He'd pinned her down, and used his knees to dig into her arms, holding her in place so she couldn't move. Then he reached up as if to choke her.

Caitlin felt an unearthly rage come over her. As she watched Cain's hands go for her throat, she let her power overcome her for real this time. She broke free of his grasp, grabbed his wrist at the last second, and spun it around. She rolled on top of him, twisting it back.

Caitlin then kicked him hard, right in the groin.

He slumped over, on the ground beside her, finished.

But she wasn't done. He had summoned her rage, and that was not something she could easily suppress. She jumped to her feet, still indignant, and kicked him again, hard in the stomach.

"Caitlin!" yelled Aiden.

But she could barely hear him. She walked over slowly and placed her foot on Cain's throat, and kept it firmly planted there. He couldn't breathe. But she didn't care. She felt the rage overcome her in waves, and wanted to stop, but knew that she could not.

Caitlin suddenly felt herself shoved hard, from the side, and felt herself stumble.

She looked over and saw Aiden, alone, walking towards her. She was confused: he was at least ten feet away from her. Then she saw his hand sticking out, and realized that he had managed to shove her without even touching her.

He scowled down at her, and she knew that she was in for a rebuke.

CHAPTER TWENTY ONE

Caitlin found herself walking with Aiden through a path in the woods. She could tell that he was silently fuming, as he hadn't spoken a word since he'd summoned her to follow him.

After the fight, he'd led her outside the circle, away from the others, and had lifted off in flight with her. She had followed, feeling like a chastised schoolboy. She didn't like the feeling. She felt that she was old enough now to be able to learn her own lessons from the fight. Besides, Cain had had it coming.

Now they tramped endlessly through forest, until finally, they came to a large clearing in the woods. The sunlight broke through the trees, lighting it up.

Aiden finally stopped and turned to her.

"I'm disappointed in you," he said.

"It wasn't my fault!" Caitlin snapped back, preparing her defense. "You saw the fight. He fought dirty, from the beginning."

"It doesn't matter. You should have transcended that."

"He was trying to hurt me. To *really* hurt me. Even when the fight was over."

"You let down your guard too quickly," he answered. "A battle is never over."

"Well, it's your job to mediate these fights. If you're mad at anyone, you should be mad at him," Caitlin snapped back, fuming with anger. She'd had enough of being chided. "Why don't you go and chastise him? Why are you chastising me?"

Caitlin realized she was raising her voice. She had lost her patience for authority figures, and it felt good to finally tell him what was on her mind.

Aiden seemed completely composed. He merely shook his head slightly, expressionless.

"I have chosen to speak with you and not him," Aiden began slowly, "as a reward, not as a punishment. You have the potential to hear what I have to say. He does not. You have the potential to become the best warrior I've ever trained. He does not."

"You're NOT my father!" Caitlin snapped back. "I don't need to be here. I don't need to listen to you!"

Even as she said it, she realized she sounded bratty. But she couldn't stop herself. She was so mad at people trying to boss her around her whole life, and she was tired of answering to people. She was also tired of taking the blame for everyone else's mistakes.

"You are correct," Aiden said calmly. "I am not your father. And you do not need to be here. Or to answer to me. You choose your path in life, every step of the way. You only need to stay here if you choose to," he reminded her calmly.

Caitlin thought about that, and slowly calmed down. He was right. She had chosen to be here. And she did want to train. She just...well, she didn't know what it was. She had just been so mad she could hardly think straight.

"Your greatest strength is also your greatest weakness," he said. "Your passion. Your fury. I'm not saying that you should have not beaten Cain. What I am saying is that you should not have beaten *yourself*."

Caitlin tried to decipher what he meant. As always, it was so hard to grasp, at first glance, what he was saying. She realized it was another one of his statements that she would have to contemplate.

"What you still fail to see is that your current powers are limited. You have, inside you, so much power—more than you ever dreamed of. I want to show you how to tap that power. You are still caught up on superficial things, like winning and losing, and anger and revenge. If you want to grow stronger, you'll need to reach the deeper levels."

Caitlin breathed deeply, and began to calm down. Whenever Aiden talk, she relaxed. The more she listened, the more she realized that he actually was *not* like all the other authority figures in her life. She realized that he was not, actually, trying to control her. He really just wanted to help her. She was grateful for that.

"What do I have to do?" she asked.

Aiden took a few steps out into the clearing, and turned and faced her. He closed his eyes and breathed deeply. He held up his staff, so that the edge of it was touching her shoulder. She could feel the wood pressing lightly into her skin.

"Take off your shoes," he said.

Caitlin did so. The soft grass felt good beneath her feet.

"Close your eyes."

She did. It seemed like minutes passed in silence; she was just beginning to wonder what he was doing, when she heard his voice again.

"What do you feel?" he asked.

Caitlin thought.

"I feel…the wood, your staff, touching my shoulder. And I feel the grass beneath my feet."

"What else?" he pressed.

Caitlin concentrated.

"I feel...the wind in my hair...I feel the warmth of the day. The humidity. It's sticky on my skin."

"Yes," he said. "Very good. Now, I want you to reach out, palm up, and hold the staff between us. Keep your eyes closed."

Caitlin reached out slowly with her hand, and grabbed hold of the staff. It was an ancient, worn, smooth wood, and she could feel the energy coming off it as she grasped it.

"Don't grasp it," he said. "Just place your hand beneath it and hold it. Don't make a fist."

Caitlin loosened her grip.

"Good," Aiden said. "Now while you hold it, I want you to tell me what you feel."

"I feel a piece of wood," she said. She felt stupid, but she was not sure what else he wanted.

"What about the wood?" he pressed. "Can you feel each individual grain? Can you feel its weight? Can you feel its thickness, its length?"

Caitlin focused harder. Slowly, she began to feel all the different textures and elements of the wood.

"Good," Aiden said. "Now, very slowly, lift the wood, high above your head. Use only your palm, not your hand. Use only the energy running through your body, coursing through your palms. Find it. Feel it."

Caitlin focused, and as she did, she felt her palm grow warm, felt a ball of energy exude from it, as she slowly lifted the piece of wood.

"Good," Aiden said. "Excellent."

He paused. "Now open your eyes."

Slowly, Caitlin opened her eyes.

She was shocked by what she saw.

There, before her, was Aiden's staff. But it was not actually in her hand. It was hovering, in the air, about ten feet above her, over her open palm.

She looked at Aiden, in shock.

As she did, the staff dropped from the sky and landed hard on the ground.

Aiden frowned.

"You broke your concentration," he said.

"How did I do that?" Caitlin asked, still amazed.

He reached down and grabbed his staff.

"It is one of your many powers. It's the only one I want to teach you for now. You have it inside you. I call it centering. You can use this to move objects a great distance from you. Or to bring them close to you.

"You see, there is no separation between you and the physical universe. As soon as you realize that, you will master the art of combat."

And with that, he turned and walked off into forest. And after two steps, he completely disappeared. Caitlin searched everywhere, but he was gone.

She stood there in shock.

But even more in shock at herself, and at what she had just done. Just how deep did her powers run? And how much about herself did she have left to learn?

CHAPTER TWENTY TWO

Sam stood in the Roman Colosseum. He was dressed in full battle gear, armed from head to toe, wearing a helmet. He looked out through it to see another warrior facing him, also dressed in full armor.

He charged, and the two of them sparred furiously.

The warrior facing him was bigger and stronger, but Sam parried with him blow for blow. Sam was getting more and more tired with each strike, and finally, his arms were too heavy to lift. He sunk to his knees, as the warrior raised his sword high, ready to plunge it into Sam's chest.

Sam blinked and opened his eyes to see that he was standing in the desert, the hard-baked sand stretching beneath his feet as far as his eye could see. In the distance was a giant mountain, and Sam found himself slowly hiking up it, using his sword as a staff. He was now dressed in a white robe.

Sam pulled back his hood, dying in the heat, and looked up the mountain. There, at the top, was a man outlined by the sun. The man also wore a white robe and hood, and held a staff. Somehow, Sam knew that this man was his father.

Sam hiked higher, excited to meet him, trying to increase his pace, determined to reach him. But it was getting harder with each step, the mountain steeper, and as he looked down, he saw snakes and scorpions slithering all around him. It was getting hotter, too, and he knew the road was treacherous, and that he wouldn't make it.

Sam, too tired to go on, looked up.

"FATHER!" he screamed.

His father smiled down at him, with a look of pure love, as he slowly pulled back his hood. The light was shining off of his face, and Sam could see that the two of them looked alike.

Suddenly, Sam stood in the cobblestone streets of Paris. It was nighttime, there was a thick fog everywhere, and amidst the torchlight, he saw a huge façade of a church—and somehow, he knew that it was the Notre Dame.

Sam opened the huge, medieval door, and stepped inside. It was gloomy and empty. He walked down the aisle, and as he did, he saw floating in front of him, a huge silver key. The light shone off of it as it floated, hanging in midair.

Sam reached out, and was about to grasp it. He knew that this was a key that he needed to have. Somehow, he just knew that this key would save his father's life.

Sam woke up, breathing hard. He looked all around, disoriented, expecting to see his father.

But he was nowhere in sight. Sam spun several times, trying to get his bearings, to realize where he was.

He was lying on the silk blanket, on top of a hill, in a field of grass, and Kendra was in his arms. They were both naked.

Sam thought back, and quickly remembered. Sleeping with her had been amazing, and he was still shocked that she had gone from showing no interest in him to wanting to be with him so quickly. Had she been playing games all along? Or was that just her personality?

Whatever it was, it felt so good to have her in his arms. He looked down at her pale, soft skin, her curly blonde hair. Her chin was nestled in his chest, a slight smile on her face.

Was she just using him? Or did she really feel as strongly for him as he did for her? And how was it possible that he could have such strong feelings for someone so quickly? Was this all real? Whatever it was, the one thing he knew for sure was that he didn't want to be away from her side.

Sam thought of his dream. It was one of the strangest and most vivid dreams he had ever had. He had never seen his father before, and the dream had felt more like a meeting. He struggled to figure out what it meant. But he had no idea.

Sam suddenly remembered something, and sat up. The afternoon sparring. He heard that Aiden would be there today, and he was determined to be there, too, to get Aiden's attention whether he was summoned or not. He looked down at Kendra's watch, and saw it was already 4:30. He was half an hour late.

Sam sat up with a start and hurried to get dressed, determined to make it on time.

Kendra sat up quickly, alarmed from her sleep.

"What is it?" she asked.

"Aiden," Sam said. "I need to see him. I'm late."

Kendra frowned back at him.

"I should imagine that your time spent with me is more important than your time with him," she said, petulant.

Sam looked at her, and saw how upset she was, and he stopped.

"Please, understand. I don't mean to offend you. It's just that—I need to see him. I can't miss him again today. And I'm already late."

Kendra looked away, clearly offended.

Sam didn't have time for this, though. He finished getting dressed and jumped onto his horse.

He looked down and saw that Kendra was moving slowly, taking her time, gathering her clothes slowly and putting them on. It appeared that she was not going to be rushed for anyone.

Sam was impatient. "Please, Kendra," he said. "I need to go now!"

"Then go!" she snapped, angry. "I'm not stopping you!"

Sam sat there on his horse, looking back and forth from her to the path, unsure what to do. It was clear that she was not going to hurry.

"GO!" she commanded, loudly.

He could hear the anger in her voice, and was surprised by her ferocity.

"Can I see you again?" Sam asked.

Kendra looked away, as she finished buttoning her blouse.

"Go see your little vampire friends," she snapped. "They are clearly more important."

Sam could see that there was no consoling her, and he didn't want to waste any more time. He would have to deal with this later.

He kicked the horse and galloped off, racing down the hill. He only hoped Aiden would still be there and that he could, finally, see him.

CHAPTER TWENTY THREE

Caitlin stood in the sparring ring, surrounded by all of her coven members, Aiden watching intently off to the side. After their training in the woods, he had brought her back to ring. She had been sparring—and winning—for hours now, and the crowd had grown considerably. She had fought nearly everyone in his coven, and had defeated them all. She was now down to some of their very best warriors.

Word had spread, and now all the royals had gathered, too. The marble steps were completely filled with them, along with tons of onlookers.

Caitlin felt as if she had come into her own. She fought with a skill unlike any she had ever experienced. She felt more fluid, more in control. She felt as if she knew what her opponent would do before he even did it. Whatever Aiden had taught her—and she still wasn't even exactly sure what that was—had sunk in deep, and as she fought, she heard his words in her head. *Your own worst enemy is yourself. The only one who can defeat you is you. This is about what you're becoming.*

She tried to sense things on a different level in battle. She even closed her eyes from time to time, and tried to feel the vibrations around her, to feel her opponent's energy. She felt how she was rooted to the earth, and felt more and more her connections to physical objects. They came at her with swords, with lances, with all kinds of weaponry, and she tried to feel her connection to each one. *There is no separation between you and the objects. The only separation is in your mind.*

She became a much better fighter than she could have ever imagined. As two of Aiden's biggest, meanest looking warriors charged her at once, one with a javelin, and the other with a long chain and ball, swinging wildly, she felt completely unfazed. For the first time, she no longer felt subject to her anger, her fury, her emotions. Instead, she waited patiently.

As the javelin was hurled at her, full speed, she merely waited to the very last moment, and dodged out of the way. It went flying by her, missing her by a millimeter, and as it did, she reached up, and managed to grab it in mid-air. She then, in the same motion, broke it in half and sent it flying back at her attacker—and its blunt tip hit him hard in the chest, sending him flying on his back.

In the same gesture, without pausing, she took the other half and caught the chain and ball in mid-air as her other opponent swung it at her. She yanked it from his hand sent it flying. She then took the butt of the javelin and jabbed him hard in the solo plexus. He dropped to his knees.

The crowd erupted into applause and admiration, as Caitlin stood there and faced Aiden, waiting for more.

"Long swords!" Aiden yelled.

An attendant appeared, throwing a long sword her way. She grabbed it in mid-air, waiting to see what opponent was left that could face her.

Aiden looked at her meaningfully, and she could tell that he was reserving someone to fight her that would truly throw her off guard.

"Blake!" he yelled out.

Caitlin's heart dropped. It couldn't be.

From out of the thick crowd of vampires and royals, there emerged a single man, holding a long sword, with a scowl on his face.

Caitlin's heart stopped. It was really him. Blake.

He looked at her with cold, impersonal anger, and it broke her heart. What hurt her most was that there didn't seem to be any recognition at all.

Aiden had chosen his final warrior well. He had clearly designed the sparring to throw her off balance, to stir up her emotions in the midst of battle. And it had worked.

She no longer felt grounded, no longer felt herself. She struggled to get back to that grounded feeling, but it was not coming. She felt unnerved, on edge. She felt unable to control her storm of emotions.

Before she could collect herself, Blake charged. He held his sword high, over his head, with perfect form, just as a good warrior should. He came in hard and fast and swung down right for Caitlin's head. Caitlin could not believe his speed. They were only wooden swords, and the blow would not have killed her. But still, it would have hurt her a lot. It was clear now that Blake did not remember her: he attacked her as he would his fiercest opponent.

Caitlin managed to duck out of the way, at the last second, as the wooden sword grazed her head.

She was stunned by it, and by Blake. But not hurt. At least not yet.

He turned and faced her again. Something in her could not get her to summon her skill as if she were facing a normal opponent. She knew she should lunge, should attack. But she just couldn't bring herself to. Instead, she found herself remembering that time, in the

Colosseum, when he gave up his life for her. Her heart broke with the thought of it. With the thought of how much she owed him.

He attacked her head-on, and she blocked his blows, blow for blow. But she did not attack back. She could not get herself to.

Finally, after several swings, their swords locked, and he came in close to her, grunting and sweating, as he tried to push her down with all he had. Just inches away, she could see the anger in his face. And she could tell that he did not remember her at all.

"Blake," she grunted, shoulder to shoulder. "It's me. Caitlin. Can't you remember?"

He looked at her and finally, after seconds of struggling, spat, "You're new here. I don't know you, obviously."

With that, he shoved her with all his strength, and he sent her back, rolling in the dirt.

Caitlin rolled and rolled, and lay there in the dirt.

That's when it hit home. Finally. He really didn't know her. He really was a stranger to her. She finally came to accept it, to accept the new circumstances.

She gained her feet with a new resolve. As he charged, ready to finish her off, she calmed herself and faced him as she would any other warrior. Finally, for the first time, she felt herself take control of her emotions. She realized that she didn't need to let her emotions control her. She realized that she could control them. That she could be bigger than her emotions.

And that realization changed her life.

As Blake swung at her, while she was still on the ground, she simply rolled back, lifted her feet up, caught him by the stomach, and sent him flying, over her head.

The crowd oohed.

She jumped up to the ground, as he landed on his back, several feet away.

Blake jumped to his feet and spun and faced her, indignation on his face. He reached back, planted his feet, and with one sharp move, hurled his sword right at her.

It was a good move, a move that few warriors would make, a quick, unexpected move of converting a sword into a spear. And it had happened so fast, so quickly, that any other warrior would have fallen prey to it.

Caitlin saw it, but even with her enhanced senses, it had happened so quick, that she had no time to dodge or parry it. It was going to hit her.

So instead, she ground her feet to the earth, and realized it was time to use her new mental power. She summoned every bit of energy she had, and willed herself to use the new skill that Aiden had showed her.

In her mind, she felt the sword as it came close, felt its particles, its energy. She became one with it. And once she did, she willed it to change direction.

At the last second, it did. Caitlin's mind changed the direction of the sword, sent it flying up in the air, far above her head, and into the dirt.

The crowd gasped, as did Blake. It was incredible. Caitlin had managed to move the object without even touching it. Clearly, she had powers above and beyond any of the others here. Everyone was stunned.

Caitlin charged Blake now, with her bamboo sword, and went to finish him off. He lifted his Shield as she struck furiously, left and right, slashing and jabbing. She tired him down, beat him back, blow after blow. He finally collapsed to one knee, holding up the Shield. And Caitlin was but a blow away from winning the match.

But suddenly, she was distracted. She saw someone standing in the distance, amidst the crowd. And despite all of her composure, all of her training, her jaw dropped wide open in shock, as she dropped her sword in mid swing.

Everyone in the crowd turned to see what she was staring at.

A boy stepped out of the crowd and walked towards her, also in shock.

He walked right up to her, reached out his arms wide, and hugged her.

She hugged him back, and felt her eyes well up with tears.

It was her brother. Sam.

CHAPTER TWENTY FOUR

As Caleb flew away from his home, from Caitlin, his heart was breaking. He had seen the hurt on her face, and the last thing he had ever wanted to do was hurt her. He had never imagined he would ever leave her side. There was nothing he wanted more than to stay there, and be with her. In fact, he had been preparing to propose to her.

But the news of his son was just too much to handle. It was not about Sera—if the message had come from anywhere in the world, he would have dropped everything and raced to see his son. Sera was, in fact, the last thing on his mind.

But Jade was overwhelmingly on his mind. He still felt crushed by guilt for letting him die back in Venice. He would do anything—anything—to have him back. And if that meant having to interact with Sera, even briefly, he would do it. And if that meant having to leave Caitlin's side, at least for now, he simply had no choice. As much as it pained him, he could not stand the idea of not seeing his son ever again.

Caleb flew along the coastline, watching the landscape change, watching the rolling hills turn to meadows then to forests, then back to hills again. He remembered, of course, where Sera's place had been, in a medieval village far in the South of France. It had been her stronghold for centuries, and he knew he would find them there.

He flew faster, wanting to race back to Caitlin, and excited to see his son alive again. He wondered how it was possible. How could he possibly be alive? He was sure that once he was dead, there was no bringing him back. After all, his son was still not a full-fledged vampire. He could not be resurrected.

He thought of the year. 1789. Only two years prior to the last time he had seen him. He wondered if that was it? Maybe it was because he had gone back such a short time? Maybe that meant that his son was still alive, just two years younger. That would seem to make sense.

But it was his understanding that for a human, if one changed the future then one changed the past—and thus one's dying in 1791 would wipe out their 1789 existence. Meaning, Jade could not be alive now.

Caleb was confused. He couldn't figure it out logically, but he didn't really care. He just wanted to see Jade again.

Caleb dove down, lower, circling the shoreline, and finally spotted it: Sera's Castle. It was stark and dramatic against the coastline, with spires reaching up into the sky, riddled with courtyards and terraces.

As he expected, Sera was there, below, standing on an upper rampart, looking up to the skies, watching, waiting for him. She lit up with a huge smile upon seeing him.

But Caleb was already annoyed. He did not see Jade by her side. And the last thing he wanted to do was smile back. He could tell by her expression that she was already fantasizing that this was more than a visit. It was the way she looked at him, like they were already together again. Would she ever change?

Caleb dove down and landed on the rampart, about ten feet away from her, and she immediately walked up to him.

"My love," she announced, triumphantly, opening her arms wide to embrace him.

But he scowled back at her, and held out a palm, stopping her from approaching.

"Sera," he said sharply. "This is not about you and I. This is about Jade. You said he is alive. Where is he?"

Caleb felt that he had to be firm. He did not want her to enter into any more of her fantasies of their being together.

Sera, ignoring his question, sighed.

"You pretend you do not care for me. But that is only because you care about me too deeply. I can feel your desire. It is like a beacon, calling to me."

Caleb shook his head.

"You still live in a fantasy. We are over. Now, where is my son?" he asked, more firmly.

But she just shook her head again.

"You and I, we always had so much potential. You were just afraid to let yourself feel your true feelings for me."

Caleb stepped closer and grabbed her by the shoulders. "Sera, I'm not playing games anymore. Where is he!?" he demanded.

She looked him right in the eyes, then slowly smiled and turned, heading down a spiral stone staircase.

"Follow me," she said, her back to him.

Caleb followed her down the staircase, through the lower courtyard of the castle, his heart beating with anticipation to see his boy again. He wondered what he looked like, how old he was.

He followed sera as she walked into a huge, master bedroom, with gigantic windows facing the ocean. But he did not see any sign of him.

As soon as he walked in, she closed the door behind them.

She walked over to the huge, four-poster bed, sat on the corner of it, and unbuttoned the top two buttons of her shirt. She looked up at him and smiled seductively.

"Caleb," she said, "you know why you're here."

Caleb looked at her, puzzled.

"What are you talking about?"

"You know as well as I do," she said. "Stop playing games. You know that Jade is not here."

Caleb felt his blood go cold. He could barely speak.

"Tell me where he is," he hissed.

She stood up, smiling wider, her shirt unbuttoned, and walked closer to him, laying one hand seductively on his shoulder.

"Stop playing dumb," she said. "You know that our son is no longer alive."

With those words, Caleb felt as if he'd been stabbed in the gut. He reflexively pushed Sera back, away from him.

She looked at him, shocked that he would push her away.

He felt his anger overflowing, as he realized, at that moment, that he had been tricked. He felt like such a fool. And more than anything, he felt crushed that Jade was no longer alive.

"How could you have done this!?" he wailed, hearing his own voice breaking. "You lied! You tricked me!"

"Oh grow up!" she snapped back. "You're not really that naïve. You knew there was no way he could live. But our love—*that* still lives. Yes, I needed an excuse to bring you here. But now that you're here, we're together. That's all that matters. And now, we can have a new child!"

Caleb wheeled and began to storm from the room, not trusting himself to even look in her direction. He was too furious, and too devastated.

But before he reached the door, he felt her icy grip on his arm, her nails digging into his flesh, as she spun him back around.

Now, *she* was scowling.

"Don't you dare walk out on us!" she hissed. "Not after all we've been through!"

He glared back at her.

"Mark my words," he said slowly, in a voice of steel, "I will never see you again as long as I live. Whether it is this life, or any other life. Nothing you can say or do will ever bring me back into your presence."

And with that, he shook off her arm, and stalked out of the room.

"Caleb!" she shrieked. "Caleb! Come back to me! I'm sorry!"

As Caleb hurried up the spiral staircase, heading to the roof, he could hear her wails and screams echoing throughout the huge, empty, medieval castle. And even as he reached the roof and flew off into the sky, he could still hear her wailing, as her screams became one with the wind and birds and crashing of the waves.

CHAPTER TWENTY FIVE

Sam walked arm in arm with Caitlin through the formal grounds of Versailles. He had been so shocked to find her here, and to see her fighting. He had been so proud, watching his big sister. At first, he hadn't realized it was her. He had just stood there, with the others, watching in awe as the tournaments continued.

He had been shocked to discover that the greatest warrior of them all was actually his big sister. He was in awe of her skills. He'd never seen anyone fight that way. It was a combination of a human warrior, and a vampire master. She moved with lightning speed, striking, slashing, dodging, doing things he couldn't even imagine. It was like watching art in motion.

After it had been over, after they had embraced, Caitlin had been surrounded by well-wishers, people congratulating her in every direction. Even Aiden had come over, and had nodded approvingly. Sam had wanted to talk to

Aiden, but Aiden didn't even look his way, and immediately disappeared. And having found Caitlin, Sam felt no reason to need to talk to Aiden anymore anyway.

Caitlin had clearly been in her element. Sam had felt a rush of admiration for her, and pride that he was related to her. And what felt even more special to him was that, despite all the well-wishers who wanted to talk to her, Caitlin only wanted to leave the crowd and walk off alone with Sam. He was delighted to see that she missed him as much as he had missed her.

Finding her here was such a great surprise. He had imagined that he'd have to travel far and wide to find her; it never occurred to him that she might be right under his nose, in the same place he was. Now, finally, he felt settled. He felt that maybe he could relax in this time and place now, and have it all: live in this beautiful palace, have his sister close by, safe, and have his relationship with Kendra. Now, they could all just live, happily, and be close again, as big sister and little brother, just like they used to be.

As they walked, Sam thought back to all the terrible places they'd had to live together growing up, to all the times their mom had moved them. There were all those awful towns in the Midwest, in New Jersey, in the Hudson Valley…And then, worst of all, Harlem. It had all just been terrible.

He looked back on their childhood now in a whole new light, knowing what Caitlin was, and knowing what he was. He had always felt, growing up, that the two of them were different. They had never quite fit in perfectly, had never quite been exactly like everybody else. He had always thought that it was just because they were always the newcomers in town. He had never imagined that the two of them were actually, truly, special. That they had special powers. Were of a special race, a special coven. That they had a destiny, a mission.

And most of all, that their parents weren't even their parents.

Sam had always felt a burning desire to find their father, and had never really known why. But now that he knew how special their mission was, it all began to make sense.

All the fights that he and Caitlin had had with their mother also made sense now, looking back. He'd always felt as if their mother had never truly loved them, that she had looked at them as if they were not really their kids. He had always wondered how they could even be related to her.

"I'm so sorry," he said finally, as they walked through the gardens, past a huge fountain. "For everything that happened in New York. For my always getting you into trouble. And for what happened with Caleb. I know that the only reason you stabbed him was because of my shapeshifting. And I am so sorry that I tried to stab you. I was out of my senses."

Caitlin looked down at him with the love of a big sister.

"Sam, you don't have to apologize," she said. Her voice sounded so much more mature, so much more confident. It was like the voice of a warrior. "That was lifetimes ago. And I know you didn't mean it."

"It was just…at the time, I was under the influence of Samantha," he continued. "She had turned me. Everything was so…different. I wasn't really myself. I wasn't thinking straight."

"Everything happened for a reason," Caitlin said. "I see that now. Caleb was meant to die. I was meant to come back for him. I was *meant* to be here, in these other times and places, and so were you. We're on a quest. A journey. It's not about us anymore. There's a greater destiny at stake.

"What I've learned is that, on the one hand, yes, we do have free will, and we have choices we can make. But on the other hand, so much of what we think we do is actually destined. I can see that now. The more I embark on this journey, the more I am starting to see that destiny is actually stronger than free will. That we don't actually make that many choices after all. We only *think* that we make them."

Sam thought about that. It rang true to him. He had been starting to feel the same thing himself, although he hadn't thought it through as carefully as Caitlin. He was in awe at how wise she had become. He felt like he was standing before a hundred-year-old warrior.

"Not to mention, I think you more than made up for any mistakes you've made," Caitlin added with a smile, as they turned down another path. "You saved me in Rome. In the Colosseum."

"I fear that we're not through yet—that Kyle may still come back for you," Sam said, with sudden worry. "That's why I came back here, to this time and place. To help you. And to make up for my mistakes."

Sam was surprised to see that Caitlin did not look worried at all.

"I'm sure Kyle is out there," she said calmly. "And I'm sure he will try to come for me. But I'm not worried about it anymore. I feel stronger than I ever have. In fact, I look forward to a fight with him now."

Sam looked at her, and could feel the strength coming off of her. He could see how assured and confident she was, and could see that she would be a worthy adversary against Kyle. He felt even more proud of her.

"Back there, in the Vatican, all those vampires in white. They gave you a key," he said. "I haven't been able to stop thinking about that. What they said. That there are three keys left to find our dad. I never used to believe that our Dad really existed. But now, I really do."

"He does exist," Caitlin said confidently. "I've seen him."

Sam's eyes opened wide in surprise. "You've met him?" he asked, astonished.

"No. I've seen him in my dreams."

Sam suddenly remembered. "My God. I know what you mean. I dreamt of him last night."

Caitlin turned and looked at Sam with a fixed gaze. He was taken aback by her sudden intensity. She stopped walking.

"What did you dream exactly?"

"I..." Sam began, but then suddenly got nervous from being put on the spot. He could feel how badly his sister wanted an answer, and he didn't want to let her down. "Um...I was climbing a mountain...and I thought I saw him...but I couldn't reach him...then I was in this huge church. There was this big key floating, and I was reaching for it...It felt like a message. Like, we were supposed to find the key there."

"Sam, think hard. Did you recognize the church?"

Sam furrowed his brow, trying to remember. At the time he recognized it, but now he was having a hard time recalling.

"It was…I knew it then…but now…it was huge…the ceilings were so high….The entrance. It had all these arches. And these three huge doors."

"Above the arches, were there carved figures? Dozens of them?" Caitlin asked excitedly.

Sam's eyes lit up. He remembered now. "Yes!"

Caitlin seemed to register something.

"Do you know it?" he asked.

"It's the Notre Dame," she said.

"Yes!" Sam answered, realizing she was right.

As Caitlin stared off into space, looking impressed, Sam wondered why it was so significant.

"Do you think it was more than just a dream?" he asked.

Caitlin nodded. "Yes. Far more. In the vampire world, dreams are always more than that. They are always messages. Meetings. Especially with someone like our father. Dad was telling you where to find him. I think that's what it was about. There are four keys we need. I think he was telling you that the second key is in the Notre Dame."

Sam thought about that. He felt honored that his father had chosen to appear to him, and to give him such an important message.

"But why did the dream come to you?" asked Caitlin, almost to herself. "Why not to me?"

"I don't know. Maybe we each get pieces of the clues, you know? We're both his lineage. Maybe it will take both of us to figure it out."

Caitlin looked at him. "I think you're right."

Sam felt more important than ever. He once again fell a surge of determination to go search for his father, to join Caitlin on the quest.

"I need to find him, Sam," Caitlin said, her voice serious. "*We* need to find him. There's a lot at stake. Not only for us. A lot of other people are depending on us. I need your help. Can you join me?"

At first, Sam felt a surge of excitement; but then, as he thought about the reality of leaving this place, he felt a pit in stomach. That would mean leaving Kendra. And, despite himself, he was still overwhelmed by the thought of her.

"What is it?" Caitlin asked. "What's wrong?"

Sam hesitated. He looked at the ground, avoiding her gaze. He was embarrassed to tell her the truth.

"Well…" he began, but stopped. He didn't know how to explain. Had he really grown so soft over a girl? Would he really let his sister down over this? What would his big sister think of him?

"Well…um…you see, him… I um…met this girl," he began.

He saw Caitlin's expression turn from confusion to recognition.

"Sam," she said, sounding like a parent, "there are more important things. This search…it's our *father* we are talking about."

But even as she said it, Caitlin knew she was being hypocritical. After all, she had been prepared to give up her search for Caleb's sake.

"I know," Sam said, still avoiding her gaze. "It's just that…well…this girl, she's different, and we…kind of just met…and I'm just not sure if I should go, like, this second…"

He saw her staring at him with disapproval. He didn't know what else to say. He wanted to go with her. But at the same time, there was something about Kendra that just made him obsessed with her.

"You *have* to understand," Sam implored. "You had someone in your life once, didn't you? What was his name? Caleb? What happened to him?"

Sam watched as Caitlin's face suddenly morphed into one of sadness and disappointment. He immediately regretted inquiring about it. Caitlin looked off into the distance, and seemed crushed.

"Yes," she said softly. "I did. Once."

A heavy silence fell between them.

"I'm sorry," he said. "I really want to help you. It's just that his girl, um, well, her name is—"

"Kendra," suddenly came a voice.

Sam and Caitlin both wheeled to see Kendra standing there, in her royal blue gown, looking haughtily down on both of them.

CHAPTER TWENTY SIX

As Caitlin stood there, Kendra took a step forward, and haughtily stepped between her and her brother. She stared at Caitlin with a defiant, territorial look, one that was clearly meant to tell Caitlin to back off. That Sam was Kendra's territory now.

Caitlin looked over at Sam, hoping that he would pick up on what was going on, that he would push her out of the way—that he would be immune to such behavior.

But alas, he was not. Caitlin was shocked to see that Sam seemed to become completely subordinate in Kendra's presence, as if she held some sort of invisible power over him. He even seemed to slump a bit, and Kendra seemed to stand taller. It looked as if he were helpless around her.

Caitlin's her heart fell at the site. She had seen this happen with other friends in the past. It was obvious that Sam was in her grip.

"Kendra," Caitlin echoed slowly, in a cool voice, looking her right in the eye. "I don't believe we have been introduced."

"We haven't," Kendra stated, in a cold tone.

"Well," Caitlin said slowly, feeling her anger begin to rise, "you're standing between me and my brother, and we were in the middle of a conversation."

Kendra stared back at Caitlin, and she could see a flash of indignation cross over her eyes. But she didn't move.

Sam stepped up from behind Kendra and stepped in between the two of them, as if sensing the confrontation that was about to happen.

"No, it's not like that," Sam said to Caitlin, in a conciliatory tone. "She just wanted to introduce herself. Caitlin, this is Kendra. Kendra, this is my sister, Caitlin."

Caitlin noticed that Sam was sweating; he was nervous for them to like each other.

But Caitlin continued to stare Kendra down with a look of steel, and Kendra did the same. Sam looked back and forth between them, increasingly nervous.

"My brother and I were just discussing a trip we are going to take," Caitlin said coldly. "In fact, we will be leaving tomorrow, so you can say your goodbyes now."

Caitlin felt that she had to take control, to take action to help break Sam from the grip of this clearly destructive woman that he seemed helpless around. It was bold and aggressive, but she felt that she had no other choice.

Kendra turned and looked at Sam. He avoided her gaze, and avoided Caitlin's, too. Caitlin had never seen him so fidgety.

"I doubt that," Kendra said back. "Sam's not going anywhere. After all, he and I have plans for tomorrow."

"We do?" Sam asked, and Caitlin could hear the hope in his voice. His tone of voice told her everything she needed to know, and she felt her heart sink. He wasn't seriously going to let himself be run by this girl, was he?

"That's right," Kendra said. "We do."

Caitlin stared back at Kendra, seething with hatred. She prayed that Sam would summon the resolve to stand up to her. As long as Caitlin had known him, he had always seemed to have this problem. He had always attracted the wrong women, women who were bossy, controlling, and always bad for him. Samantha had been the latest example. And now, Kendra. Sam just had bad luck in this area. Caitlin wasn't surprised.

But she was still mad. She had hoped that Sam would have changed, would be strong enough to tell her No. That he would join Caitlin on their mission.

But Sam turned and looked at Caitlin with sad, guilty eyes. She could see in those eyes that deep down he wanted to go with her, but was unable to say no to Kendra.

"I'm so sorry Caitlin," Sam said, in a broken voice. "I… I don't think I can go tomorrow."

Caitlin nodded, keeping a calm composure. But deep inside, her heart was breaking. She could see the victorious smile on Kendra's face, and she felt her anger rising. But she knew there was little she could do. She had learned from past experiences that, when it came to affairs of the heart, at the end of the day, one could never really have any influence or control over a friend's relationships. That was always something that they just had to work out on their own. If Sam was going to make any changes, it would have to come from him.

Caitlin took control of her anger and immediately turned and walked away, before she did anything rash.

"Caitlin, wait!" Sam called out after her.

But she wasn't going to stop. He had made his decision, and it was clear.

And truth be told, deep down, she felt that she was no one to judge. She knew what it was like to be in love, to want to forgo the mission. He would just have to let his own destiny take its course.

As she walked, she realized all the more, that this mission was just something that she was meant to do alone.

*

Caitlin retreated back to her room, closing the door firmly behind her. She wanted to be alone, and she wanted privacy. It had been such a long, overwhelming day. She had learned so much from Aiden, had risen to the heights on the battlefield, performing better than she ever thought she could. She had been overwhelmed at seeing Blake, hurt by his not remembering her—and then overwhelmed at seeing Sam. As if all that were not enough, she had to meet Kendra, too, and had been overwhelmed at seeing her brother in her grip.

So many conflicting thoughts and feelings raced through Caitlin at once, she barely knew how to process it all. It had felt like ten days in one.

As sunset fell, Caitlin took off her clothes and soaked in her tub. She felt every muscle in her body relax. Ruth sat patiently at her side.

Caitlin's mind raced. She thought of Sam, of how much he had changed. She thought of Aiden. Of her new skills. She thought of her dad, her mission. She thought of Sam's dream, of the floating key. Of the Notre Dame. As all these thoughts blended together, she felt more determined than ever to fulfill her mission.

Versailles was filled with every luxury, but she felt that her mission was calling her elsewhere. All the people that she loved and knew were here (except for Caleb), but they were all distracted. Polly seemed to be in the grips of her singer boyfriend. Sam had Kendra. Blake didn't even remember her. And she felt that, already, she had taken her training nearly as far as she could for this time and place. She didn't know how much was left for her here, and she felt it was time to move on.

Caitlin got out of the tub, dried herself with a huge towel, then changed into the casual wear that had been left by her bedside. It was a silk bathrobe, white and gold, intricately designed, and as she put it on, she'd never felt anything more luxurious.

She lay back in her huge, four-poster bed, sinking into the endless pillows, and sighed.

Ruth jumped onto the bed and set her head in Caitlin's lap.

After a few moments, she reached over to her bedside table and picked up an object and held it.

The encased scroll.

She sat up slowly in bed, staring at it, holding it with both hands. She ran one hand slowly along its edge, feeling the encrusted jewels. She closed her hands around it, trying to feel her father's energy. It was electrifying. She felt as if she held a piece of him.

Ruth looked up at Caitlin and whined, as if asking her to open it.

Caitlin finally decided. It was time.

She reached over, grabbed the locks on both sides of it, and pushed them in.

There was the slightest click. She pulled back the lid, and there was a slight hiss, releasing air that had been trapped for centuries.

Caitlin opened it slowly, its hinges creaking, and as she did, she could not believe what she saw.

CHAPTER TWENTY SEVEN

Kyle stood beside Napoleon, a huge army of supporters behind them. Napoleon had summoned his entire coven, all his people, hundreds of vampires strong, and along the way, they had all agitated in the streets and encouraged the citizens to join them and storm the Bastille. It had been easy: there had been such discontent hanging in the air anyway among all the French citizens, such anger towards the royal authority, and the prison in the Bastille happened to be the perfect symbol, the perfect representative of everything royal. The further they had gone, the more the mob had grown.

And Napoleon, of course, looked to Kyle for direction.

Kyle felt himself surge with power, relishing the feeling of being in charge of an army once again, relishing the destruction and bloodshed that were about to happen. As he stood with his men in the cobblestone plaza opposite the Bastille, Kyle stared up at it. The castle-like fort, with its drawbridge and turrets, was well-defended by soldiers, looking as formidable as he remembered. But having been inside, Kyle already knew it strengths and weaknesses. And he knew now how to bring it down. He carried in his pocket a chemical that would counteract the effect of the titanium, and free the savage seven for good.

Kyle smiled at the thought. Once he unleashed those creatures, there'd be mayhem spreading across Paris unlike any the city had ever known. Indeed, he knew, it would spark an entire revolution.

This huge mob was exactly the distraction Kyle needed to breach its walls and get to work. And the revolution was the bigger distraction he needed to get to and isolate Caitlin. With such havoc unleashed across the city, he felt certain that it would free her from her royal protectors, and that in the chaos, he could find and kill her much more easily. He salivated at the thought. There wasn't a second left to lose.

"NOW!" Kyle screamed.

As one, the huge mob suddenly burst into action, sprinting across the plaza, heading right for the Bastille. They stormed its walls as one, and within moments, shots were already being fired, and the drawbridge raised. The mob returned fire as it charged. It was already a bloody mayhem, and they weren't even near its walls.

Kyle took advantage of the confusion. He broke from the crowd and lifted into the air, flying off to the side, over the moat, and around the other side. He hid behind a stone embankment, and watched as all the guards streamed around to the front of the building. As they did, Kyle saw his chance. He flew across, and in one quick motion, he knocked out the remaining guard, grabbed his keys, and snuck inside.

Kyle was familiar with the building now, from his first excursion, and he knew exactly where to run in the darkness. He ran down the spiraling stone staircase, and then suddenly ducked into a recess he'd found previously in a wall. He stood there and waited, remembering how many guards there had been below. He knew that if he just waited, they would race past him, to help defend the gate.

He was right. Moments later, dozens of vampire guards raced by, oblivious to his presence. He waited several more seconds, until the coast was clear, and then took off at a sprint, heading lower and lower.

He first reached a large iron gate and, without pausing, tore it off its hinges with a single hand.

He descended deeper, and reached a large silver gate, and this time, he extracted the guard's key and unlocked it. The gate opened quickly.

Now Kyle was in utter blackness. He kept descending, sprinting lower and lower. He could already sense the stench of the savage seven as he ran deeper, and he knew he was getting close, nearing the lowest possible level.

Kyle finally reached it. It was cavernous down here, and he saw the titanium bars. He had to recoil from the metal, even from where he was, the energy of it so strong.

But Kyle was prepared. He reached into his bag, extracted a powder, and threw it on the bars. Sidnius Moroxide. The only compound which could dissolve the titanium.

Kyle waited several moments, and as he watched, the titanium turned colors, from a glowing silver to a pink. Once it all turned, he knew was ready. He reached out, grabbed the bars, and yanked with all his might.

Even with the effects of the powder, it took considerable strength. But as he pulled and pulled, he eventually tore the thousand-year-old bars from their hinges.

The moment he did, the savage seven stepped forward, only feet away from him, snarling. They were the most evil demons he had ever seen, preachers from hell, ones that made his entire race look like fairies. Their gnarled faces were thousands of years old, and they lifted up their huge claws, and snarled at him, ready to pounce even on him, their liberator.

He knew that these creatures would not be grateful. On the contrary, they would kill him if they could.

He admired that. And he wanted them to kill. But he didn't want to fight them himself. That would defeat his purpose.

Kyle turned around and took off at a sprint, then broke into flight, knowing they would follow on his heels. He headed up higher through this through the circular fort.

The savage seven where as quick as they were rumored to be, and within moments, Kyle sensed them flying on his heels, right after him.

Good, Kyle thought. *They're ready.*

He flew and flew, and finally burst out onto the main level, through the front door, and right to the drawbridge. As he hoped, the seven followed him, like a pack of hornets, but now, as they saw a glimpse of freedom, they got distracted. They lost sight of Kyle and instead, tore the heads off all the guards in the post.

Kyle flew out into the open, relieved to have them off his tail. He had a huge smile on his face. Below him, thousands of citizens were fighting to the death, storming the building. On the other side, the savage seven were tearing apart the guards from the inside. Within minutes, they would be free, roaming the streets with the others, and they would weak destruction of a scale that Paris had never known.

Kyle hadn't felt so giddy since he was a boy. This was exactly what he had needed. Now he could find and kill Caitlin quite easily.

Now, his revolution could begin.

CHAPTER TWENTY EIGHT

Caitlin sat on her bed, staring down at the open container in surprise. Inside it lay a delicate scroll, curled up, and sealed in wax. On the wax was an insignia of a small, ancient cross, one which Caitlin immediately recognized as identical to the design of the small silver cross that she wore around her neck. Caitlin reached down and felt her necklace now as she looked at the symbol, and felt comforted to know that it was still there.

She reached out and took hold of the scroll. It was brittle, written on a hard parchment, and yellowing. It looked ancient.

She gingerly broke the seal, and unrolled it.

The first thing she noticed was that the scroll ended abruptly as she was halfway through unrolling it. She looked at the bottom, and saw the torn ridges, and she could tell right away that this was an incomplete scroll, apparently torn in half. She only held the top half.

She looked at the scroll, and observed the elegant handwriting. It reminded her of the script she had once seen when looking at a copy of the Declaration of Independence: it was so perfect, it was hard to imagine it had been done by a human hand.

She felt her hands trembling as she stared at it, realizing that this was the script of her father. That he really existed. That he'd really left something for her. That he cared enough about her enough to do so. She felt her heart lift, and felt more determined than ever to fulfill her mission—and to find him. She read each word with utter fixation:

My dearest Caitlin:

If you are reading this, you have already surpassed many obstacles. It means that you have already chosen to travel the road less traveled, to take the difficult path. For that, I commend you. You are truly your father's daughter.

You must forgive all the riddles, codes, letters, and keys, but the secret that I guard is most powerful, and must be broken into fragments, to prevent others from decoding it. Only the truly worthy—only yourself—are meant to decode the secret that you ultimately will.

If you are reading this, you already have one key in your possession. You must obtain the final three to reach me.

The second key is your focus now. To find it, you will first have to go to the Fields of the Scholars—

The letter was torn right there, in mid-sentence.

Caitlin read it a second time, and a third time, then finally set it down.

She leaned back, her mind spinning. Holding this was overwhelming. Her mission felt more real, and more pressing, than ever.

But she was also confused. The Fields of the Scholars? Where on earth could that be?

She was more determined than ever to embark right away, to embrace her mission, to head there immediately, wherever it was, and to find the second key.

But before Caitlin had any more time to dwell on where this place may be, there was a sudden knock at her door.

She started to get up from bed, but before she could even reach it, the door swung open by itself.

In strutted Polly, a huge smile on her face, beaming. She was dressed in a lavish, formal outfit, a long, satin pink gown with white trim, her hair pulled back in a bun, and her face carefully made-up and powdered.

Ruth ran up to her, so happy to see her, jumping at her feet.

"Oh my God, why are you not dressed!?" Polly began. "The concert is tonight!"

She rushed into the room and immediately began to ruffle through Caitlin's wardrobe, as if to prepare an outfit for her.

Caitlin sat on the edge of her bed, confused.

"What concert?" she asked.

"Didn't I tell you? He's singing tonight. My boyfriend. You *have* to come. Everyone will be there!"

Polly came running over excitedly, grabbing Caitlin's arm and pulling her up off the bed and onto her feet.

"Not to mention, dinner is starting now," Polly continued. "There's always a feast before a concert. Everyone's going to be expecting you!"

Caitlin withdrew her hand from Polly's grasp, and slowly shook her head.

"I'm sorry, Polly," she said. "But I can't go. I'm actually about to leave Versailles."

Polly looked incredulous.

"What are you talking about? We barely had time to talk to each other! What do you mean leave? Where!? You just got here!"

"I'm sorry," Caitlin answered, "but I need to find my father. I'm going back to Paris. To the Notre Dame. I feel that he's there, or that there might a clue there to lead me to him."

She watched Polly's face fall in disappointment.

"And we haven't had time to talk because you've been so wrapped up with this singer,"

Caitlin added. She felt that she had to let her know how she was feeling.

Polly looked down, looking sad for the first time Caitlin had ever known her.

"I'm sorry," she said. "I didn't mean to hurt your feelings. I just..." She looked up, and her eyes were suddenly beaming again. "This guy is just *so* amazing. You *have* to meet him. *Please.* I promise, after tonight, things will be different. We'll hang out a lot more. It's just the beginning. He hasn't met any of my friends yet. I want you to be the first!"

Caitlin sighed, not knowing what to do. On the one hand, she wanted to leave right now. But on the other, she certainly didn't want to let Polly—or anyone else—down. Especially since everyone had been so hospitable to her here. After all, it was already night, and she didn't see the harm in waiting until the morning. And looking at Polly, she could see how much it meant for her to meet this guy. She could understand. If the situation were reversed, and it were about Caleb, she might feel the same way, too.

Most of all, Polly always managed to touch a soft spot in her heart.

"Okay," Caitlin said, "but I'll just stay tonight. Tomorrow, I leave."

"Yeah!" Polly screamed, jumping up and down, excitedly rushing about the room. Caitlin marveled how much she was like a little kid. She went through all of Caitlin's clothes in a rush, and picked out a long, elegant yellow skirt, with a red trim.

"This one," Polly said. "Yes, this is perfect. You *have* to wear this."

Caitlin looked at it, and shook her head. She'd never worn anything remotely like it before. It was so long, heavy, formal, and had so much material. It looked like it had enough material to make drapes for an entire house.

"I don't know, Polly," she said. "I don't think it's me."

"Nonsense," Polly said, running around and holding it up against her. She gasped. "Oh my God! It's beautiful!"

Caitlin decided it would be futile to resist. Clothes were clearly Polly's thing. She figured she'd letter be happy with what she wanted, especially since Caitlin didn't much care for all these fancy clothes anyway.

"Okay, I'll wear it," she said.

Polly practically screamed with giddiness, clapping her hands. Ruth barked excitedly, joining in.

And Caitlin realized she was in for a long night.

CHAPTER TWENTY NINE

After what felt like hours getting ready—far longer than Caitlin would have liked—Polly was finally satisfied with the way that the two of them looked. Because they couldn't see themselves in mirrors, they had to rely on each other. According to Polly, Caitlin looked ravishing. Caitlin wasn't so sure. She had never thought of herself as ravishing, in any outfit.

But she had spent more time putting on makeup, and getting into this outfit, than she had in any outfit of her life. There had been layers and layers of fabric, each more uncomfortable than the next, and in this July heat, she felt her body temperature rise with each added later. She had no idea how they did it.

If that were not enough, Polly had caked her face with layer after layer of thick, white powder. Caitlin didn't understand why this generation thought this to be attractive. And even if for some reason they did, wasn't one layer enough? She was pale to begin with, but now, she was sure she looked ridiculous.

As if all this weren't enough, as if she weren't already boiling over and ready to tear off every item of clothing in this heat, her outfit had to be topped off with a huge, heavy hat. Caitlin was so warm and stiff that she could scream. She felt like a plaything, dressed up to be shown off to people. She hated it. She preferred loose, simple clothing, that she could throw on and off easily, and she preferred not having to wear any makeup. And she hated spending hours getting ready.

That said, she tried to put on a big smile. She didn't want to ruin Polly's excitement, which, as usual, was brimming over.

"Oh my God, you look gorgeous!" Polly said again. "You're going to be the talk of the night!" Without another word, she took her arm, and the two of them walked out of the guest house, and began to cross the grounds.

They crossed through the perfectly trimmed formal gardens, heading for the main, marble palace of Versailles, Ruth trailing on their heels.

As they headed up the marble staircase, immediately several servants rushed to open the doors for them. Caitlin had never felt so regal.

They glided through the open doors and down a marble hallway, and in the distance, several more servants opened doors for them.

They entered a grand, magnificent, dining room. Caitlin had never seen anything more opulent. The room was dominated by an enormous dining table, which looked like it sat at least fifty. This was surrounded by thick, grand velvet armchairs, decorated in a light blue velvet with white arms. The table was covered in flowers and burning candles. Everywhere was real silver, real china.

There were heaps and heaps of food all throughout, and each guest already had a plate brimming over. Dozens of servants hovered around them, waiting on their every whim, pouring glass after glass of wine into the finest crystal she had ever seen. Above the table were several magnificent crystal chandeliers, reflecting light off of everything.

And this was just the beginning. Everyone was dressed in fineries more opulent than Caitlin had ever seen. There were gowns and dresses and suits of every shape and size and color imaginable. The table was a rainbow of color. And this was topped by extravagant hats, and even more extravagant jewelry, women and men wearing rings the size of golf balls, long glittering earrings, draping bracelets. The table positively sparkled.

Off in the corner of the room was a harp and a cello, and the performers played lightly, providing pleasant background music.

Caitlin surveyed the group, and there were so many faces she didn't recognize. But there were several that she did. She spotted Sam, sitting way too close to Kendra, who leaned into his shoulder as he fed her chocolate-covered strawberries.

As she scanned further, she saw Blake sitting at the far end, and beside him, a beautiful, tall blonde girl. Caitlin could sense that she was human, and seeing Blake together with her, and seeing the two of them so happy, felt like a small dagger in her heart.

She immediately looked away, trying to focus on anyone else. She saw the twins, Taylor and Tyler, and then, to her relief, she saw Lily. That was the only face that set her at ease. She was even happier to see that there was an empty seat beside her. Caitlin hurried over, Polly at her side.

"Mind if we join you?" she asked Lily.

Lily looked up, and her eyes opened wide in delight.

"Who else do you think I saved it for?" Lily asked with a smile.

Caitlin sat beside Lily, and Polly sat on Caitlin's other side.

Caitlin tried not to look in Blake's direction. She turned her head the other way, and saw Sam and Kendra. But seeing those two so enmeshed upset her, too, so she looked away from that end of the table. She fidgeted, not knowing where to look, already impatient to leave.

"Where is he?" Caitlin asked Polly, as she scanned the table for Polly's new boyfriend. She was eager to meet him, to see what all the talk was about—and then, to leave. She had been surprised not to find him at the door, waiting to greet Polly and bring her to her seat, as the other men did.

"He's performing tonight," Polly said with great pride, "so he won't be joining us at the feast. He always needs to prepare before his performances. He needs time alone. Backstage. That's because he's a very great artist."

Caitlin looked at Polly, and wondered if she were serious. She was. She had never seen her so smitten by a guy, and she worried for her once again. Everything she said about this guy gave Caitlin the creeps, made her feel as if something was off about him. He sounded so vain, so megalomaniacal. Caitlin could care less that he was performing—she still thought that he should have greeted Polly and escorted her to the table, and dined with her, especially since Polly was so enthusiastic about him.

Caitlin once again felt moved to tell Polly exactly what she thought—but, reluctantly, she bit her tongue. She didn't want to get involved and ruin her good time, especially since she didn't think it would do much good. At the very least, she'd wait until she met him first.

Several servants appeared, placing dish after dish on Caitlin's plate, and filling her glass with a thick, red liquid.

Caitlin felt herself getting hungry as she saw what was in the glass: blood. She held it up, and realized that this blood was an even lighter shade of red than any she had seen.

"It's refined," Lily explained.

Caitlin looked at her.

"They take all the impurities out of it," Lily continued. "It's supposed to be healthier for your kind. Remember, this is Versailles: everything is extravagant here."

Caitlin tasted it, and was surprised at how much lighter it was, and how it went down so much more smoothly. She was also surprised by the immediate kick she got, and by how she felt so rejuvenated so quickly. Whatever it was they did to it, this blood was definitely of a greater quality.

Caitlin took a piece of raw meat off of her plate, reached down, and slipped it to Ruth, who was hiding beneath her legs. Ruth jumped up and snatched it from her fingers, and happily gulped it down. She looked up at Caitlin, ready for more, and Caitlin slipped her another piece.

Caitlin looked around the table and could see that there was a large mix of vampires and humans here. There was a lot of interaction between the two, and the relationship felt very harmonious.

"Quite a scene, isn't it?" Lily asked.

Caitlin nodded back. Everyone seemed happily engrossed in chatter, and light laughter spread throughout the table.

"I envy your life," Lily said. "Our royal life is one of forced idleness. This. All the time. I'd rather be out there, sparring, traveling, whatever. Anywhere but here."

Caitlin was surprised to hear Lily say that, because she had just been thinking of what an amazing life it must be to live here.

"But this place is so beautiful," Caitlin said.

"No place is beautiful if you're trapped in it," Lily answered.

"But you're not trapped. You're royal. You can go anywhere you want."

"I'm trapped by my class," Lily said. "I can't travel with commoners, or on common roads, or by myself. Everything must be formal. There are layers and layers of etiquette. Yes, I am free to go. But where? I'm trapped by this life."

"So why don't you leave it?" Caitlin asked.

Lily sighed.

"I've thought about it. Many times. Maybe one day I will. But for now…golden handcuffs, I guess."

Lily smiled and raised her glass, and Caitlin did the same. They cheered, and both drank more.

"Caitlin!" came an excited voice.

It was Sam, from down the table. He was smiling and surprised to see Caitlin there, and was raising a glass towards her.

"It's so great to see you here!" he said.

Caitlin smiled and raised her glass back at him.

Beside him, Kendra scowled back at Caitlin, not hiding her hatred for her.

"Oh my God, how do you know him?" Polly asked.

Caitlin looked at her, confused. "Who? Sam?"

Polly nodded.

"He's my brother!"

Polly's eyes opened wide in shock.

"Your *brother*? I had no idea! Oh my god! When I first brought him here, he said he was looking for his sister. I had no idea it was you! Wow! Your brother. That's intense!"

Polly seemed to be thinking about it, curling her hair with her finger as she did.

"Well, in that case," Polly said, "you should warn him."

Caitlin looked at her with concern. "About what?"

"About that witch," Polly said. "Kendra. She's only after him to get turned. She's tried to get all of our guys to turn her at some point. They know it's forbidden, so they won't. Sam is playing a dangerous game. He can never turn her. So he should stop leading her on. And he should know what she's really out for."

As Caitlin studied Kendra, across the table, she got angrier and angrier. Now her general distrust and anger towards Kendra turned to something more: protectiveness of her brother.

She was about to get up, to go around the table, and excuse herself and Sam and have a good talk with him—but just as she slid back, there was a sudden loud clinking of crystal, and the whole table stood. As one, they all got up and moved away from the table, heading into the other room.

"Where is everybody going?" Caitlin asked.

But before she could answer, Polly suddenly got super excited, her eyes opening wide, nearly jumping up and down where she stood.

"Yay! You get to meet him. My boyfriend! He's up. He's about to sing. Come quickly," she said, grabbing her arm. "Let's get a good seat!"

The crowd slowly filtered into the next room, and Polly led her, excitedly tugging at her, leading her through the crowd. The huge, formal sitting room adjacent to the dining room was large enough to act as a small concert space.

The room was filled with dozens of small couches, chaise lounges, and overstuffed armchairs.

Polly led Caitlin to a small couch, in the front row, and the two of them sat together, Lily sitting with them. Before them was a raised stage, covered in a beautiful, black and white, tile marble, above which hung a huge chandelier. On its edges sat musicians, one sitting behind a harp, one behind a harpsichord, one holding a cello, and another a violin. All that was missing was the singer.

Caitlin looked around, and saw everyone taking their seats with excitement and anticipation. She saw Sam sitting in a loveseat with Kendra, holding hands. She looked the other way, and on the other side saw Blake and his girlfriend sitting together. She looked all around, and nearly everyone seemed to be a couple. Everyone but her.

Caitlin felt more self-conscious than ever, and already was uncomfortable. She couldn't help thinking of Caleb, and her heart dropped further. She wanted to leave this place. She hoped that Polly's boyfriend would appear soon, so that he could give his concert, and she could go.

The only solace to her in the room was Lily, sitting beside her. She had become a true and fast friend, and she wished that she'd had more time to talk with her. Caitlin reflected on how much life had changed: she would have bet that Polly would have been the one who was her closest friend, but already things had changed so quickly.

The room suddenly quieted, as a huge velvet drape moved in the back of the stage, and several of the candles were snuffed out by the servants. A man, wearing a long, black velvet coat, high collars, and a white shirt with huge cuffs, strutted dramatically out onto the stage. The lights were dim, so it was hard for Caitlin to get a good look at his face. But already, she could see that he walked very dramatically, full of himself, and that he had a huge shock of black, wavy hair.

As he walked closer, right to the edge of the stage, only feet from her, Caitlin got a good look at his face.

Her heart stopped, as her entire body when cold.

No. It couldn't be.

"I am going to sing for you tonight a series of motets by Vivaldi," the singer announced dramatically.

He turned and nodded to the musicians. He opened his mouth and on cue, the musicians played.

Caitlin studied his face closely, praying she was wrong. But she wasn't. It was definitely him. She was beyond shocked. She was horrified.

Standing before her was one of her greatest enemies. Sergei. Kyle's sidekick. The man who had stolen the Sword from her in the King's Chapel in Boston. The man who had stabbed her in the back. The man who had worked closely with Kyle to help make her life hell.

She recognized the scar across his cheek. It was definitely, absolutely him. There was no doubt about it.

Caitlin felt her entire body start to shake. She wanted to lunge forward and take revenge, kill him with her bare hands.

But of course, she couldn't. He was singing, performing, and the room was filled with people who had been hospitable to her. For whatever reason, they had taken this man in. Didn't they have any idea who he really was?

Worst of all, Polly sat there beside Caitlin, her best friend, filled with desire for this creature. Caitlin couldn't conceive it. Polly was clearly completely hypnotized by him.

Caitlin didn't know what to do. First and foremost, she felt a burning desire to warn Polly. And then, to warn the others. There was no way that this was just a coincidence, she felt. Clearly, Sergei had come back in time. Probably looking for her, Caitlin. Probably still looking for the Shield. Probably sent by Kyle. He probably infiltrated all these people, and had been playing them all to his purposes. He would probably feign forgetfulness, loss of memory. He would probably insist that he was not the person she thought.

But Caitlin knew. Every ounce of her body knew. The scar she still bore in her back, by her kidney, throbbed at the sight of him. That scar had never gone away. And this was the man who had to pay for it.

It took every ounce of Caitlin's will to sit there while he continued his song.

What was worse, worse than everything, was that, despite it all, Caitlin had to admit that his voice was beautiful. It was, in fact, the most beautiful thing she had ever heard. It was like the voice of an angel, come down from heaven. And the song, it was so peaceful, so medieval. It sounded like something that could be sung in a monastery somewhere.

How was it possible? Caitlin wondered. How could such a hideous creatures could produce such beautiful music? Was life so paradoxical?

Despite everything she knew and felt about this man, Caitlin found herself getting hypnotized by the music, too. It was strange, as if he'd had an unearthly power. She had to force herself to snap out of it.

Finally, after what felt like hours, the songs ended, and the room erupted into huge applause, everyone jumping to their feet, clapping. She couldn't believe how ignorant they all were.

Polly turned to Caitlin, eyes shining.

"So? What did you think? Isn't he amazing? Isn't he gorgeous? Oh my God, wasn't that incredible? Don't you just *love* him!?"

Not waiting for an answer, Polly grabbed Caitlin's arm, preparing to drag her to the stage, to meet him.

But this time, Caitlin resisted.

Polly stopped and looked at her, confused.

"What's wrong?" Polly asked.

Caitlin tried to collect yourself, to stay calm.

"Polly, we have to talk."

"You have to meet him first," she said. "We can talk after—"

"No!" Caitlin snapped. "We have to talk now. *Right* now!"

Polly looked shocked as Caitlin reached out and dragged her against the direction of the crowd, into the other room.

The two of them were soon in the adjoining empty room.

"Caitlin, what are you doing? I need to go see him—"

"Polly!" Caitlin said firmly. "That singer, your boyfriend, Sergei—he's not who you think he is."

Polly looked back at her, confused, not registering.

"He's a very, very bad man, Polly," Caitlin said. "He's a dark and evil vampire. He is a loyal member of Kyle's Blacktide coven. He's come back here from another century, probably sent back to find me. I'm sorry to say this, but he's using you. And you have to stay away from him."

For the first time ever, Caitlin watched Polly's face contort with anger.

"You don't know what you're talking about," Polly snapped back. "Sergei's not like that. You've got him mixed up with somebody else. Sergei is perfect. Yes, he's a vampire, but he's from a good coven. He didn't come back for another time. He's always been here. He told me. He's from Russia. He's a singer. He's not out to get anyone. Least of all you. You just think this is all about you, that the whole world is about you!"

Caitlin was stunned by that. She had never seen Polly act this way.

"Polly, please understand—"

"No, I understand already. You're just jealous. You want him for yourself. And you can't stand to be happy for me. What's wrong with you? I thought you were a good friend."

Polly suddenly brushed passed her, heading back to the room—and Caitlin reached out and grabbed her wrist at the last second.

"Polly, I'm telling you. *Please.* I know it's painful to hear it. But you have to listen. You have to trust me. Stay away from him."

Polly looked back at Caitlin, locking eyes with her, seething with rage.

"Take your hand off of me," Polly said, slowly and firmly, with such venom in her voice, that it actually took Caitlin aback.

Caitlin slowly released her grip.

"Our friendship is *over*!" Polly said.

And with that, Polly marched off, into the other room, slamming the huge door hard behind her.

Caitlin stood there, feeling hollowed out. She felt so sad to see her relationship with one of her best friends crumbling before her eyes. She hated the fact that a guy got between them. That he had changed her best friend. The Polly wasn't the same person she used to be.

And she hated the fact that there was nothing she could do about it. That, no matter what she said or did, she knew that Polly would never listen. She was too clouded by love to see straight.

And she felt worried that Polly was in for trouble. That she would have her heart broken.

More than ever, Caitlin knew that her time at Versailles was up. She had lingered for Polly's sake, and that had clearly been a mistake. She felt there was no more time to waste. It was time to find her father.

As Caitlin walked out of the room, suddenly, the door opened behind her. She turned, and saw Lily approaching.

"What happened?" Lily asked, as she walked up beside Caitlin, the two of them walking together away from the room.

Caitlin was embarrassed. She hoped she hadn't made a scene storming out of there, and she wondered how much everyone else had seen. But she couldn't have stood to be in front of Sergei a moment longer, and she didn't trust herself to be in his presence without taking revenge.

Caitlin shook her head, not sure how much to tell Lily.

"Polly and I…we…had a disagreement."

She could feel Lily looking at her.

"It's over Sergei, isn't it?" she asked.

Caitlin turned and looked at her. Lily was very perceptive.

"How did you know?"

Lily sighed, as the two continued walking down a new hall.

"Polly's completely changed ever since she met him. It's been unbearable, really. And he's such a…creep. So full of himself. Personally, I can't stand him. I don't know what she sees in him. What anyone sees in him. I don't even know where he came from. It was just like, one day he was here."

"Well, I do," Caitlin said.

She stopped and turned to Lily.

"I met him before. Unfortunately. In another place and time."

Lily's eyes opened wide. "You mean another century?"

Caitlin nodded. Lily look fascinated.

"He's an evil vampire. The right-hand man of an even more evil vampire, Kyle. And what's worse—I'm the one that turned him."

Lily's eyes opened wide in shock.

"That is something which I will always regret. So I know that whatever he's up to, it's no good. And somehow, he's using Polly."

Lily shook her head. "I tried to tell her to stay away, but she wouldn't listen. The strangest thing is, he doesn't even seem to like her."

Caitlin sighed, wondering.

"You're leaving, aren't you?" Lily asked.

Caitlin looked back at her, and she could see her sadness. Once again, she was surprised by Lily's powers of perception, and at how close friends they had become so quickly.

Caitlin nodded back.

"I have to. I have to find my father. And the Shield. I'm on a mission. One that I've been ignoring for way too long."

"So where will you go to next?" Lily asked.

Caitlin thought about that. She thought of the letter, of her father's reference to the Shield, of the next clue. She kept thinking of that phrase. *The Field of the Scholars.* But for the life of her, she couldn't figure it out.

"My father left me a letter. A direction for where to look for him next. He mentioned a place, but… I'm not sure exactly where it is."

"What place?"

"The letter mentioned a place called the Fields of the Scholars."

Lily's eyes opened wide, and Caitlin was surprised at her reaction.

"Do you know it?"

"Yes," Lily said breathlessly. "It was an area in Paris in the middle ages. But it's code. It's not really a field. It's really referring to a church, to a portion of land that they leased out hundreds of years ago. It must be referring to the Abbey of Saint Germain Des Pres. It's the oldest church in Paris."

Caitlin's mind reeled with the information. That would make perfect sense, given its location, and how old it was. The moment Lily named the church, she felt it was the right place.

"I can't thank you enough," Caitlin said.

"There is more," Lily said.

Caitlin looked at her. Lily still looked shocked, as if she'd seen a ghost.

"That code you used: The Fields of the Scholars. When I was young, I was told that one day a person would come here, asking about it." Lily turned and looked both ways, secretively. "I was told to guard the secret. Not to let anyone know, or to show it to anyone, until someone asked specifically about it. I was told that whoever came along and asked, would be the One. And ever since then, I've been appointed to guard over the artifact. The one that will lead you exactly where you want."

Caitlin looked back at her in shock. She knew that Lily was royalty, but she had never guessed that she was guarding a precious artifact. Or that any human would be important enough to be entrusted with guarding a cherished vampire secret. She realized again what a special person Lily must be.

Caitlin was so curious as to what it was.

"What is it?" Caitlin asked breathlessly, her heart pounding.

Lily again looked in both directions, saw that no one was watching, and quickly took Caitlin's arm and led her away.

"Follow me," she said.

*

Caitlin walked beside Lily, down the endless marble hallways, passing servant after servant, all standing at attention along the sides of the walls. They approached another huge set of double doors, and several servants rushed to open them, bowing especially low in the presence of Lily.

Caitlin looked at her again, and marveled at how royally she was treated in this palace.

They descended a set of marble steps, turned down another hallway, then descended yet another flight of steps. Finally, Lily stopped, and looked over her shoulder.

There was no one in sight.

She removed a small key from inside her dress, inserted it into the door, and unlocked it.

They walked down another long marble hallway, and Caitlin was confused as it seemed to end in a marble wall. It looked like a dead-end.

Lily reached up and ran her hand along the wall, as if searching for something.

Finally, she found a hidden latch. She pressed, and as she did, the wall suddenly opened up, spinning open, and revealing a secret passageway.

Caitlin watched in surprise.

"I haven't opened this wall since I was a child," Lily said. "No one knows about it in the palace but me."

The two of them entered the dark staircase, Lily grabbing a torch off the wall before they did, and headed down into the darkness.

It was dark and damp down here, lit only by the torch that Lily held before them. They turned down twisting and turning passageways, and entered a subterranean level covered in stone.

"At one time, this was the wine cellar," Lily said. "It hasn't been used for centuries, though."

They turned down yet another corridor, and again, it seemed to end in nothing but solid stone. Lily reached up, combing the walls, as Caitlin held the torch for her. Finally, she found a patch of mildew, scraped away at it, and pulled at a small knob.

Out of the wall, their opened a small drawer.

Lily opened it, and began to extract something.

Caitlin held up the torch, and was shocked at what she saw.

It was a large, silver cross, bigger than the size of Caitlin's hand, and as Lily held it up and put it into Caitlin's palm, Caitlin could feel how heavy it was.

"It's the cross of the Alutic," Lily said. "It's been in the royal family for centuries. It's meant for you."

Caitlin marveled at its weight.

"How do you know?" Caitlin asked.

"You asked about the Fields of the Scholars. It could only be meant for you. I don't know how this will help you in your search, but I know that somehow it will."

As she spoke to, Caitlin felt it to be true.

"But there's one thing I don't understand," Caitlin said. "My brother, Sam, he dreamt of the Notre Dame. I was thinking that was my next stop. But after reading the letter, and seeing this cross…it all seems to be pointing me to the Church of Saint Germain Des Pres. So how is that connected to the Notre Dame?"

"Maybe you are meant to go here first. And whatever you find there will lead you to the Notre Dame. I don't know. But I do know that this church is your next stop."

That felt right to Caitlin, too. She turned and looked at Lily, and her eyes filled with gratitude.

"I don't know how to thank you."

Caitlin reached out, and the two embraced, like long-lost sisters.

"Whatever I find may just lead me back in time," Caitlin added, with worry. "If it does, I won't see you again."

Lily smiled back. "You'll see me. Humans have many lifetimes, too. And I'll tell you a secret: some of us know how to time travel, too."

CHAPTER THIRTY

Polly stormed back into the room, pushing her way through the crowd, eager to be by Sergei's side. She could not believe how rude and jealous Caitlin had been. She had thought she was a close friend. Now she saw that Caitlin, like everybody else, was just jealous. She had probably taken a liking to Sergei, too, and probably just wanted to steal him away.

Either that, or Caitlin just couldn't stand the fact that Polly had such a great man in her life. Whatever her reasons, Polly certainly didn't need any advice from her. She knew, deep down, that Sergei was the one for her.

Polly pushed her way through, and got close to Sergei. He was surrounded by a dozen admiring girls, and Polly felt her jealousy rise. She shoved her way in, right in front of his face, forcing him to look at her.

Finally, he did. He looked somewhat resentful, though, as if she were interrupting him.

But Polly felt that she knew the real Sergei, deep down, and that he was just putting on a show, for other people, that he was afraid to publicly show his true feelings for her.

"I loved your concert," she gushed.

He merely raised an eyebrow and looked away, and began talking to someone else.

Polly knew that, too, was just part of his act. She knew he was hopelessly in love with her, and that he was just trying his best not to show it.

It was okay. Polly had staying power. She would wait until all these hangers-on disappeared, and then she would talk to him, one-on-one, and know how he truly felt.

*

Sergei finally left his backstage area, and Polly positioned herself in the hallway so that when he walked out, he had to see her. He stopped, surprised.

"Have you been waiting for me all this time?" he asked.

Polly nodded. "These are for you."

She reached out and handed him a bunch of flowers.

He took them without a word, and began walking quickly away.

Polly joined him, walking alongside him.

Finally, he broke the silence. "You can tell me again about my voice," he said, as they walked.

Polly was thrilled that he wanted her opinion.

"It was amazing."

"Is that all you have to say about it? Just amazing? Wasn't it greater than that?"

Polly raced to think of better adjectives.

"It was magnificent. The best I've ever heard."

Sergei nodded his head with something like approval.

"I know," he finally said. "It was one of my better performances."

Polly raced to think of something else to say to him, some excuse for them to spend time together. She walked quickly, trying to catch up.

"I was hoping…" she began, "I was hoping that we could celebrate your performance."

Sergei suddenly stopped, turned and faced her. His blazing eyes seemed to stare right into her. There was a long silence.

"What did you have in mind?" he asked.

Polly thought. She really hadn't had anything planned. She had just been desperately looking for an excuse to spend more time with him.

She shrugged. "I don't know," she said hesitantly.

He stared at her for what felt like forever, and finally, he sighed, as if resolved.

"Very well then," he said. "You can follow me to my room, if you wish."

Polly stood there, her heart pounding, overwhelmed with excitement. Had she heard correctly?

Sergei turned and walked away, and she hurried to catch up.

"I'd like that," she said, as she walked. "Very much."

CHAPTER THIRTY ONE

Sam couldn't get over the concert. He had never heard classical music before, and he couldn't get over that guy's voice. The guy seemed like kind of a jerk, but he had to hand it to him: he really could sing.

More importantly, his night with Kendra had been amazing. She hadn't stopped cuddling up to him the whole night. He never knew what to expect with her: she was hot and cold. It seemed that once she'd gotten sight of Caitlin, she'd become super territorial and possessive. She barely left his side since.

He didn't mind. He felt like she was totally into him, and nothing made him happier. He felt completely glued to her side.

As soon as the concert ended, she'd taken his hand and led him out the room, away from all the people—and he hadn't resisted. She didn't want to stick around and talk to the singer. She wanted him to herself. And she clearly had plans for them for the night. With a mischievous smile, she led him away, and he had been thrilled.

She led him down a back hallway, through a huge chamber, and up a flight of steps.

"You haven't seen my room yet," Kendra said with a smile. "It's the grandest in the palace, except maybe for Marie's. Of course, it should be."

Sam couldn't wait. He thought back to his time with her, after horseback riding, and how amazing it had been.

They ascended another flight of marble steps, and a servant opened a set of double doors for them, and then, as they entered, closed it behind them.

They barely got a few feet, when she turned and began tearing off his clothes.

She covered his face and neck in kisses, and he reciprocated, caught up in her whirlwind of passion.

"Sam," she whispered in his ear, as she pulled off his shirt. "Will you do something for me?"

Sam could hardly think straight.

"Yes," he said, kissing her neck.

"Anything?" she asked.

He nodded, as he kissed her.

"I want to be with you forever," she said, kissing his neck.

"So do I," Sam said, and he meant it. He'd never been so obsessed with a girl. He couldn't help thinking back to his time with Samantha. That had been intense, too. But nothing like this. She was the whole package for him. In fact, if he were given the choice to marry her on the spot, to spend his whole life with her, he would do it.

"I know how we can spend forever together," she said.

"How?" he asked her, between kisses.

She pulled her head back, took his face in her hands, and stared at him. Her aqua eyes transfixed his.

"You can turn me," she said.

Sam was shocked at her request. Immediately, he sensed that would be forbidden. That if he did it, he would be an outcast. That they would both be on their own. He remembered the one rule he had been given when first introduced to this place—and he certainly didn't want to break it.

On the other hand, it seemed so natural, like the perfect way for them to be together, forever. And it was what she wanted—and she was the one asking for it.

"I…" Sam began, not knowing what to say. "I'm not sure if it's…allowed."

Kendra suddenly pulled back and frowned, a storm of emotion crossing her face.

"Of course it's allowed!" she snapped. "The only people who say it's not are just jealous—jealous they don't have a human they love that *they* can turn."

Sam had never thought of it that way. Maybe she was right. Maybe he had just been misled.

"I…" he began, then stopped, still not knowing what to say.

She suddenly looked down, and her eyes welled with tears. She looked so sad, Sam could hardly stand it.

She slowly nodded.

"Now I see," she said. "You don't really love me, as I love you."

Sam felt his heart breaking. He never wanted to hurt her.

He took her by the shoulders, and pulled up her close and looked into her eyes.

"Kendra, don't say that," he said. "I do love you. I really do."

Even as he said it, he knew the words to be true. It felt surreal to him, that he would feel that strongly about her so quickly, but he did.

Her eyes suddenly filled with hope again.

"But you don't want to be with me forever?" she asked.

"I do," Sam said. And as he said it, he realized it was true.

"So what's wrong then?" she asked. "Is it that you are afraid? Afraid of what others will say? Afraid that they will punish you?"

Sam scowled. "I'm not afraid of anyone. And I don't have to answer to anyone."

She smiled back, looking victorious.

"That's what I thought about you. That's the man that I thought you were."

The more she spoke, the more Sam felt that she was right. After all, why should he have to answer to anyone?

"Then *show* them," she said. "Prove it. Prove it to me. Turn me. Make me yours forever."

She came in and kissed him hard on his mouth, and as she did, he could no longer resist the primal instinct overwhelming him.

He suddenly leaned back, and with a primal snarl, his front teeth extended, longer than he ever imagined they could.

And he plunged forward and sunk his teeth deep into her neck.

She cried out with a gasp of pain—but it was too late now. His teeth were deep in her neck, and as she leaned back, he held her head with one hand, and with the other plunged deeper, unable to stop himself, as he felt her life force fill his veins.

He drank and drank and drank, as if there were no tomorrow.

CHAPTER THIRTY TWO

Polly lay in bed, besides Sergei, both of them naked, beneath the sheets. She rested her cheek on his shoulder, and looked up at him, studying his face. He lay there, eyes open, staring at the ceiling, expressionless.

His features were so perfect, so chiseled. She wondered how she had gotten so lucky.

She thought back to what a wonderful experience it had been, sleeping with him. Now, more than ever, she knew that they were meant to be together forever. She would do anything for him at this moment.

She reached up, and ran her hand along his chest. Finally, he turned to her.

"Tell me about your friend," he finally said.

Polly was confused.

"The one that stormed out after my concert."

Caitlin. Polly was annoyed. Why did he have to bring her up now? Why did she have to ruin a moment like this?

"That was nobody," Polly said. "I'm sorry she ran out."

"What's her name?" he pressed.

"Caitlin," Polly said.

Polly saw what looked like recognition in Sergei's eyes. It made her think, made her wonder about everything Caitlin had said. About how she had known Sergei before. Had any of it been true? No, of course, that was ridiculous. But why was he asking about her now?

"And where was she going, in such a rush?" he asked.

Polly shrugged. "I don't know. Who cares about her?"

Sergei suddenly turned to her, with complete intensity.

"I do," he said harshly, "or else I wouldn't be asking."

Polly was taken aback. She didn't know what she had done to offend him. "I'm sorry," she said.

"Then answer my questions," he pressed.

"What do you want to know?" Polly asked.

"Where exactly was your friend going?"

Polly shrugged again, thinking.

"I have no idea. She probably went looking for her father, I guess. She always is."

"Did she mention any place specific?"

Polly racked her brain. She suddenly remembered something.

"Well, she did mention something about a dream. About her brother. About some kind of key in a church."

Sergei's eyes opened wide. Polly was surprised at how interested he was. He suddenly sat up, and grabbed her shoulders fiercely.

"What church?"

Polly was scared by his intensity. She didn't understand what was going on.

"I don't understand. Why does it matter? Why's it so important?"

He shook her, roughly. "Tell me!"

"It was the Notre Dame," Polly said, suddenly scared. "She said something about the Notre Dame."

Sergei suddenly threw her across the bed, and she landed hard on the floor.

He then threw off the covers, dressed, and hurried across the room.

Polly burst into tears.

"What's wrong with you?" she cried. "Why are you being so mean? Where are you going?"

Polly couldn't understand what was happening. Just a minute ago, her world had been perfect.

Sergei stopped before the door, turned, and smiled at her for the first time. But it wasn't a smile of love. It was an evil, crooked smile.

"Stupid girl," he said. "I've gotten all I need from you. You are as useless to me now as you were the first moment I met you. And now your friend will pay the price."

And with that, Sergei stormed out, slamming the door behind him.

Polly sat up, put her head in her hands, and cried and cried and cried.

All she could think, as tears poured down her face, was how stupid she had been. How mad at herself she was for believing in Sergei. How, all along, her friend, her only best friend in the world, Caitlin, had been right.

And worse, how she had returned the favor by putting her in danger.

CHAPTER THIRTY THREE

Sam lay there, in Kendra's huge bed, sprawled naked on top of the most luxurious covers he had ever seen. She lay in his arms, and they both reclined in a huge mound of silk pillows. He felt like he had died and gone to heaven. He'd never been with anyone remotely like Kendra, and he hoped they could stay together forever.

His mind reeled, as he thought of the implications of what he had just done. He had really turned her. She lay there, sleeping with her head on his chest, peacefully enough, and for all the world to see, she was just as she had been before. But he knew that when she woke, she would be different. Changed forever. Turned. One of his race. Just as Samantha had turned him.

He recalled how difficult it was for him when he first woke, and came to the realization. But then again, it wasn't something he had asked for. It had been thrust upon him. In her case, she had asked for it, had begged him to turn her. And she had received her wish.

He wondered what she would be like when she awoke. If she would still love him as much. Or hopefully, even more.

But he still couldn't escape the gnawing feeling that he had done something wrong. That he had transgressed some sort of sacred vampire rule. That somehow, he would have to answer for this.

Before Sam could finish the thought, Kendra suddenly opened her eyes, and sat bolt upright, immediately awake. She stared at him, her eyes wider than he had ever seen them. Her eyes seemed to be glazed over, like the eyes of a wild animal. Alert. As she stared right through him, he began to wonder if she even recognized him at all.

"Kendra?" he asked, sitting up in bed. "Are you okay?"

She suddenly jumped up from bed in a single leap, landing halfway across the room, surprising him.

She quickly got dressed, her back to him, and she moved so fast, faster than anyone he had ever seen. It was unnatural. Clearly, she already had the speed of his race.

He slowly got out of bed, began to get dressed, and came over to her.

"What's wrong? Is everything okay?" he asked again.

But she kept her back to him as she dressed, and he wondered why she was acting so strangely.

"Why don't you come back to bed?" he asked.

She suddenly turned and faced him, and he saw the wildness in her eyes, and was almost afraid.

"Why would I?" she spat back.

"What do you mean?" he asked.

"I already have all I need from you."

Sam felt as if he had been punched in the gut. He could not believe her words. Had she really said what he'd thought she had just said?

"What are you talking about?" Sam asked with more urgency, and he could hear the fear in his own voice.

She suddenly headed for the door, and he reached out and grabbed her arm, to stop her.

But she spun around, and with her incredible new strength, roughly threw his arm off of her. He was shocked. She stared at him with a ferocity he had never imagined, her aqua eyes glowing and unearthly.

"Don't you ever put your hands on me," she snarled in a low, guttural voice.

"Kendra," he said softly. "It's me, Sam. What's happened to you? Don't you recognize me?"

She suddenly broke into a laugh, a demonic laugh, right in his face, mocking him.

"Of course I recognize you, you pathetic little thing. And I never loved you. I was just using you. You gave me what I wanted. Now, I'm done. I'm only going to spare your life because you turned me. But if you get in my way again, you will suffer—the same way that your people, and your sister, are about to suffer."

With that, she wheeled, grabbed the huge oak door, and tore it off its hinges.

The two servants stared back at her, in shock, and she spun the wood and knocked them both off their feet with it.

Then suddenly, like a wild animal, she bounded down the hall, leaping twenty feet at a time, tearing down the corridors of Versailles, smashing candelabra as she went. She was like a one-woman wrecking machine.

Sam could not believe what he saw. He looked at the destroyed hallway, the unconscious servants, and wondered, with dread, what he had created.

He bounded off after her, chasing down the hall. As he did, he felt how much her words had stung. Had she just been playing him all along? Had he fallen perfectly into her trap? And what did she mean about Caitlin? What was her agenda, exactly?

As Sam ran down the corridor, using his full vampire speed, he caught a glimpse of her, far down a corridor, tearing through a room. As she did, she hurled human beings to the left and to the right, to terrible screams of mayhem.

Sam picked up speed as he followed. She smashed through yet another door, down yet another corridor, then finally, entered the main entry parlor of Versailles. She ran right for the main doors.

About a dozen guards, apparently alerted to her presence, stood before the door, blocking it with their bayonets. As she approached them, they lowered them towards her.

"Stay where you are!" one of them yelled.

As Sam watched, she leapt up, high in the air, over their heads, and with a single kick, knocked open the huge double doors. They went crashing down with a bang.

She landed out the other side, and with one more leap she was flying in the air, heading off into the night.

Sam wanted to follow her, but he suddenly spotted something on the horizon, and his heart stopped.

There, racing towards the palace, was an angry mob of thousands of citizens.

They were charging right for the palace steps.

CHAPTER THIRTY FOUR

As Caitlin flew across the French countryside, far away from Versailles, the silver cross and her dad's scroll in her pocket, clutching Ruth in her arms, she finally, for the first time in this place, felt as if she were on the right track. She felt deep in her bones that she was finally doing exactly what she was supposed to be doing. Searching for her father. Searching for the Shield. Following the clues, doing what she was destined to do.

As she flew and flew, her head cleared even more as she got further away Versailles. She was mad at herself for not doing this sooner. She knew all along what her mission was: why couldn't she just embark from the beginning?

She thought of Caleb. Her heart pulled as she remembered how much she loved him, at how bad she'd felt when he'd left. At the same time, now that she was on her mission, she realized that if he hadn't left, maybe she would have just settled down, and never sought out her father. She realized once again that, no matter how painful things seemed while they happened, if she looked back upon them in retrospect, over time, she realized that everything happened for a reason. That reason wasn't always easy for her to see while it was happening. But the more distant she got from events, the more that reason started to become clear.

As Caitlin raced towards Paris, she started to feel a tremor of nervousness, of anticipation, at the idea of possibly meeting her father. Could it be that he had been waiting for her in Paris all this time? So close? That he would be at the Saint Germain Des Pres church? Or at the Notre Dame? Would he embrace her, be proud of her? Would he give her the Shield?

Caitlin hoped that he would indeed be proud of her, that he would recognize what a woman, what a warrior, she had become. That he would acknowledge all that she has sacrificed to find him. He would open up a whole new world for her, introduce her to his coven. And maybe she could finally have a place in the world, a people to belong to, a place to settle down. She would like that.

Caitlin also thought about Sam, with a pang of regret. She wished that he was with her, at her side, helping her on her quest. But she realized that he was too caught up in his relationship, and there was simply nothing she could do about that. Sometimes, people just had to come to their own realizations, in their own time. She just hoped that everything would be okay for him. She had a sinking feeling, though, upon looking at Kendra, that it would not.

More than anything, Caitlin wished that Caleb was here with her now, at her side, as he had always been on her search. She missed him desperately, missed having him there, missed not being able to share her ideas with him. And whatever she found, she wanted to find it together with him. And if once again, for some reason, she had to go back in time, she desperately wished that he would be by her side.

But as Caitlin flew, she realized that she was much stronger now. She had become a warrior. And part of what it meant to be a warrior was to be unafraid to go it alone if need be, to carve your own path in this world. To forge forward, even when no one else was willing to forge forward with you. It was about individual strength, and courage. And sometimes that meant the courage to do what no one else was doing.

Caitlin felt a new wave of strength come over her, emboldened by all of her training with Aiden, all of his lessons, and all of the sparring she had done. She wanted Caleb there, but she felt strong enough to handle this mission on her own.

As Caitlin flew, the landscape changed, and the thick forest of the French countryside began to give way to the urban landscape of Paris. Beneath her, Caitlin recognized the buildings, the tall church steeples, the occasional medieval church and abbey, and the more fashionable recent construction of the 18th century townhouses. From up here, it was a breathtakingly beautiful city.

But at the same time, as she looked down, real concern overcame her. Despite the late hour, the streets were flooded. They were absolutely packed with mobs of angry citizens, carrying torches. The tension and anger in the air was palpable; she could feel it, even from this height. People screamed and ran throughout the chaotic streets, and worse, they were destroying property, throwing stones through windows, throwing torches into buildings. The crowd seemed to particularly center around the huge Bastille prison, and spread out from there. She couldn't believe it: it looked as if a war had broken out.

Caitlin had not expected this. She'd expected to simply fly to Saint Germain Des Pres, find what was she was looking for, and continue her search. She had not expected having to navigate an angry mob of citizens in the streets. She didn't want to hurt anyone. But then again, she couldn't let them get in her way.

As Caitlin flew over the left bank of the city, she spotted the tall, square tower of the Saint Germain Des Pres church. It was distinctive, especially from this bird's-eye view. In addition to its tall rectangular tower, it was attached to a large monastery, with a long, sloping roof. Its walls were arched along its ends, giving a beautiful, cylindrical shape to the complex. It looked like other medieval churches she had seen in the countryside, and it was shocking to see such a medieval masterpiece here, right smack in the middle of the city.

Luckily, the crowds weren't as intense in this part of the city. Caitlin chose a dark alley in which to land, where no one could see her, and descended quickly.

Still clutching Ruth, not giving her time to walk or to relieve herself, Caitlin made her way quickly into what looked like a back entrance to the church. The huge front doors, she noticed, were locked and barred, and she didn't want to enter through the public square, and give any rowdy humans a chance for an encounter.

Instead, she went around the rear of the building, and saw a small, arched door, probably used by the priests. This, too, was locked. But Caitlin, stronger than she'd ever been, simply looked at it, closed her eyes, and breathed, focusing on becoming one with the doorknob. When she finished, she heard a click, and saw it open by itself. Aiden's techniques had finally sunk in.

Caitlin walked into the open door, proud of herself for not having to kick it down, and closed it firmly behind her, locking it.

It was dark in here, with just a few lingering candles, dwindling down, spread on the altar, probably the remnants of some evening worshippers. The only other thing that lit up the interior was the moonlight, streaking in through the immense stained-glass windows, which soared all the way up to the ceiling.

Caitlin looked up and took it in. It was some of the most beautiful glass she had ever seen, rows and rows of it dominating the walls, culminating in a high, arched ceiling with Romanesque columns. On the walls were painted huge, ancient frescoes. The stone, too, looked ancient, and she could tell that this church was different, that it had been around forever.

She remembered Lily having told her that this was the oldest church in Paris, thousands of years old, and as she looked at it now, she could tell that it was. It was incredible to her. Here she was, in the year 1789, standing in a place that was already ancient. It made her feel insignificant in time.

Caitlin walked down the long aisle, feeling drawn towards the altar. Her footsteps echoed on the immaculate, shining black and white tiled marbled floor. There were hundreds of small wooden chairs set out in neat rows and this place looked big enough to hold thousands. Along the walls were small arches, and small statues of various medieval saints.

As Caitlin finally reached the far end, she came to a single, simple altar, recessed into the wall. It contained a large statue of Mary, holding a cross, built upon a marble pedestal.

Caitlin took out the large cross that Lily had given her. She held it up and examined it. As she did, she was shocked to see that it appeared to be the exact size of the cross in the statue's hand.

As she looked closer, she was also shocked to realize that the cross the statue held was actually empty. As if waiting for a cross to be inserted into it.

Could it be? Caitlin wondered.

She climbed onto the pedestal, reached up, and held up her large silver cross. She inserted slowly, wondering if it would fit. As she inserted it, she was shocked to see that it was, indeed, a perfect fit.

As she pushed her cross, locking it firmly into place, she heard a noise, and looked down to see the pedestal of the statue swing open.

Caitlin hurried down, and pulled open the secret compartment. The marble opened slowly, with a scraping noise, letting out ancient air and dust.

Caitlin reached in, grabbing hold of something. She pulled it out.

She couldn't believe it. It was another encased scroll, the same size and design as the one that had held the first half of her father's letter.

She opened it slowly, hands trembling, and her mouth dropped open as she realized what it held.

CHAPTER THIRTY FIVE

As Sam stood there, in the entryway of Versailles, watching hordes of masses storm the steps, he broke into action. He ran to help all the guards, who were scrambling to restore the huge double doors. But the human guards weren't strong enough to lift them back up in time.

Sam leapt forward, and, using his strength, pulled them up by himself, restoring them back into place. He quickly scanned the room, and spotted a huge, wooden beam mounted above the fireplace. It looked like the size of an ancient tree trunk, and like it would take twenty men to lift.

Sam ran over to it, and to the shocked look of the guards, he hoisted it alone, carried it across the room, and slammed it in front of the doors, barring them.

Just in time. Moments later, there came the pounding of hundreds of fists at the door, as the masses tried to get in.

Thanks to Sam, the door seemed to be holding. At least for now.

As Sam stood there, he was soon joined by Aiden, the twins, and all the other coven members. Guards, too, flooded in from all over the palace, and soon Polly and Lily, and even Marie Antoinette, joined the room. Everyone was in shock at the chaos.

"What has happened?" Marie asked.

"There have been reports that the Bastille has been stormed, my lady," one of the guards yelled, frantic. "The masses are in disarray. They're destroying everything in the streets. And now, it has spread here. I think it is a revolution!"

Sam could see the horrified expressions on the faces of Marie and her entourage.

Aiden stepped up, and mobilized his team.

"Taylor and Tyler, you protect the East wing," he ordered, and they burst into action.

"Cain, you cover the Western entrance. I will help hold these doors myself. And Lily, please accompany Marie back to her quarters. The rest of my men will guard you."

Sam walked up to him. He turned and looked at Sam, and Sam felt as if he was staring at him with disapproval.

"Go help your sister," Aiden ordered, disapprovingly. "You have harmed her enough already."

Sam felt a pang of guilt race through him, as he thought of Kendra and her ominous words about Caitlin.

Polly ran up to them.

"It's all my fault!" she cried. "I was deceived by Sergei. He asked where Caitlin was going. I told him about the Notre Dame!"

Aiden shook his head. "Go and join Sam. She will need all of your help. And no matter what happens, make sure nothing stops her from getting the Shield."

Sam turned to Polly. "I made a mistake," he said. "I need to make it up. I need to try to rescue Caitlin."

"Me, too," Polly said. "I'm coming with you."

The door shook, as several more people banged against it.

"GO!" Aiden yelled.

Sam took off at a running start, and felt Polly right behind him. He leapt high up into the air, through an open window, and flew into the night.

Soon, the two of them were high in the air, racing towards the horizon.

He was determined to do whatever it took to save his sister.

And if that meant killing Kendra, then so be it.

CHAPTER THIRTY SIX

Caitlin unrolled the new scroll with shaking hands. Her heart pounded as she realized that it was the second half of her Dad's letter.

She quickly took out the first half of the letter, unrolled it, and held it up to this one. As she put them together, she saw that the ridges fit perfectly, and that now, finally, it was one complete letter.

She read the entire letter again, from the beginning:

My dearest Caitlin:

If you are reading this, you have already surpassed many obstacles. It means that you have already chosen to travel the road less traveled, to take the difficult path. For that, I commend you. You are truly your father's daughter.

You must forgive all the riddles, codes, letters, and keys, but the secret that I guard is most powerful, and must be broken into fragments, to prevent others from decoding it. Only the truly worthy—only yourself—are meant to decode the secret that you ultimately will.

If you are reading this, you already have one key in your possession. You must obtain the final three to reach me.

The second key is your focus now. To find it, you will first have to go to the Fields of the Scholars—

Now Caitlin lifted the second half of the letter:

—and you will need to visit the Notre Dame and retrieve the key. The dagger will point the way. And don't forget: the island is a big place.

We will be together soon.

I love you.

Your father.

Caitlin read the letter again and again, completely bewildered. The dagger will point the way? What dagger?

Caitlin checked back inside the marble compartment, wondering if she had missed something. She reached in deeper than she had at first, combing its walls with their hands.

And then she felt it. Something was attached to the back of it.

She pulled hard, and out came a small, silver dagger. She was shocked. She had almost overlooked it.

Now she had the dagger, and she assumed that she would need to use it, somehow, in the Notre Dame, in order to find the key.

But what did he mean when he said that the island was a big place?

All the clues seemed to indicate that the Notre Dame was the last stop. But then again, something bothered her about his letter. It felt too obvious, too straightforward to her. She felt that there was some embedded message in there she was missing.

At least Caitlin knew where she needed to go next.

As she stood to go, there was a sudden bang at the door, followed by the smashing of stained glass all around her.

She heard a chorus of angry shouts, and knew it was the mob. The humans, in the midst of their revolution. Her heart broke to see such beautiful precious, ancient glass shattering, falling to pieces all around her.

But this was not her war. Not her revolution. She had another war to wage. One far more dangerous.

And it began in the Notre Dame.

CHAPTER THIRTY SEVEN

Caleb flew through the night, determined to rush back to Caitlin's side. He hated himself. He didn't understand how he could have been so stupid, so naïve. So easily misled.

Worse, he had left Caitlin for nothing. He had ruined their moment, the very time he was about to propose, the very peak of their love, to run off for an illusion. For a false belief that his son was still alive.

He would never forgive Sera for what she'd done. For ruining his life—again.

But more importantly, he would never forgive himself for being so stupid. He should have listened to Caitlin, and stayed put.

As he flew, Caleb closed his eyes, and the image passed through it again: he recalled his arriving back at his castle, and the sinking feeling of finding it empty. Caitlin gone. He had run through empty room after empty room, and had finally realized that she had left him.

Ever since then, he had combed the skies, had looked for her everywhere. Now he was combing Paris, block by block.

As he did, he received a sudden signal, like an electric shock to his system. It was the signal of Caitlin. Of her presence. Of her being in distress. He could feel it, in every pore of his body. She was in trouble, he was certain of it. And he could now feel where it was coming from. From deep inside Paris.

Caleb changed course, heading towards a different section of Paris with new speed, new resolve. He was determined to find her this time, and to make wrongs right.

This time, it would be different. This time, they would really make a new start of it. Truly be together forever. This time he knew, there would be nothing to stand in their way.

And when they finally did get a moment together, alone, he would ask her the question he'd been dying to ask her from the start.

He would ask if she would be his wife.

CHAPTER THIRTY EIGHT

Caitlin flew the short distance from Saint Germain Des Pres over the Seine river, and then over the Ile de la Cite. She circled the small, narrow island slowly, trying to take it all in. There, of course, was the Notre Dame, huge, enormous, towering over everything, the largest building on the island. It was an overwhelming structure. The thought of finding whatever it was she needed inside it seemed daunting.

She circled the island again, trying to take it all in context, and noticed that the Notre Dame wasn't the only building on it. There were rows of medieval houses, crooked alleyways, cobblestone streets, and other buildings spread throughout. She looked down to see if the mobs were here, too, as they seemed to be everywhere else in Paris. Strangely enough, they were not. In fact, the square in front of the Notre Dame was completely empty. She found that to be odd. Why would the masses revolt everywhere else in the city, but not in its most famous place? Who was controlling them, exactly?

Caitlin swooped down lower, looking more carefully. All was eerily silent. Was it a trap?

Caitlin landed in the huge, stone plaza before the church, having it to herself, and set Ruth down. The church was lit up by dozens of torches, and she stared up at its edifice in awe. It was massive, with huge, arched doors, and dozens of figures carved over it. She had been to many churches on her journey: she thought of the Duomo in Florence, St. Mark's in Venice, and dozens of others—but she had never been to a church as large as this. She also couldn't help remembering that she had begun her journey here: did that hold some significance? Was she coming full circle?

She walked right to the front door, and tried the knob, just in case.

To her surprise, it was open.

She turned and looked over her shoulder, sensing some danger. But she saw nothing there.

She turned and went inside, not liking the feel of this. Everything was too quiet. Everything seemed too easy.

Caitlin looked inside the church, and was blown away by its size and scope. Here, the pews stretched as far as the eye could see, and the aisle seemed endless. On either side were enormous stone columns, the size of tree trunks, reaching high into the sky, culminating in a series of arches. Between them were enormous candle chandeliers.

At the end of the aisle sat an immense altar, crowned with dozens of statues. Caitlin wondered how anyone could worship in here—it was so large, it seemed like it could hold an entire city.

Caitlin reached down and felt the dagger in her hand, and wondered where on earth she should begin her search. She sensed danger again, and spun, but saw no one. She suddenly felt that time was of the essence.

Caitlin closed her eyes, and summoned her inner power. She allowed her senses to take over, to lead her. She willed herself to get calm, to get quiet, and to tune in to where the key might be. She knew that there was a key to be found, from the letter, and she knew that the dagger would play a part in it. But other than that, she had no idea where to look.

After several moments, her senses began to take over, and she felt a strong sudden impulse to head into the lower levels of the church.

She found herself walking to her left, through a large marble corridor, then turning down another corridor. She followed a series of statues along the wall, until she found herself led to a small, narrow staircase.

Caitlin descended, twisting and turning, and finally, it lead her into a wide-open, low-ceiling, underground crypt. It was even more solemn down here, with only a few candles burning, and Caitlin could see that this was a mausoleum of some sort. All along the walls, as far as she could see, were sarcophagi. It looked like the perfect place for an ancient vampire coven.

Caitlin let her senses take over, and felt herself being led. She walked down the long corridor, in the dank, musty air, passing one sarcophagus after another. Finally, she felt herself wanting to stop before one of them.

She examined it, and saw nothing out of the ordinary.

Caitlin was about to look elsewhere, but Ruth sat there, whining at it, not letting her leave. Caitlin looked again.

As she examined the intricate design of the lid, the small figure of a knight carved into it, the folded hands outlined on the stone, the armor, the belt, she realized something. There was a slot in the belt, notched into the stone. Just wide enough, she realized, to hold a dagger.

Caitlin held up the small, jewel-encrusted dagger, and gently inserted into the slot. It fit perfectly. Encouraged, she pushed it all the way in.

A stone lever suddenly sank down, and a small compartment opened on the statue's palm.

Caitlin was amazed. A small, gold key was now sitting in the statue's palm.

Caitlin held it up, inspecting it, thrilled to have found it.

But she was also stumped.

This could not be the second key. This key did not look anything like the other one: it was small and gold, not large and silver. It appeared to be a key to something else.

Caitlin suddenly heard a noise somewhere, high above, in the upper level of the church.

She quickly stashed the key into her pocket, grabbed Ruth, and hurried out from the crypt.

She ran up the steps, and onto the main floor of the Notre Dame. She checked both ways for danger, but saw none.

But suddenly, as she watched, the main front doors of the church were kicked open. To her shock, there suddenly rushed in a huge, unruly, screaming mob.

Caitlin sensed immediately that this mob was different from the other. These were vampires. And at the center was a figure she recognized from the history books: Napoleon. She was surprised to discover he was of her kind—and that he was leading an entire coven, hundreds of vampires, charging right for her. She was vastly outnumbered.

It had been a trap, she realized. They had been waiting for her to come here, to find what it was they needed. And now that she was boxed in, they were determined to kill her off for good. She had been setup.

As the crowd charged, Caitlin thought quick. She closed her eyes, and focused on summoning her primal energy. Her rage. She focused on her new powers, and she knew that she could fight off an army. She *knew* it.

As the hundreds of vampires charged, Caitlin suddenly charged *them.* At the last second, right before they collided, she leapt high into the air, higher than she ever imagined possible, and grabbed hold of a huge, dangling chandelier, fifty feet off the ground. She immediately climbed its chain, scaling it faster than she could have imagined possible, heading straight for the ceiling. From there, she figured she could break her way through one of the huge stained-glass windows, and escape through the roof.

Just as Caitlin was getting close, suddenly, one of those huge ceiling windows shattered.

She looked up, and there before her, looking down, snarling, was one of the most evil looking creatures she had ever seen.

Six more stained-glass windows suddenly shattered, and she saw that there were seven of these creatures—huge, enormous, disfigured vampires. They blocked her access to the roof.

Caitlin was cornered in from both directions. She had no choice but to stand and fight.

She didn't wait a moment longer. She grabbed hold of the chandelier's chain, and snapped it off from the ceiling. The huge iron chandelier, twenty feet wide, plummeted straight down to the crowd below, Caitlin plummeting with it.

It landed on dozens of Napoleon's vampires, crushing them beneath its weight.

Caitlin activated her wings at the last moment before she hit the ground, hovering in the air, and landed softly. On the ground, she then took the enormous candelabra by the end of its chain, and with her Herculean strength, she swung it over her head as a weapon. She swung in larger and larger circles, and as she did, the enormous iron knocked out dozens more of Napoleon's men. She was a one-woman wrecking machine, and no one could come within fifty feet of her.

But then she heard an unearthly screech, and saw the seven evil creatures plunging down towards her. She took hold of the chandelier and with one last swing, hurled it, aiming right for one of them.

It was a perfect shot, and it took him out, sending him flying backwards and embedding him in a wall.

But that left six more of those things, and before Caitlin could react, one of them came down hard and kicked her, sending her halfway across the church. The creature had strength unlike anything she had ever fought. She smashed against a wall hundreds of feet away, the wind knocked out of her.

Caitlin felt that she could handle Napoleon's men. But she didn't possibly see how she could handle six of these things on her own.

Still, she jumped back to her feet, ready to fight. And just in time. One of them was already in the midst of swinging for her head, and as she ducked, his large fist went right into the wall. Caitlin reached over, grabbed the sword off of his belt and decapitated him.

Sword in hand, Caitlin faced off with another of those things, which was already lunging for her. She ducked just in time, then swung around and chopped him in half.

But that still left four of them, and she was just not quick enough to handle all four at once. She felt herself being kicked hard from behind, right in the kidneys, and she went flying through the air, and smashed headfirst into a wall.

She got up, but now her world was blurry, and those things were bearing down on her, along with dozens of Napoleon's vampires. She needed some time to regain her strength, but there was no time to be had. They were closing in fast, and she just didn't have more left in her. It was one of the few moments in her life when she felt that it was over. And she resigned herself to her fate.

At just that moment, another huge stained glass window smashed, and another vampire plunged down, aiming right for her.

As he came into focus, she saw who it was.

Her eyes opened wide in shock. It was Caleb.

Caleb dove in just in time, swooping her up in his arms, and flying her off into the air just before one of those evil creatures stomped her with this foot, crushing a huge hole in the floor were Caitlin had been lying.

He carried her up high, to one of the upper balconies of the Notre Dame, and placed her safely on a seat. He then turned and leapt off the balcony, meeting one of those evil things in midair. The two of them grappled with each other, struggling; eventually, Caleb gained the upper hand, and threw the creature across the church, smashing him into a wall.

But Caleb was suddenly jumped by the other three creatures, who dragged him down to the main floor.

Caitlin snapped out of it. She felt her primal energy return to her, especially as she saw Caleb in danger. She leapt off the balcony and dove to help him, feeling stronger than she ever had.

As she flew through the air, she saw the three evil creatures smash Caleb into the floor, pounding and kicking him in the back of the head—and fury overcame her. It was a fury unlike any she had ever known. She felt the rage course through her feet, her arms, up through her head—and felt herself alive with a primal battle fury.

She increased her speed, diving for all she was worth, aiming right for one of the creatures. Without slowing, she dove right at him. At the last second, he turned his disgusting face, and she punched it so hard, she snapped its neck in half.

Caitlin then wheeled and elbowed the other creature right in the face, knocking him back. Before it could get to its feet, she leapt and kicked it under its chin with such force, she sent it flying halfway across the church. It landed on a huge spike, impaling it.

There was but one of those things left, and as it charged at Caitlin, she closed her eyes, and tapped her new power. Using her mind only, she lifted it way into the air, then sent it flying, across the church, and out a glass window at the speed of light.

Caleb looked up at her in awe.

Napoleon's vampires, too, were in shock that anyone could kill such evil things. Caitlin faced them and roared, ready to bear down on them next, and as she did, they all suddenly turned and fled. Napoleon fled with them, not willing to face Caitlin after what he had just witnessed.

Caitlin reached down and picked up Caleb and brought him to his feet. He smiled back at her, and she knew he would be all right.

"You saved me," he said, through his smile. "It was supposed to be the other way around."

She smiled back.

"You saved me, too," she said.

But before the two of them could collect themselves, suddenly, there was another crash.

They turned to see, in the far corner of the church, several more windows get shattered. She could not believe it. Who could it be now?

In flew Kyle, Sergei, and Kendra. The three of them spread throughout the air, each holding unusual weapons, and flying right for them.

At the same time, the huge doors opened from the rear of the church, and in poured hundreds of new vampires, all clearly loyal to Kyle.

Caitlin didn't care. This was the faceoff she'd been waiting for. She hated Kyle, Sergei and Kendra with a passion and fervor she reserved for few others. And as she saw Caleb stand up proudly beside her and prepare himself for the confrontation, she knew he shared the same feelings.

"It's time for you to pay for my son!" Caleb screamed, as he dove in the air, right for Kyle.

"And it's past time that I killed you for good!" Kyle retorted.

The two of them met in the air with a vicious sound, the sound of their bodies crashing into each other echoing, as they wrestled each other, fangs out.

Caitlin wasted no time. She flew right for Sergei, relishing the idea of attacking her nemesis, the one who, literally, stabbed her in the back, and who spurned her girlfriend.

"You will pay!" Caitlin screamed.

He snarled. "Have you forgotten? You are my maker!" he screamed back. "If anyone will pay, it's going to be you!"

The two of them met in mid-air. Sergei lunged for her throat, but Caitlin saw it coming. She dodged at the last second, and instead tackled him in midair, plunging with him right down to the ground, and smashing with him into the floor. She reached up and began to choke him, ready to kill him on the spot, for what he had done to her, for what he had done to Polly, for everything he had done to help Kyle. She had him in an iron grip, and she felt she was winning—when suddenly, she felt a horrible kick in her back, knocking the wind out of her, and forcing her to let go.

She rolled over to see Kendra looking down at her, snarling. Kendra extracted a small silver dagger, and quickly lunged right for Caitlin's heart. She was quick, and sneaky, and Caitlin only dodged it at the very last second.

Caitlin spun around and back-handed Kendra hard, knocking her down.

But then Sergei was back on her, punching her hard, and knocking her across the floor. She could handle either of them on her own, but the two of them together was becoming too much for her. She looked over and saw that Caleb was still struggling with Kyle, the two of them wrestling on the ground, first one having the upper hand, then the other. They fought viciously, punching, elbowing, choking. It was an epic battle.

Behind them, Caitlin saw hundreds of more vampires rushing towards them, and she knew that they couldn't win. They just couldn't fight them all—and these three—at once. Once again, she felt that they were losing, and that this could be their final resting place.

Suddenly, there was yet another crash through the windows.

There appeared, flying right for her, two more vampires. She couldn't believe what she was seeing.

It was Sam and Polly, both diving right for her.

Just in time. Just as Kendra was gearing up to kick Caitlin again, hard in the kidneys, Sam dove between them, and knocked Kendra back with a vicious elbow to her throat. She went flying back, hard against the wall, and it saved Caitlin at the last second.

And as Sergei jumped up and prepared to stomp Caitlin in the head, Polly dove in faster, kicking Sergei hard, planting both feet in his chest, and sending him flying across the room, smashing into the altar, and breaking the marble monument into pieces.

Caitlin jumped to her feet, so happy to see them, and so grateful for their help.

"Caleb!" she yelled, and the three of them jumped into action.

They hurried over, and each took turns kicking Kyle so hard that they finally knocked him off of Caleb.

Caleb spun over, got on top of Kyle, and grabbed him by the throat, choking him. It looked like he had him for good this time.

Caitlin looked over and saw the masses charging them; she also saw Kendra and Sergei slowly starting to recuperate.

"Caleb!" Caitlin cried. "Let him go! There's no time! We have to go!"

But this was clearly the face-off that Caleb had been waiting for. Caleb squeezed for all he had, the veins bulging in his face, as Kyle turned purple. Caitlin didn't think he would ever let go.

"CALEB!"

Finally, reluctantly, Caleb let go. He spit in the unconscious Kyle's face.

"Another day!" he spat.

Caitlin turned to Sam and Polly.

"I found a key," Caitlin said. "But it's not meant for here. It's meant for some other place."

"Go!" Sam said. "Find it. Bring Caleb. Go now! We will stay here and hold them back for you."

"We can't let you fight alone!" Caitlin cried.

"You have to," Sam said. "This is no longer about you. It is about our mission. GO! The mission is more important."

Caitlin instantly knew he was right. This was her chance, and she had to take it. There wasn't a second left to lose.

"But how can the two of you fight them all off?" she asked worriedly.

Sam smiled, and as he did, Caitlin was shocked to watch him shapeshift before her eyes. Within seconds, he looked exactly like Kyle.

"I have a few tricks up my sleeve," he snarled, in Kyle's voice. It was eerie.

At that moment, Caitlin realized they'd be just fine.

She turned and grabbed Caleb's hand, reached down and grabbed Ruth, and they leapt into the air, taking off, for the opening in the ceiling.

She looked back one last time, and watched Sam, looking like Kyle, give orders to Kyle's people, and tricking them—and she knew that they would be just fine.

CHAPTER THIRTY NINE

Caitlin and Caleb flew out of the ceiling of the Notre Dame, and into the night air. They flew together over the small Ile de la Cite. As they did, Caitlin was wracking her brain, trying to think where to go next, where that key might lead. She kept thinking of the letter, kept turning her father's words over and over in her head.

Don't forget: the island is a big place.

It had bothered ever since she'd read it. *The island is a big place. The island is a big place.*

Was there somewhere else on the island, she suddenly wondered, *that could hold the final key? Some place close to the Notre Dame?*

Her adversaries—Kyle, Sergei and Kendra—had managed to infiltrate her coven, and had discovered to meet her in the Notre Dame. But no one else had seen the second half of that letter. And no one else realized that it led to something else. To one final clue. One final place. Everyone else thought the Notre Dame was the final destination, Caitlin realized. But it wasn't.

"Where now?" Caleb asked, flying beside her.

Caitlin suddenly dove down, Caleb following, and examined the island more closely.

It was filled with twisting and turning alleyways, with medieval houses. As she flew to the other end of it, the island tapered in a point, and she noticed something that made her pause.

There was another church. Not as grand as the Notre Dame, but still large, and extraordinarily beautiful. There was nothing else remotely like it on the island, and she suddenly felt certain that whatever it was she needed, it was there.

The island is a big place.

Caitlin pointed. "There," she said.

She dove down, Caleb by her side, and landed before the church.

It had a massive limestone edifice, reaching high into the sky, and coming to a point. Its façade was ornately carved, covered with gargoyles in every direction. It had a single, tall, arched door, and as she faced it, she knew this was the place.

"Do you know it?" she asked.

Caleb looked at her.

"Yes. The Cathedral of Saint Chapelle," he said. "A very sacred place for our kind. It's been around for thousands of years. Most people do not know of it. They know only of the Notre Dame."

Caitlin turned to him.

"I feel that this is it. Whatever it is I am meant to find, I feel that it is here. My father, he said that the island was a big place. I think that what he meant was that the Notre Dame was not the only place on the island to search. That our final clue is *beside* the Notre Dame."

They walked to the door, preparing to open it, when suddenly, the door opened wide, startling them.

Before them stood a tall, strikingly beautiful vampire, wearing a white robe and hood. She pulled it back, revealing light blue eyes and long, brown hair.

She looked right at Caitlin and smiled.

"Caitlin," she said. "We have been awaiting you. Welcome."

Caitlin and Caleb exchanged a glance. The woman stepped aside, and they entered.

As they did, she closed and barred it behind them, using a type of metal Caitlin had never seen, three huge bars covering the doors.

"Titanium," she said. "Invincible to vampires. No one can attack us here. You're completely safe. You can rest at ease now."

Caitlin sensed the woman's positive, healing presence, and she knew that what she was telling her was true. For the first time in she didn't know how long, Caitlin felt herself relax. *Safe. Finally.*

"But still, we have little time to lose," the woman said. "I trust you have the key?"

Caitlin looked back at her surprise. She wondered how she knew.

The woman smiled further, "Of course I know. We are of your father's people. We watch everything that you do."

Caitlin extracted the small, gold key from her pocket, and reached out to give it to her.

The woman pulled back her hands.

"No. I don't want it. That's yours to keep. Only you can open it."

The woman suddenly turned and walked quickly down the long, marble aisle of the church.

Caitlin and Caleb began to follow her in the huge, empty edifice, their footsteps echoing.

Caitlin looked up and noticed the soaring ceilings, tapering to a point; she saw the endless rows of arched, stained-glass windows, hundreds of feet high, and was overwhelmed by the beauty of this place. It felt like they were walking inside an enormous kaleidoscope.

As they walked down the aisle, Caitlin wondered where they were going, and Caleb turned to her.

"I'm so sorry," he said softly, out of earshot of the woman. "For Sera. For leaving you. For everything. I hope that you'll forgive me."

It felt so good to hear those words. She was overwhelmed with emotion. She didn't trust herself to speak at that moment, so she just held out her hand.

Caleb took it, and his skin felt so good to her. She felt comforted by his presence, as they walked together down the aisle.

"This church was built thousands of years ago," the woman said. "A very special place for our race. It was built specifically to house the most important and valuable of treasure. Here, among many other treasures, we have fragments of The Cross, along with the real Crown of Thorns."

The woman turned down another corridor, then down a flight of wide, marble steps.

They entered the lower level of the church, and it took Caitlin's breath away. It was the most beautiful thing she'd ever seen. It had a low, arched ceiling, painted a vibrant, celestial blue, and interlaced with shining gold arches. This place looked like a treasure chamber, and in the torchlight, it was positively glowing. It was spectacular. Caitlin felt as if she had just entered King Tut's tomb.

"Down here, we keep the most valuable of artifacts. A special silver chest was built to hold them all, a chest which took twenty years to build. Inside of that chest, you will find what you need."

As they continued, the room opened up, and Caitlin was shocked to see standing before them, waiting, dozens of vampires, all dressed in white, all with white hoods. They each held a silver goblet, each one filled with a white liquid.

In the center stood a single vampire, a man with a long silver beard and piercing green eyes. He stared kindly at Caitlin and Caleb, holding a small silver goblet for each of them.

The woman gestured for them to approach.

They walked right up to him, and Caitlin felt herself starting to tremble. Was her father here?

"Drink," he said softly.

They each took a goblet and drank the white liquid.

Immediately, Caitlin felt restored. She recognized it as the white blood of her father's coven. She also grew lightheaded.

The man stepped aside, and revealed behind him a huge, glowing silver chest.

"Your key," he said softly.

Caitlin handed him back the goblet, stepped forward, knelt, and inserted her key into the small lock on the chest.

It turned with a little click, and slowly, she opened the heavy lid.

Inside, nestled amidst piles of jewels, was a second chest, with an even smaller lock.

Caitlin was puzzled.

"I'm sorry," Caitlin said. "This is the only key I have."

The man shook his head. "You also have another key."

Caitlin racked her brain, but had no idea what he was talking about.

He pointed at her neck.

She reached down, and suddenly remembered the antique, silver cross she wore. Could that be it?

She gingerly took it off, and inserted it into the lock of the smaller chest.

She was shocked to see that it fit.

She turned, and it opened.

There, in the small chest, was one large, silver key. The same exact size key as the one she had received in the Vatican. She knew immediately that this was the second key she needed to reach her father.

She was ecstatic.

But at the same time, she was frustrated, hoping she would find all three keys at once, to find her dad here, in the room.

She took it, rose and stood beside Caleb, feeling increasingly lightheaded, as she faced the man.

"There are but two keys left," the man said. "And then you can unlock the gates, receive the Shield, and meet your father for yourself. We are proud of you. And so is he.

"Your father, though, waits for you in another time and place. I am sorry to say it is not here. Are you willing to go back again? To continue your journey?"

Caitlin turned to Caleb, but she already knew her answer. She was prepared to go back, and she saw from his eyes that he was, too.

"Then kneel."

The two of them knelt, holding each other's hands.

"Lower your heads."

They did so, and as they did, Caitlin felt her heart pounding. There were so many questions left unresolved. Where would they end up? Would they be together? What about Sam? Polly? Ruth? She had so many questions she was burning to ask Caleb.

She felt the entire coven gather around, and felt several of them laying their hands on her head.

"We hereby lay thee down to rest," echoed the chorus of vampires. "Caitlin and Caleb, to resurrect another day. In God's ultimate grace."

Ruth came in and lay beside her, whining. As the words were repeated a second time, then a third time, Caitlin felt her world grow lighter.

At the last second, before it all disappeared, she turned to Caleb, and saw him turn to her. She looked deeply into his eyes, and knew, just knew, that next time, they would be together forever.

"I love you," she said.

"And I love you," he answered.

And those were the last words she heard, as she felt herself growing ever lighter, dizzier, drifting into the ceiling—until her entire world was blackness.

COMING SOON…

Book #6 in the Vampire Journals

Please visit Morgan's site, where you can join the mailing list, hear the latest news, see additional images, and find links to stay in touch with Morgan on Facebook, Twitter, Goodreads and elsewhere:

www.morganricebooks.com

Also by Morgan Rice

turned
(book #1 in the Vampire Journals)

loved
(Book #2 in the Vampire Journals)

betrayed
(Book #3 in the Vampire Journals)

destined
(Book #4 in the Vampire Journals)

Lightning Source UK Ltd.
Milton Keynes UK
UKOW041041020513

210101UK00001B/2/P